THE AU PAIR

JANE RENSHAW

Published by Inkubator Books
www.inkubatorbooks.com

Copyright © 2024 by Jane Renshaw

ISBN (eBook): 978-1-83756-323-4
ISBN (Paperback): 978-1-83756-324-1
ISBN (Hardback): 978-1-83756-325-8

Jane Renshaw has asserted her right to be identified as the author of this work.

THE AU PAIR is a work of fiction. People, places, events, and situations are the product of the author's imagination. Any resemblance to actual persons, living or dead is entirely coincidental.

No part of this book may be reproduced, stored in any retrieval system, or transmitted by any means without the prior written permission of the publisher.

PROLOGUE
23 JULY

Faking a drowning isn't as easy as you might think. You can't just rock up at the beach with the girl's clothes, dump them on the sand and hope for the best. A bit of forward planning is required; a bit of thinking things through.

Even on a remote beach like this, a wide, wild expanse of sand and rocks and scrubby dunes, doing it in daylight is a bad idea. No matter how early in the morning or late in the evening, guaranteed there'll be some meddler in the offing, some birdwatcher called Derek or Malcolm whose idea of a good time is lying on his belly in the marram grass, sweaty little hands clutching a pair of high-powered binoculars.

So cover of darkness is crucial. Unfortunately, at this northerly latitude in July, dusk doesn't fall until after eleven o'clock, and dawn comes ridiculously early, some time between 3 and 4 a.m., leaving a pretty narrow window of opportunity.

The sand is another problem. There's no way to avoid leaving footprints, so you must time your visit to coincide with an incoming tide. If you walk close to the water, both to and from the scene, the waves will soon swallow up all traces that you were there and the girl – let's call her Alice – was not.

All right. So you've timed it to perfection, there's no chance of being observed, the tide's coming in... You mustn't blow it now by leaving the clothes somewhere stupid where they'll be in danger of being washed away. At the same time, the place you choose has to be accessible by a route that will soon be underwater.

The big rock at the end of the bay is ideal.

It's a round, chest-height boulder of ancient gneiss forged in the fiery furnaces of the primeval Earth – oh, maybe two billion years ago. In the light of your torch, you'll see it's covered in an array of interesting lichens, but you mustn't be distracted. Concentrate on the task in hand.

Modest little Alice would have ducked down in the shadow of the rock to strip off and pull on her bathing costume (a navy one-piece that you've already burnt to ashes), before bundling up her clothes and leaving them safely on top of the boulder.

They attest to her innocence, these clothes. Not for Alice the crop tops and sexy little skirts favoured by many teenage girls her age. Alice's clothes consist of a baby-blue cotton bra and panties, loose indigo jeans, and a cap-sleeved white T-shirt with a cartoon dog on the front. All these you bring in your bag, but also – because you've thought this through – her rather battered pink walking sandals, which you must remember to scuff in the sand, and a colourful beach towel from the house. Easy to imagine Alice jogging here through the gently foaming shallows, the demure navy bathing costume rolled up in the towel tucked under one arm. Easy to imagine her impatience as she pulls off her clothes, eager to sprint down the pristine expanse of sand and into the sea.

All too easy to imagine her getting into difficulties, her strong young limbs fighting a losing battle against the current pulling her far from shore; her shouts for help becoming fainter and fainter until they stop altogether; her body drifting away, pulled beyond the point by the running sea and out into the wide expanse of the Atlantic Ocean.

If you've set it up right, if you've been careful and done all your forward planning, no one will question that narrative.

Why should they?

There will be no reason to doubt it.

No reason for the police, the public, or even the family to dwell on the possibility of any other end to the tragically short, sweet life of Alice Snyder.

1

ALICE - 24 DAYS EARLIER, 29 JUNE

Alice Snyder bounced on her toes like a little kid as the train rolled in to Achnasheen station. *Achnasheen* – even the name was like poetry! And all around her was just the kind of wilderness she'd been hoping for, windswept fields and heathery hills and far-off mountains so grey and smudgy you couldn't tell where they ended and the clouds began.

All that was missing was a lone piper up on one of those hilltops to send the mournful wail of the bagpipes echoing around the place. An old lament for fallen soldiers or some such.

Alice already knew a whole lot about Scotland, but she couldn't wait to totally immerse herself in the culture. As she stepped onto the platform and hauled her case down after her, breathing in the pure Highland air, she felt a huge guilty smile tug at her cheeks.

Not a soul in Branchfield, Indiana, even knew where she was!

Well, in the note she'd left, she'd told Mom and Daddy

she was going to the UK, and they might have shared that around, but no one knew where she was *exactly*. No one knew that right now Alice Snyder was standing on the platform of Achnasheen railway station in the beautiful Scottish Highlands!

That silly, thoughtless, selfish girl.

That runaway.

That *thief*.

Although she guessed Daddy wouldn't have shared the thief part.

The station building – and there was only one building – was cute and probably historical. It was like some of the other houses she'd seen from the train, with white walls and a slate roof that had upside-down V-shapes sticking out from the front.

As the train pulled away, she realised there wasn't another human being in sight. And apart from the station – which seemed to be closed – not another building.

She lifted her arms in the air and did a happy dance. *Dance like nobody's watching.* Well, nobody was! Do this in Branchfield and two minutes later someone, probably Mrs Miller, would be calling Mom to say she just saw Alice acting strange. Branchfield was one of those little farming towns where you couldn't scratch your ass without someone having a conniption.

There was quite a breeze blowing off those hills.

Alice unzipped the outer compartment of her case and pulled out her Gap hoodie, the grey one Mom had bought her last time they'd visited Aunt Ruth in Chicago. As she pushed her hands into the soft material, warm against her bare arms, a little flutter of *I wish Mom was here* went through her stomach, like she was eight years old rather than eighteen, an adult person who had taken control of her life.

Yeah. It was *her* life, wasn't it?

She had every right to be doing this. Apart, she guessed, from the stealing. But she was going to pay back every cent.

And she didn't regret it one bit.

Five minutes later, though, five minutes of pacing up and down the platform and round the back of the station, she was beginning to get antsy. Apart from the station building, there was just a parking area, some grass, a pond, and a little wooden hut that seemed to be a shop and café, but it was closed too. Through the trees back here she could see a few houses, which was a little reassuring, but then the moorland began again.

Achnasheen really was in the middle of nowhere.

What if it was all some sort of cruel joke? What if the Davidson family didn't even exist? What if Caro Davidson, the classy lady who'd been so much fun on the video call, was a sociopath who got her kicks from luring unsuspecting teenagers halfway across the world with the promise of a fake job?

Alice wheeled her case over the short, springy grass to one of the picnic tables by the pond and sat down. She took out her phone and scrolled through to Caro Davidson's number, but then stopped, finger poised, reluctant to take this step that could bring everything crashing down. What if the number turned out to be unobtainable? It was late afternoon, and she was almost out of money. She had eighty-five pounds left in her wallet and just a little more in her bank account. That night in London had been *expensive*.

What if she ended up having to make a phone call to Daddy? How would she find the words to admit that she'd messed up big time and he was right about her being too immature to be let loose in the world?

There were little bright blue flying insects, maybe dragonflies, darting around over the water of the pond. It was all right for them! Alice often felt jealous of animals. They didn't have to worry about a thing – not school, parents, jobs, money, nothing.

Free as the wind.

'Alice!' a voice shouted.

A hand was waving out of the big grey car coming towards her on the little dead-end road that led down to the station.

It was Caro Davidson!

Thank the Lord!

Mrs Davidson ignored all the empty parking spots. She just stopped the car at the nearest point to the picnic table and jumped out, pushing her sunglasses up into her mane of wavy hair.

'You poor thing! Did you think we'd abandoned you? I'm *so sorry*! I was ambushed in the supermarket by the biggest gossip in Torridon and *could not* get away! And then when I tried to text you to say I'd be late, my phone was out of charge. I'm such a ditz, as you would probably say!' She pulled Alice into a hug.

Caro Davidson evidently didn't conform to the reserved Brit stereotype.

Alice grinned. 'No problem. I figured you'd be along soon enough.'

Mrs Davidson held Alice away from her and gave her a look that said *I know that's a big lie. I know you must have been fretting.*

In person, she was even more striking than on the video

call. She wasn't tall, but she was so thin she looked it, and her clothes were the simple kind you just knew cost more than your whole clothes budget for the year: a white shirt with pearly buttons, a chunky silver bangle, dark green skinny jeans and chestnut-brown suede sneakers. Her face was a little too bony to be beautiful, but with those sparkling eyes, high cheekbones and glossy, highlighted hair, Caro Davidson was an attractive older lady. She was maybe – fifty?

'I'm *so* sorry,' she repeated. 'In compensation, how about a Coke and some crisps? I'm all too familiar with the teenage appetite!' She had the trunk open now and was rummaging in a shopping tote.

She shoved a huge bag of chips at Alice along with a can of Coke. 'Not chilled, I'm afraid.'

'Thank you so much, Mrs Davidson.'

'Oh *God*, no, you mustn't call me *Mrs Davidson*, like I'm a hundred years old! It's Caro. Now, I'll have to make space amongst the chaos in here to stow your case.' But she just stood for a moment, looking at Alice. 'You're a very pretty girl,' she said at last, almost like it was a bad thing.

Alice could feel herself blushing. 'Thank you.'

She guessed everything was relative. On the video call, she hadn't been looking her best because it had been late at night and her face had been puffy from crying. Plus, she'd locked herself in her en suite bathroom to make the call, in case Mom or Daddy had heard the crying and came to see if she was okay. The light in there was a little harsh and unflattering.

'It's a long way to come on your own,' Caro went on. 'Your parents are okay with it?'

'Oh, sure. When I told them all about you and your family and your lovely home, they were, like, *go for it!*'

'Well, good.' Caro turned back to the trunk. 'Right, let's squeeze your case in here and get going.'

Caro drove fast, and one-handed, with both windows down and rock music blaring. With her other hand, she held a cigarette out of the window. Alice soon gave up trying to drink her Coke and eat her chips. She tucked the can and chip bag into the well of the passenger door and gripped the armrest for dear life.

But as she realised the road was straight, wide and empty, the car handled like a dream and Caro had complete control, she began to enjoy the sensation of rushing through the wild scenery. On Caro's side were trees and on Alice's a lake – no, a *loch* – its choppy water reflecting broken pieces of the long hump of the hill on the other side and the clouds, from which the sun suddenly broke, its silvery rays moving on the water like a spotlight.

Alice let go of the armrest and put her own hand out of the window, then her elbow, and soon she was bopping in her seat to the rhythm and singing along in her head. It was like they were flying, like she'd stepped straight into a Harry Potter movie and Caro was one of the cool teachers with amazing magical powers that she didn't always use responsibly.

Up ahead, an elderly couple were walking by the side of the loch. Caro didn't slow down, and the man shouted something at them. Caro laughed and flipped him the bird while still managing to keep a hold of the cigarette, and Alice couldn't help laughing too.

She felt like one of the bad kids from home.

Well, she guessed she *was* a bad kid now.

. . .

HALF AN HOUR LATER, they turned off the 'main' road, as Caro called it, and onto a narrow little one that had wider semicircles spaced along it with signs saying *Passing Place*. There was grass growing through the middle of the surface here and there, and when Alice mentioned this, Caro said, 'Yep, we're literally off the beaten track now. Some days, even in summer, you don't meet another vehicle the whole way to Scallan Lodge.'

Alice really hoped this was one of those days. She didn't like to think what would happen if they zipped round a corner and there was a big truck coming the other way. But oh my, it was *gorgeous*! They passed through a shady pinewood and then out into the sun, and on their right was the blue water of the sea loch, the mountains rising up all around.

Finally, 'Here we are,' said Caro, and slammed on the brakes.

There were big old stone gateposts in amongst some trees, a sign saying Scallan Lodge and another underneath saying Private.

Now the surface was just a dirt track, and the ruts and potholes meant Caro had to slow right down, but even so they bounced around like crazy, like on a fairground ride. The track came out of the forest, and Alice could see it winding ahead of them up a hill, the land on either side heathery and wild.

'What are those little white pompoms on stems?'

They were everywhere, dancing in the breeze.

Caro shrugged. 'Don't know, don't care.'

At the top of the hill, the land changed again. Added to the heather and pompoms were reeds, and pools of dark water everywhere, the colour of the Coke she wasn't drinking. There was just this high bog, and then the distant sea, and then the sky. It was like she'd truly come to the edge of the world.

'But... where's your house?'

Caro was lighting another cigarette. 'We've another mile or so to go yet.'

The bog gave way to more trees, and Alice breathed their resiny scent as the car descended a series of Z-bends that had her grabbing the armrest again. Then they were right down at sea level, looking across the moor and dunes to a little cove, to the dazzle of the sun on the water and the bright sand.

She whooped. 'A *beach*!'

'Do you like to swim?'

'Uh...'

The family would want Alice to supervise the kids in that cove.

'Not so much,' she admitted. 'I'm not a strong swimmer. I guess it wouldn't be safe for me to take the kids in the water. Is that a problem?'

She held her breath. What if Caro sighed and shook her head and said that wouldn't work?

Cue phone call to Daddy.

Caro blew smoke out of the window. 'No, no. Christina, my eldest, swims like a fish, but the littlies still don't go above their ankles in the sea – can't trust them not to get swept away by the currents. We only let them swim in the pool, and never alone.'

Oh, thank the Lord!

'But you should learn to swim properly, Alice – it's an important life skill. We'll have to get you in the pool and put you through your paces.'

Alice's heart sank back again. 'Oh – okay. Great! Thank you!'

And now she could see the house.

Oh my goodness, it was a mansion, rising up above the next headland like it was rising out of the rocks. Its walls were grey stone, its roofs slate – roofs plural, because there were a lot of them on all the different parts of the building and on the turrets and towers that stuck up from it.

'You live in a castle!'

Caro laughed. 'A Victorian mock-up of a castle, built in the nineteenth century as a shooting lodge for a wealthy family. The style's called Scottish Baronial, and you get it all over the Highlands. Generally favoured by Victorians who made their money in trade wanting to pretend they were members of the aristocracy.'

'Are *you* a member of the aristocracy?'

She laughed again. 'No! I grew up in a nice but perfectly ordinary semi in Linlithgow. We have – well, *had* an events business that made us some money.'

Alice definitely felt she was in a Harry Potter movie now, arriving at Hogwarts! There were more stone gateposts and lawns with bushes all around them, and a gravel driveway sweeping up to the house. A big arched stone porch shaded the front door, so at first she didn't see the little girl standing there. She wore a brown dress, and her hair was in two strawberry-blonde plaits. This must be their seven-year-old.

'Isabel's been so excited to meet you, bless her. She was up at five o'clock this morning making that.' Caro pointed. Far above Isabel's head, looped over the door, was a banner of sorts made from sheets of paper strung together and saying, in wobbly capitals:

WELCUM ALICE!

Alice was tearing up.

Her heart felt like it was swelling in her chest with joy, with the feeling that this was what she'd been looking for, that God himself, maybe, had guided her here, to this place and these people. And she couldn't help thinking that Mom would never have allowed seven-year-old Alice to make a banner like that and stick it up for all to see. At the very least, she'd have made her do it over without the spelling mistake.

She waved madly to Isabel with both hands, and, almost before the car had stopped, she was out of it and running to meet the little girl and begin her adventure at Scallan Lodge.

2

MELANIE - 34 DAYS LATER, 2 AUGUST

Melanie Macfarlane eased the car off the potholed track onto a piece of rough ground and got out, shielding her eyes with her hand against the sun. Was that the beach where Alice's clothes had been found? It matched the images in the press and on the internet – a gentle semicircle of sand hemmed in by rocks and dunes.

She opened the boot and pulled on her walking shoes.

There was a path through the dunes, or maybe it was a sheep track. Their shiny black droppings were everywhere, and in the rough field behind the dunes, a dozen or so shorn ewes and their fluffier, almost grown-up lambs lazily cropped the grass.

The beach itself was deserted, the sand stretching down to turquoise water.

Melanie walked slowly, almost reluctantly, along the curve of the sand to the big boulder at the far end of the cove. When she reached it, she set the flat of her palm against the rough stone.

Hikers, a retired couple in their sixties, had found eighteen-year-old Alice Snyder's clothes on top of this rock.

Pants and bra, T-shirt, jeans. Sandals. A towel, unused.

The theory was that she'd gone into the sea for an early-morning swim and never come back. The search for the 'missing American teen' had gone on for days and involved the coastguard, police and a posse of locals, to no avail. Alice Snyder's body had not been recovered.

Melanie walked down to the edge of the water and stood watching the waves creep up the sand. What had been her fate? Had she swum out too far and realised she didn't have the strength to get back to shore? Did she fight as the end came, her lungs desperate for air as they tried to breathe through the seawater that pushed its way into her nose and mouth? Melanie could almost see it happening, out there in the constantly heaving water. The beautiful face that smiled from newspapers and internet pages contorted in desperation, in terror, the long, straight caramel hair a tangled skein –

She pushed those thoughts away and released the breath she'd been holding; took another.

Drowning was only one possibility and, in Melanie's view, a remote one, although the police seemed to have little doubt about it. Officially, of course, they were still treating Alice Snyder as a missing person. They'd sent no report, as yet, to the Procurator Fiscal; there had been no setting in motion of the procedures and processes required in Scots Law in the case of any sudden or unexplained death. And Alice's parents, Warren and Tonya Snyder, were adamant that their daughter, a weak swimmer, would never have gone into the sea in the first place. They'd been in Scotland ever since Alice had first gone missing, and had appeared at several press conferences, urging anyone who had seen Alice to get in touch with the police.

Alice could have left her clothes here to make it look like she'd drowned. She'd run away from her home in Indiana – was it too much of a stretch that she could have run away from Scallan Lodge?

But she'd taken nothing – not her phone, not her passport, not her purse with her bank card, not any other belongings, as far as could be ascertained. In the press conferences, the Snyders had been equally adamant that their daughter wouldn't have run away again without letting them know she was all right. Even at her most rebellious, Alice was a kind soul who wouldn't want them worrying.

No.

The Snyders believed that it hadn't been Alice who'd left her clothes on this beach. That there had been foul play. That someone, some predator, had taken her.

Their girl.

So young, so beautiful, so very *desirable* to the sort of scum who preyed on kids like Alice, innocent young people who had no experience of the world and its dangers and no possible way of knowing evil when it came for them.

'She's the light of our lives,' Tonya Snyder had said tightly in one of the appeals for information. 'Everyone loves Alice. She's such a sweet, open-hearted girl... We just want her home.'

She was probably dead, of course.

Not that the Snyders accepted that, and Melanie supposed they never would, unless and until Alice's body was found.

She turned to the south. Beyond the curve of the cove and the rocky promontory that bounded it, she couldn't see the next headland. But between the sweep of shore and the sky, a jagged interruption to the natural landscape, were the uncompromising grey Victorian roofs and chimneys and towers of Scallan Lodge.

The sight of it, the name itself in her head, sent warring emotions rushing through her. She turned on her heel and marched back up the sand and through the dunes to where she'd left the car, hardly seeing her surroundings now as fury won the battle and all her senses, all her store of energy was concentrated in a needle-sharp focus on what she had to do now.

3

ALICE - 29 JUNE

The little girl was adorable, looking up at Alice with big blue eyes.

Alice crouched to her level. 'Hi! I'm Alice. It's so good to meet you, Isabel! Did *you* make this?' She pointed at the banner above their heads.

Isabel nodded.

'That's so kind of you! I sure do feel welcome!'

A tiny smile lifted the soft mouth, and she held out an envelope with 'Alice' carefully printed on the front.

'For *me*?'

Another nod.

It was a home-made card, again with 'Welcum Alice' on the front, along with a sunflower and some mutant people with outsize heads. Isabel had given them huge smiles that went from one side of the face to the other. Inside, she'd written, 'We are happy you are our o pear.'

Alice was tearing up again. She'd been worried that the kids might not like her – that they might be brats, like her friend Jasmine's little sisters, who had once run away from her when she took them to the park. Alice had got in *so* much trouble for that, completely unfairly.

If the Davidson kids took against her, she guessed she'd be fired.

Cue phone call to Daddy.

But Isabel, her main charge and so the most important kid to keep onside, was obviously just darling.

'Thank you, sweetheart. It's such a great picture! Is this you?' Alice pointed to the smallest of the manically smiling mutants, which had bright orange hair in bunches.

Another nod.

'And who's everyone else?'

It was funny to watch the struggle that was obviously going on in Isabel's little head. She was too shy to speak, but she needed to tell Alice that information. Alice helped her along.

'Is this your sister Christina?' She pointed to one of the figures.

'That's Mummy,' Isabel whispered. 'That's Christina.' She pointed at the figure with hands on hips and frowning eyebrows above the big smile, giving the face a rather psychopathic look. 'And that's my other sister, Tess, and that's Daddy.' Daddy was two circles, the upper one with a shock of brown hair, the lower with only arms, like a snowman. 'Oh. I forgot Uncle Gray.'

'You could add him later,' Alice suggested.

A tiny nod.

'I love my card. Thank you!'

'They're just cartoons. I can't really do people.' The words were suddenly tumbling out. 'But the flower's not *too* bad.'

'It's a beautiful sunflower. And the people are *cute*, Isabel!'

Well, apart from Christina.

A big, grinning man in a khaki sweater emerged from the house behind the girl and put his hands on her shoulders. 'She's captured our essence, hasn't she? Who ate all the pies? Couldn't you have shaved a few inches off my waistline, Izz?'

Isabel squinted up at him. 'It's a cartoon, Dad. Tess said you have to make people exa... exasperated?'

The man laughed, the tanned skin around his eyes crinkling. 'Exaggerated. Well, that's a relief. I needn't order the hoist just yet.' He held out a hand to Alice. 'I'm Ken. Christina's staying with a friend and won't be back until tomorrow, but the rest of the gang's all here – somewhere! Welcome to the madhouse!'

And *phew*, Ken was obviously lovely too!

'You have a beautiful home,' Alice said as he took her hand and squeezed it with just the right amount of friendly enthusiasm. He was like a middle-aged boy, with that thick, untamed hair, sunny smile and bouncy energy.

'It's a money pit, but it's worth it.' He released her hand and gestured around them. '*My heart's in the Highlands, my heart is not here...* Or I should say *there*. We were in London for seven years before we made a break for it – returned to the land of our birth.'

Caro rolled her eyes as she trooped past them with a shopping bag in each hand.

'Oh, let me help you with those!' Alice exclaimed.

'Thanks, Alice. There's more in the boot.'

Alice must have looked startled, because Ken laughed and said, 'Otherwise known as the trunk. But I'll get them. And then I'll haul your case up the hundred or so steps to the Tower Room or, as the girls call it, the Princess Room.' He waved at the rooftops.

'Thank you!' said Alice. 'But I can do that.'

'No, no – it's good for me, so I'm told. Mitigates the effects of the pies.'

Alice tried not to look too relieved. Her case was heavy.

'And it's only *forty-two* steps,' said Isabel. 'Which is still a lot. But it's worth it,' she added quickly. 'It's the *best* room.'

'Izz, why don't you show Alice around before dinner?'

Isabel gazed up at Alice with a sweet, hopeful expression.

Alice gave her a big smile. 'I can't wait to see *everything*! Where should we start?'

The little girl soon lost her shyness as she showed Alice her treehouse, the 'jungle', which was a rewilded part of the garden beyond the lawns, and the Frog Fountain – a dried-up round pit made of stone in the middle of the rather overgrown flower garden at the back of the house. It had an urn on a sort of plinth in the middle.

Isabel sighed. 'The frogs keep jumping in, thinking it's still full of water, and we have to rescue them.' Suddenly, she started waving frantically in the direction of the jungle. 'There's Tess!'

A pale, pinched little face appeared amongst the leaves and then was gone.

'Tess!' called Isabel. '*Alice* is here!'

'Oh, never mind,' said Alice loudly when the face failed to reappear. 'Maybe Tess can get her gift later. I've brought you both something from the States.'

Still no Tess, but Isabel clasped her hands together, as if in an effort to contain her excitement. 'What?' she breathed.

'Nothing much,' said Alice quickly, wishing she'd brought the kids nicer gifts.

As they made their way into the house, tiful garden room full of frondy plants and w ings, Isabel said, 'Sorry about that. Tess is a bit of a character.'

Alice did her best not to smile at this obvious repetit of an overheard adult's comment.

'But she's a good person,' Isabel hurried to say, pushing open a door into a big lounge room and looking round at Alice anxiously.

'I'm sure she is, honey.'

The lounge room was very grand, with a high fancy ceiling, wood-panelled walls and, dominating the space, a huge oak fireplace carved with shells, waves, ships and what looked like sea monsters. There were three huge old windows looking out to sea, the middle one itself divided in three, like half a hexagon jutting out beyond the wall and giving views on all sides. The furnishings were suited to the scale of the room – long couches, winged armchairs and heavy oak tables and sideboards. But it was homey, with a jigsaw half-completed on the table in the jutting-out window, colourful throws on the couches, an abandoned shoe on the hearth rug.

Isabel didn't stop to let Alice look around – she was on a mission, marching across the room to the far door. Alice hurried after her into a big hall and found herself suddenly right back home, right back on a summer Sunday morning in Branchfield, stepping with her parents into the cool, calm space that was so dearly familiar but at the same time just a little terrifying.

Church.

Okay, so the stuffed animal heads and antlers and swords on the walls here were not decorations generally oured by Lutherans, but there was the same feeling of peace, the same smell of polish and old paper, even a stained-glass window on the landing that flung jewels of light tumbling down the imposing, massive oak staircase. In Branchfield Lutheran Church, the central window featured a full-length Jesus looking down on the congregation with an expression that said, *I love you, but I'm watching every move you make.*

This window was blue and green, mainly – it was the sea, with a boat on it, and fishermen casting a net. As she followed Isabel up the stairs and got near enough to read the fancy lettering around the edge, Alice saw it said, *Follow me, and I will make you fishers of men.* One of the people in the boat had a halo around his head.

'Fishers of *men*,' said a voice from the hall.

She looked down.

A tall guy was standing there, his facial features similar enough to Ken's to tell her that this was probably Uncle Gray. But he didn't look like anyone's uncle – he couldn't be more than thirty. He had Ken's thick head of hair, but it was darker and much longer, falling to his shoulders in a glossy sweep. He had dark, dark eyes, like a pirate's. In fact, he looked just like Johnny Depp in *Pirates of the Caribbean*. There was a braided bracelet around one tanned wrist, and a glint of silver at the open neck of his shirt.

Daddy didn't trust guys who wore jewellery, and felt this policy had been vindicated when Arnold Rogers, a lawyer in Branchfield, had gone to jail for fraud. Daddy couldn't understand why anyone in their right mind would put their legal affairs in the hands of a man who wore earrings.

'The casual misogyny of the Bible,' the pirate added, coming up the steps. No earrings – but they would suit him!

'I'm Graham Davidson – Ken's brother. Everyone calls me Gray. You must be Alice.'

'Yes I am! Pleased to meet you, sir.'

He grinned, but didn't offer her his hand as Ken had done. He stood close to her shoulder, looking up at the window, and Alice felt her body go all hot and uncomfortable. He even smelt like a pirate. Kind of spicy and a little sweaty, but it wasn't a BO smell. It was fresh sweat, like he'd just been working out.

Or running across a deck with a knife in his teeth.

She bit down on a giggle.

'Misogyny mainly by omission, of course,' he went on. 'Only about ten per cent of the people mentioned in the Bible are women. And of those – well, name me one who isn't either a madonna or a whore.'

'Um,' said Alice, feeling herself blush.

She was already wondering how to work into the conversation the fact that she was class valedictorian and not the airhead she might appear, but probably a guy like this wouldn't be impressed by that information anyhow. Branchfield High School wasn't exactly known for producing intellectual giants.

'Well, now.' She thought frantically. 'Lot's wife?'

'Whore!' said Gray.

Alice blinked.

He guffawed. 'She looked back at Sodom, didn't she, after being explicitly told by the angels not to?'

Alice nodded warily.

'Thus making it clear that she didn't really want to escape, that she was sorry to leave all the fornication and perversity behind her. Thoroughly deserving of being turned into a pillar of salt. And note that she isn't even named – she's only referred to in relation to her husband. *Lot's wife.*'

Alice suddenly wished her boyfriend Skip were here. His daddy being minister of the church, Skip knew pretty much everything about the Bible and could have debated this with Gray, put up a proper defence. In fact, Alice and Skip had once had a similar conversation about women in the Bible. She had complained that they didn't get much airtime, and Skip had said...

'Um... most women then were homemakers,' she parroted.

'And that makes them less worthy of mention?'

'No,' said Alice slowly. 'But I guess it means they weren't out and about so much. When Jesus did meet a woman, he never treated her like she was any less than a man. Not even if she *was* a... prostitute.' She must be blushing again. 'So if there *is* discrimination in the Bible, it's coming from the people who wrote it, and the people who lived then, not from Jesus himself or his teachings.'

For a long moment he looked at her, eyes narrowed. He was older than she'd first thought – maybe mid-thirties?

'Good point well made, Alice.'

'Thank you.' No way was she going to make herself look like any more of a dumb-ass, not to mention a traitor to feminism, by admitting that she was just repeating what her boyfriend had said.

Gray nodded. 'You're going to be fun to have around.'

That was a subtle way, she guessed, to indicate that this conversation was over. He wouldn't want to waste his time chit-chatting with the hired help. But Alice didn't want it to end. She wanted him to keep throwing awkward questions at her, like she was a rookie baseball player and he was her coach throwing curveballs, and she was determined to impress him by hitting them out of the park.

She found she was smiling at him goofily – somehow she couldn't look away from those deep, dark eyes in that gorgeous tanned face. Slowly, he smiled back, a little like he was laughing at her.

'Alice?' came a small voice from above them.

'Oh, sorry, Isabel! Nice to meet you,' she muttered at Gray, and headed on up the stairs to where Isabel stood, hands on hips, waiting on the landing.

'I'm never going to find my way back,' Alice protested as Isabel led her along passageways and across another landing with stairs leading down from it. Then more passageways and another few steps, and they were in a dark hallway with more heavy old furniture and a steep staircase leading upwards. People were clattering down the stairs, the sound reverberating around the stairwell with its bare wooden steps.

Ken appeared and stood grinning at them. The noise on the stairs had stopped, and Alice realised that there hadn't been a whole lot of people, just Ken.

'Done the grand tour, then?' He beamed at Alice.

'We sure have! It's such an *amazing* place – and you're all being so kind! I – I met your brother just now. Gray?'

Ken's face changed. 'Oh. Yes.'

She could feel herself blushing all over again, but managed to say lightly, 'He's already tried to engage me in intelligent conversation.'

'Don't worry, I'm not even going to attempt that. I was going to tell you that the loo in your shower room – it's under the stairs there – is a bit temperamental. You have to give the handle a good old yank when you're flushing it.'

Alice grinned. 'Good to know.'

Isabel pushed past her daddy, turning back to frown at Alice. 'Come *on!*'

It hadn't taken long for the shyness to vanish, Alice reflected happily as she followed her upstairs. She didn't count the steps, but she was sure there were at least forty-two. There wasn't a door at the top – the staircase led straight into the room.

Oh my!

It was like stepping into the sky.

The big, square room had three windows on each side and seemed to be filled with the sky, *blue, blue, blue* all around. Alice laughed and ran across to one of the windows. There was an amazing view right over the ocean! She ran right around the room, the panorama of sea, rocks, trees and moorland flashing past almost giving her vertigo, making her head spin. There was no other house in sight, just nature, everywhere. She imagined Gray out there on the ocean, scrambling up the rigging, the wind tugging at his glossy locks.

Isabel was standing in the middle of the room laughing too, jumping up and down and clapping her hands.

'I *love* it!' said Alice, taking Isabel's hands and jumping with her.

She'd just *known* she was going to love Scotland!

It took a little while for the two of them to calm down enough that Alice could take a proper look at the room itself. The floor was polished wood, and backed into one of the corners that faced the sea was a big bed with a wooden frame and white bedclothes. A wardrobe had been built across the opposite corner, and under one of the windows was a low, wide antique dresser with a mirror on top. There was also a comfortable-looking couch patterned in heathery colours, and a couple of armchairs and little tables.

Alice wondered if she'd have the dream here, like she'd had every night since she'd decided to come to Scotland. Maybe she wouldn't. Maybe this room was special enough to fill up her head with good things.

'It's the Princess Room,' said Isabel.

'It sure is.'

'*You're* like a princess,' Isabel said softly, the shyness returning as she looked up at Alice through her long, pale eyelashes. 'You're so pretty and nice.'

'Why, thank you, Isabel! But I'm kinda average. *You*, on the other hand, are a little doll!'

Ken had left her suitcase by the bed. Alice flipped it onto its belly and opened it, removing a small box, which she handed to Isabel. 'It's nothing much.'

But Isabel seemed delighted with the two pairs of hair clips, one with a row of tiny cats and one with flowers. They had belonged to Alice herself when she was a kid but were as good as new. It was one thing Mom always said she never had to reprimand Alice about – looking after her things.

'Can you put them in for me?' said Isabel.

'Which would you like? The cats or the daisies?'

Isabel was holding the hair clips in her palms as if they were precious jewellery, staring at them in wonder. 'I can't decide.'

'Why not have both?'

As Alice arranged all four clips in Isabel's silky hair, Caro appeared at the top of the stairs.

'Oh, darling, how chic!'

'*Alice* gave me them!' Isabel danced to the mirror on top of the dresser.

'That was very kind.' Caro smiled at Alice. 'Dinner will be in half an hour, which leaves just about enough time for a paddle on the beach, if –'

'*Yeah!*' from Isabel. 'Let's go!' She grabbed Alice's hand.

Alice laughed. 'Hold your horses, Isabel. First, I think the Princess Room needs... the finishing touch.'

'*My card!*' screamed Isabel in delight as Alice set it on one of the bedside cabinets, turned so she'd see that *Welcum Alice* whenever she came into the room.

'Perfect!' pronounced Alice.

And it was!

Everything about Scallan Lodge was just perfect.

4

MELANIE - 2 AUGUST

Scallan Lodge was grim as hell. A huge grey Dracula's castle. Up close, the signs of neglect were obvious: the gravel was full of weeds, the paintwork on the windows and doors was flaking, and one of the panes in an upstairs window had been replaced by a bit of hardboard. The granite walls were streaked with green from choked gutters, and there was even a buddleia bush growing from one of them.

A house like this, of course, cost a fortune just to live in, never mind maintain, and the Davidsons' current income was no doubt inadequate to the task.

Melanie parked her car by the front door and was hauling out her case when a man's voice called out, 'Donna? Hello, hello!'

It was Ken Davidson, striding towards her, an insincere smile plastered to his fleshy face. The photographs of him on the internet showed a younger version of the man, a slightly slimmer, better groomed, suited version. They all dated, of course, from before their high-end events management business, the cringily named Bring It On, went bust two years ago.

'Hi.' She took the hand he offered and shook it, making her own hand floppy in his manly grip. Melanie's alter ego of Donna MacKenzie was no sort of force to be reckoned with.

'You found the place all right, then!'

Duh?

'Yes. You are very remote here, though, aren't you?' She let the smile waver. Donna was the kind of person to be spooked by this.

'Nearest neighbour approximately three miles in that direction!' He waved a hand vaguely.

She turned away from his gaze. It was very unlikely that he, or any of the family, would find anything to recognise in Donna MacKenzie, but it was a slight risk.

Another man was approaching them across the gravel. He raised his eyebrows at Melanie. 'Would have been a different story once, of course. You probably saw all the old abandoned houses on your drive from Torridon.' He was the type of man she despised on sight, all surface sheen with those perfect white teeth, long, glossy, subtly highlighted hair, just the right amount of stubble and a silver chain snaking across the tanned skin at the open neck of his white linen shirt. 'The population was once a lot larger, before they were all cleared out to make way for sheep in the 1830s.'

Ken sighed. 'This is my brother Gray.'

'Right,' said Melanie, the Donna act slipping momentarily as she let the hand he stuck out towards her hang in the air, before making herself grasp it and not flinch as his thumb grazed the back of her hand. 'Hi. I'm Donna.'

His eyes were all over her, like a wolf sizing up its prey.

She simpered up at him. Donna MacKenzie had no idea

that Graham Davidson had been charged with sexually assaulting a woman at one of their events, the fiftieth birthday party of a TV presenter, or that a former staff member had then come forward to say he'd attempted to rape her one night when she'd been working late in the office. After that, Bring It On had been dropped by most of their corporate clients, and presumably the Davidsons had found it hard to drum up any business from private individuals too, despite the charges against Graham Davidson later being dropped after both women withdrew their accusations. Not exactly a selling point, was it? How would you market that?

Experience the ultimate adrenaline rush as you desperately try to avoid the attentions of our in-house pervert!

Fury rushed through her.

Men like this...

Melanie would have liked to have slammed 'Gray' to the ground and smashed that smug handsome face on the gravel until he told her what he knew, what he'd done.

If he'd done anything.

The Snyders were convinced he was responsible, but it was important to look at every angle. It was possible, *just* possible, that Gray Davidson wasn't involved in whatever had happened to Alice.

'You're just in time for lunch,' Ken went on. 'Although don't get your hopes up – Caro isn't exactly Jamie Oliver. Just one of the many reasons we're so glad to see you!'

What, so Donna was expected to cook their meals as well as look after the kids?

All for only just above minimum wage?

Nice.

The kitchen was at the back of the house and would have

had a sea view if it weren't for the overgrown rose bushes strangling the windows. Although it was a bright day, the lights were on, all the better to showcase the mess strewn everywhere – kids' toys, socks, jumpers, newspapers, batteries, boots, dirty dishes. The island was spattered with what looked like soup, and an encrusted hand mixer lay next to a large chopping board heaped with potato peelings and onion skins.

The room seemed to be full of people, but none of them was making a sound.

Melanie was very conscious of Gray standing right behind her. He smelt musky and sharp at the same time, like she imagined an actual wolf might smell.

'Here's Donna!' exclaimed Ken with false jollity.

The gaunt, fortyish woman frowning down at the pots on the Aga turned with an impatient expression, swiftly amended to a smile.

'Oh, Donna! Great! Lovely to see you! How was your journey?' And without waiting for an answer, she pushed her hands through her cloud of unkempt hair and then clapped them together. 'Everyone, here's Donna!'

The two little girls on the sofa at least looked at Melanie. This would be Tess and Isabel. Tess was pale, skinny, puny for an eleven-year-old. Her short, choppy brown hair looked as if she might have cut it herself. Her expression was blank, dead. Isabel, the little one, wore a fluffy, grubby white onesie despite the heat and looked feverish, strands of hair sticking to her forehead. She'd obviously been crying, but managed a small smile.

'Hello, there!' Melanie racked her brains for something to say. She always found kids tricky, ending up either talking down to them or burbling on about things they could have no interest in. 'Nice to meet you,' she settled on.

The other occupant of the room was a pouty teenager standing by one of the windows. She didn't look up from her phone or acknowledge either her mother or Melanie in any way. Christina, presumably. Comical false eyelashes, heavy make-up, peasant blouse, short skirt.

At last, still without looking up, she spoke. 'Whatever.'

There was a short laugh from behind Melanie, and Gray's voice said, 'Antisocial little buggers.'

Without warning, Caro smacked a serving spoon down on the island, making Melanie jump. 'Let's everyone give Donna a proper welcome, please. She's had a long journey to be here –'

'I want *Alice*!' Isabel wailed, her small features seeming to collapse in on themselves.

'Alice is dead,' said Tess, her voice filling the room, very loud and strident for such a puny child.

Isabel began to cry in earnest, and Caro looked as if she might join her. She dropped to the sofa and put an arm around her youngest child, who buried her face in her mother's scrawny bosom.

'We don't know yet what's happened to Alice,' Caro said weakly. 'The previous au pair...' She gave Melanie an apologetic grimace. 'She's gone missing. I don't know if we said...'

'Uh, *no*?'

Melanie had expected either Caro or Ken to mention it, in the video call that had served as a job interview. But no. All they'd said was that they found themselves suddenly in need of an au pair, and how soon could Melanie start?

'Terrible thing,' said Gray briskly, going to the worktop and picking up the kettle, flicking back his flowing locks with a toss of his head. 'Looks like the poor girl got into difficulties in the sea. We all searched for days, as did the police, the coastguard... A bad business.' He started to fill the kettle at the tap. 'Tea or coffee, Donna?'

'No,' said Melanie abruptly. 'Thank you,' she added belatedly.

'How about I show you your room so you can unpack before lunch?' Caro gave Isabel a final squeeze and stood. 'Christina, look after your sister, please.'

On the trek through the house, Caro told Melanie that the previous au pair had been a very young, very naïve, rather headstrong girl from America.

'She was warned about the currents off the beach,' she said, stopping on the landing above the huge Gothic hallway.

Melanie supposed it was an appropriate place for a conversation about death. It was classic old hunting-lodge style, exposed rafters and dark oak panelling, dimly lit by a huge stained-glass window. There were dozens of old swords arranged in circles on the walls around the obligatory stags' heads whose glassy eyes stared back at her, antlers meant for skewering opponents in the white-hot fever of a long-ago rut now collecting dust and cobwebs. The place was filthy. One particularly long string of cobweb dangling from the high rafters swung sinuously back and forth in the draft.

Caro lifted her shoulders helplessly. 'But... teenagers. They think they're invulnerable, don't they?' Her gaze slid away from Melanie's. Did her guilty demeanour indicate that she was feeling bad for failing to protect a young person in her care from the dangers of the sea – or from something worse? 'Gail, our previous housekeeper, and the daily help we employed for a while after Gail left – they were both mature women.' She narrowed her eyes at Melanie.

Was she seeing something that was familiar?

But then she asked, 'How old are you, if you don't mind my asking?'

Shit.

What age had Melanie settled on for Donna, on the CV she'd emailed Caro last week? She'd knocked a few years off her real age of thirty-four, worrying that that was too old to fit the bill as an au pair working for peanuts. But how many years?

'Twenty-six,' she tried.

She was confident she could pass as mid-twenties. Melanie was athletically built but slight, and her round face, curly bob and smooth skin meant people often thought she was much younger than she was. She'd even been asked for ID on her last night out with colleagues, much to the amusement of all. But that had been in the dim light of a bar.

The lighting in the hall wasn't much better, of course, and the corridors Caro guided her along were similarly gloomy. But the Tower Room, as Caro called it, was dazzlingly bright, making Melanie squint at the 360-degree views. They were truly spectacular, and it was surely perfectly acceptable for Donna to turn her back on Caro at this point to gaze out of a window.

'I'll leave you to settle in,' said Caro, and Melanie flashed her a quick smile and a 'Thanks!' before turning back to the sea view.

Just as well Caro had gone. Melanie's mouth was so dry she was sure she couldn't have got any more words out. And her lungs were labouring, like all the air had been sucked from the room. She fiddled with the window, trying to open it, but it was one of those UPVC ones with lockable catches, and she couldn't see a key. So they didn't have money to fix the gutters, but they'd splashed out on replacement windows?

With her palms on the double-glazed glass, she looked down.

And down and down, past the rooftops below to the gardens at the back of the house. They were full of flowers, but all growing through each other, out of control. And the lawns down there seemed to be knee-high and weedy.

Despite its panoramic view, this light-filled room in the sky managed to seem horribly claustrophobic. Like Rapunzel's prison.

She tried each of the windows in turn, but they were all locked. Even if they hadn't been, there'd be no escape possible from any of them, this high up – any attempt to jump onto one of the roofs below would probably prove fatal.

Was this even legal?

Surely an employee's accommodation should have an alternative means of egress, in the event of a fire?

But there was only the staircase.

She ran lightly down it and investigated the rest of her accommodation – a little shower room with a loo under the stairs. No window. No window on the stairwell, either.

The door to the rest of the house had a keyhole, but no key.

Back up in the Tower Room, Melanie unpacked quickly, arranging practical T-shirts, walking trousers and fleeces in the chest of drawers. She'd brought nothing she needed to hang in the wardrobe. At the bottom of her case, safely stowed under everything else, was Frog. She lifted him out and set him on her palm, smiling down at his worried expression. The imaginatively named beanie frog was green, of course, and had seen better days. Melanie had restitched him along his seams several times over the two decades they'd been together.

'Well, Frog,' she said, 'here we are.'

The top of the chest of drawers, she decided, was the ideal spot. She settled him there, back legs crossed, hands – did frogs have hands? – planted on the wooden surface.

'I can do this,' she told him.

But Frog didn't seem so sure.

5

ALICE - 30 JUNE

This time in the dream, Alice arrived at the cute little cottage to find there was a high spiky fence between her and the garden. She gripped its metal bars and shook them, but they were solid and too slippery to climb. She walked all the way around the fence, but there was no gate. She called out, again and again, but no one came to let her in.

Boy was she glad to wake up!

The dream was Mom and Daddy's fault. They had put it into her head with their negativity – no, it was more than that. It was more like *hostility*, ever since Alice had first started talking about coming to Scotland.

It was very early, not even six o'clock. After tossing and turning for a while, she got dressed in her running gear and perched on the heathery couch with a view of the ocean before steeling herself and switching on her phone.

Of course it went crazy, buzzing with a whole new crop of missed calls and voicemails and texts that had come in overnight. Mom, Daddy and Skip had been blowing up her phone ever since she'd left home, but she hadn't had the courage to call them back. Instead, she'd sent regular text messages to let them know she was okay.

Texting was definitely the way to go.

She tapped in a message for each of them, saying she'd arrived at her (unspecified) destination and the family were just lovely – very welcoming and kind. She was *so sorry* for stressing them out like this, but they mustn't worry because she was just fine! Her UK summer was going to fly by, and then she'd see them all in the fall! She peppered the texts with her usual strings of emojis – hearts, grimacing faces, faces blowing kisses, turtles and chipmunks (for no reason other than that those were her favourites), faces with sunglasses, waving hands, thumbs up, autumn leaves.

In Daddy's last text message, he'd told her quite sternly that they needed to know where she was. But Alice couldn't oblige him – if she did, he'd be on the next flight over, hauling her ass back home.

She looked at the message she'd just sent him, and then quickly composed another, reiterating that she would pay back every cent she'd taken. Was an emoji appropriate here? She decided to limit herself to a turtle and a grimace. And three hearts.

All done!

Well, that was a huge weight off her mind. Now she could relax and enjoy herself.

She slipped out of the house and into a mist that was soon seeping into her clothes and hair. She ran up the track towards the road, breathing in the damp scents of the pines and those other trees. She imagined all the people who had lived here through the centuries, breathing this same air. Crofters and the like. The draw Alice had felt to Scotland, long before she'd known she was coming here, meant she'd spent hours on the internet finding out all she could about it. She'd pored over old photographs of the poor people's houses back in Victorian times – black houses, they were called. Rough stone walls, and thatch made from turf and heather that the smoke from the fire percolated through because there were no proper chimneys.

But they were all gone now.

It was as if she were the only person in the world! She couldn't see far in the mist, just to the edges of the bubble that moved with her as she ran. When she reached the road, she turned back – how embarrassing would it be to get lost out here?

It was mainly downhill now. She started humming her favourite old Thanksgiving song, 'Over the River and Through the Wood'.

'*The horse knows the way to carry the sleigh, through the white and drifted snow,*' she sang in time with her feet. '*Through the white and drifted mist,*' she amended.

Suddenly, there was something in front of her.

Something big.

A man.

She screamed, he grabbed her, she pulled away –

'No need to be alarmed,' said an amused voice. It was Gray! Oh, thank the Lord! 'But it is a bit *Hound of the Baskervilles*, isn't it?'

Alice put a hand to her chest and breathed. 'I didn't expect anyone else to be out here this early.'

Gray was also dressed in running gear, a blue V-necked T-shirt and black Lycra shorts that emphasised his lean, muscular frame. His mane of hair was tied back and slick with sweat or mist, or maybe both. Wiry chest hair sprouted from the point of the V-neck, and Alice was having a hard time not staring at it. There was something so primitive about a guy's chest hair, like it was a feature that belonged on an animal or at most a very early hominid that had just started using tools.

He was breathing heavily as he came closer and put a hand on her sleeve. There were tiny beads of mist on his straight eyebrows, on his long dark lashes...

'Are you all right?' He squeezed her arm, his face concerned.

She swallowed. 'Sure! I'm fine. You just startled me for a second.'

He kept hold of her arm, like she was about to fall down or something. She looked down at his strong hand, at the delicate braided friendship bracelet, incongruous on that masculine and, yes, *slightly hairy* wrist.

'Really, I'm perfectly fine.' She gave him a big smile.

If this were a movie, he'd take her in his arms right here and –

Oh my goodness!

What was she thinking?

'Well, I'll come with you back to the house,' said the real-world Gray. 'Make sure you don't get lost in the mist and – what was it happened to the chap in *Hound of the Baskervilles*? Sucked down into the morass, wasn't he? Actually, the bogs can be treacherous. I did once step onto what I thought was solid ground, and next thing I knew, I was taking a vertical mud bath, right in over my head. Popped up again like a cork, but could have been nasty.'

'Oh my!' She imagined what a sight that would have been, Gray covered head to toe in slick, shiny mud. 'Uh, don't worry, I'm not going to venture off the track. But some company would be real nice.'

'If an old codger like me can keep up with a young thing like you!' He swept an exaggeratedly polite arm through the air to indicate she should go ahead. 'Ladies first. You can pull me along in your slipstream!'

In fact, Gray was a great runner – of course he was! – and Alice was conscious of him right there behind her as they ran. She almost imagined she could feel his breath on the skin of her neck that was exposed by her ponytail, but that was just the mist. A few times she tried to run alongside him, but he always somehow fell back, and she found herself ahead of him again. She guessed he was just being a gentleman, but she wished they could be side by side.

It was hard not seeing his expression when he said things like, 'In pursuit of Alice Snyder! I do pity the young male population of Branchfield. You leave them all floundering in your dust, I'll bet!'

She chose to take this literally. 'I usually go running with my friend Kimmy and my boyfriend Skip.'

'*Skip!* Priceless!' She really did feel a puff of air on her neck as he laughed.

She jinked to the side and looked around at him.

'Sorry,' he said. 'But you Americans and your nicknames. What's yours? No, let me guess –'

'I don't have one.' She smiled. 'But some folks call me Ali.'

'Ali! I like it! Right up my *alley*.'

Alice rolled her eyes, and he held up his hands as if surrendering to the joke police. She loved that he was obviously super-intelligent but had a goofy sense of humour just like hers. As they both laughed, Alice at Gray and Gray at himself, she treacherously thought of Skip and how he couldn't laugh at himself *at all*, although he was quick enough to mock Alice when she said or did something wrong.

'How wonderful!' said Caro, peering into the depths of the pot.

'It's only vegetable soup.' Alice gave it another stir. 'I thought everyone might like something hot for lunch, seeing as the temperature's dropped about fifty degrees!'

'That's a Scottish summer, I'm afraid. Four seasons in one day. We had hail last week, didn't we, Izz?'

Isabel nodded. 'It hurt your head.'

Alice was feeling smug. Isabel was drawing happily at the table, and okay, so Tess had disappeared off again, but at least Alice had gotten words out of her. She'd appeared in the kitchen doorway about half an hour ago, as Alice was getting Isabel settled with paper and crayons, but Alice had pretended not to notice her. The girl seemed to flit about the place like a little silent ghost. Alice had the weird feeling that if she looked at her straight on, she'd vanish, like a wisp of misty Scottish air.

So she'd carried on talking to Isabel. 'I saw a lovely plant this morning growing in a crack in the wall of the house.' Someone, maybe Ken, had mentioned yesterday that Tess loved everything to do with nature. 'It had little pink flowers like stars! I've no idea what it was. Here's the photo I took.' She put her phone on the table. 'Maybe you could draw it, and we'll try to find out its name later.'

'That's English stonecrop,' said Tess, suddenly at Alice's

elbow. 'But it grows in Scotland too. Obviously. And Ireland and Wales.'

Alice didn't make a big deal of it, the fact that these were the first words Tess had offered her. She just smiled at the girl and said, 'Oh, is that so? English stonecrop – what a great name! Thank you, Tess. Isabel, you could write that on the drawing when it's done.' As she helped Isabel select the right green crayon for the leaves, she was conscious of Tess staring at her. And then, just as suddenly as she'd appeared, she was gone.

But Alice was pretty sure she had found the way to her heart.

Everyone had a heart eager to open wide, Mom had always told her. You just had to find the key. Alice imagined literal keys, Tess's one safely in her pocket now along with Isabel's.

'I'm so glad you're a proficient cook,' said Caro.

So was Alice, as it seemed one of her tasks was to prepare meals for the family.

'But as far as the cleaning is concerned,' Caro went on, 'you needn't go all out. As you may have noticed, I'm not overly house-proud. Just as long as the place isn't an absolute health hazard... The whole north wing is closed up, and no one ever goes there, so it's not quite such a daunting task as it might seem.' She looked around. 'Concentrate on the bathrooms and the kitchen. Which I see you've already made a start on.'

'Uh-huh, but I meant to ask you where you keep the cleaning cloths?'

'Under the sink.'

'I found some dish cloths under there.' Which were

currently boiling away with a whole lot of baking soda in the other big pot Alice had found. 'But no cleaning cloths.'

'We just use the same ones.'

Alice hoped her shock wasn't showing. But along with the shock was a little bubble of laughter trying to push its way up. Caro was such a bad housekeeper! No wonder she was so happy Alice was here, and no wonder she hadn't made it clear in the interview that the au pair would be expected to cook family meals and clean this huge house, as well as look after the kids. This maybe also explained why Alice had got the job – someone from the US couldn't just up and leave. Well, she could, but getting home wasn't just a case of hopping on a bus.

'Oh my God, the *stench* of garlic,' said a tall girl as she sashayed into the kitchen and flung down a shoulder bag. She had Caro's long wavy hair, but there the resemblance ended. Christina, as this must be, had so much make-up on that you couldn't see her skin.

'Hello, darling!' Caro pulled her into a hug but wisely didn't attempt to kiss the thick layer of foundation. 'You're back early. This is Alice. Alice, my eldest daughter, Christina.'

'Hi!' Alice beamed at her. 'I'm so pleased to meet you!'

'Yeah, hi,' said Christina, wrinkling her nose. 'Whatever that is, it's a no from me.'

'It's lovely soup Alice has made,' said Caro. 'But if you don't want it, you can get your own lunch. It's not fair to make Alice prepare different things for everyone.'

Christina shrugged and sashayed out again.

It seemed the key to Christina's heart was going to be more of a challenge to locate. But everyone expected sixteen-year-olds to be difficult, didn't they, so it wouldn't be a big deal for Ken and Caro if she and Christina didn't connect?

As if reading her mind, Caro made a face. 'She's at that age.'

Alice didn't know what to say. 'Your children are all very different,' she settled on, dipping a wooden spoon into the soup to fish out a chunk of carrot. She set it on the chopping board, wafted her hand over it a few times, and popped it in her mouth to test for softness.

Caro perched on one of the island stools. 'Hardly surprising, given that they all have different dads.'

Alice almost choked on that carrot chunk. 'Oh. Right,' she managed.

'I was a bit of a wild one when I was younger. I've no idea who Christina's father is. Tess is probably my ex-boyfriend's.' She lowered her voice. 'And Isabel is *probably* Ken's.' She gave Alice a slow wink.

Oh, good Lord!

There was no one like Caro Davidson in Branchfield, Indiana! At least, no one Alice knew.

She was certainly seeing life here in Scotland.

6

MELANIE - 2 AUGUST

It was shocking how much their slave, aka au pair, was expected to do. After lunch, Caro showed Donna around – the house was a maze of passages and small hallways and rooms, some leading off each other. At one point Caro opened a door onto a dusty corridor and said, 'That's the north wing. We don't use it except for storage, so don't bother cleaning in there.'

They ended the tour in the 'laundry', a room at the end of the passage off the kitchen.

'I'm afraid there's rather a build-up...' Caro waved a hand at the dirty clothes and sheets piled up on the big table in the middle of the room. A linen basket against the wall was full to overflowing. 'I'll leave you to it, shall I?' She indicated the washing liquid on the worktop by the sink. 'Just shout if you need anything.'

The washing machine and tumble drier, thankfully, were large and efficient, and Melanie made use of the line strung between two poles by the back door to dry some of it too. By the end of the day, she'd worked her way through most of the backlog in addition to cooking the evening meal and making a start on blitzing the kitchen.

Between tasks, she attempted to make friends with Isabel and Tess, but the girls remained pretty much mute in all their interactions. She managed to elicit the information from Ken that Tess's favourite foods were oatcakes, strawberries and mashed potato ('But not all at once,' he remarked, making Donna giggle appreciatively) and Isabel's were macaroni cheese, chocolate buttons and rice cakes, so perhaps she could bribe them with those. She needed to get the little brats onside to find out what, if anything, they knew.

At ten o'clock, she decided the rest of the kitchen could wait until tomorrow. Passing the small sitting room off the hall, she saw, through the half-open door, that the light was still on, although there was no sound from inside. Before switching off the light, she poked her head in to make sure no one was there.

Caro and Ken were slumped in armchairs on either side of the cold hearth, glasses in hand, three empty wine bottles on the coffee table between them. Caro raised her eyes as if this was something that took a tremendous effort.

'I'm off to bed,' said Melanie. 'Unless there's anything else...?'

'No no,' said Ken. 'You've done sterling work. Sterling. Thank you, Donna.' He lurched to his feet at the same time as attempting to set his glass down on the table. Wine slopped over the brim onto the already stained and ringed surface, which suggested this might be a regular occurrence.

'I'll get a cloth,' Melanie suggested half-heartedly.

'Tissue,' said Ken vaguely, looking about the room, turning not just his head but his whole body. 'There!' he shouted suddenly, triumphantly, pointing at the box of tissues on the table behind the sofa.

Melanie plucked a few from the box and blotted up the wine.

Caro now seemed to be asleep.

'Good night, then,' said Melanie.

'*Night night, Donna!*' boomed Ken.

Despite being bone weary, she didn't sleep. At midnight she stopped trying, got up and dressed, and made her way down through the quiet house. She looked into the little sitting room, but Caro and Ken were no longer there. The empty bottles attested to the fact that Melanie hadn't dreamt it, that the Davidsons had been in here getting pissed as newts. What if one of their traumatised children had needed them? She supposed that duty, along with everything else, would have been subcontracted to Donna.

She left the house by the back door and crossed the triangle of grass to stand by the washing line. It was a magical scene, moonlight touching the tops of the trees, the rooftops, the grass, and on the water it was a silvery road to the horizon, but there was no light of human origin and no sound apart from a brief scuffling in the trees. A fox, maybe, finishing off its prey.

Then silence again.

The night air was sharp with salt and the faint stench of rotting seaweed.

The tide must be out.

Before she was conscious of seeing or hearing anything, her subconscious, her instincts were telling her to *go*, get back to the safety of the house. She turned and ran across the grass to the door, hands stretched in front of her to guard against cannoning into anything in the dim light, all her senses straining.

And now she heard it: a tiny *scrinch, scrinch* sound, like a mouse was tiptoeing over the gravel of the parking area.

Looking over her shoulder, she realised that one of the vehicles was moving, as if of its own accord – the big Range Rover. She shrank back into the shadow of the doorway, expecting to be raked by headlights at any moment, but it reversed and then headed off round the side of the house without switching on its lights. Not even side lights.

And it must be electric, or at least hybrid, because it made not a sound.

With the beginnings of hysteria, she realised that she was thinking of the vehicle as a sentient thing. But *someone* was driving it. Someone was leaving, in the dead of night, and taking pains not to alert anyone in the house to their movements.

Why?

For a mad moment, Melanie considered following them, running up to her room for her own car keys and taking off after that Range Rover. But she'd be too late. By the time she'd done that, they'd be away.

Instead, she stationed herself at the window of the utility room. She'd wait here until they got back, and then, if the moon was still up, she would see who it was. She pulled a chair to the window, propped her elbows on the sill, and rested her chin on her hands.

Next thing she knew, she was being woken from a deep sleep by a voice saying behind her, 'Donna?'

She jumped up, the chair clattering to the floor.

In the cold, early morning light, Gray Davidson was looking at her with a knowing smile and raised eyebrows.

His hair was pulled back from his face in a ponytail, emphasising the sharp lines of his handsome features.

Melanie scanned the room. He was blocking the only exit.

She simpered at him. 'I thought I'd make a start on a bit of a deep clean. I just sat down to watch the sunrise, and I must have dropped off!'

'Caro isn't that much of a slave-driver, is she?'

'Oh – no, I... First night in a strange place! I couldn't sleep, so...'

'So you decided to make the most of your wakefulness.' His smile widened, showing those strong white teeth. 'What a good little au pair you are. But I wonder if I can persuade you into bed?'

'What?'

He opened his eyes wide at her. 'Oh, no, no! I didn't mean...' He threw back his head and laughed, and Melanie was again reminded of a wolf, baying at the moon that had just left the sky. Abruptly, he stopped and fixed her with an amused look. 'I meant your own bed, Donna – and unaccompanied.'

The way he spoke, the way he was smiling at her – if Melanie really had been a meek little thing like Donna, she'd almost have believed that it had been her mistake, that she'd jumped to a ridiculous conclusion from a perfectly innocent remark.

'Oh!' Donna giggled, as if embarrassed.

'It's only six o'clock. You've a couple of hours before anyone else surfaces.'

'Oh. Yes. Right.' Donna nodded, flustered.

He winked. 'Sweet dreams.'

And then he was gone.

Her legs were shaking. She righted the chair and subsided onto it.

When he had returned, he must have seen her at the window, slumped asleep. She glanced out of it now. The Range Rover was back in its place as if it had never left.

What had he been doing out there in the night?

Had he gone to Alice? Was he keeping her somewhere, locked up? While Melanie shrank from the thought, it was probably the only scenario in which Alice could still be alive. She wanted to run to her car, to drive around all the possible places Gray could have gone last night – but that would be hopeless.

The police had searched the area, every possible place Alice could be, for miles around. If Gray was keeping Alice prisoner, she had to be somewhere far away from Scallan Lodge. Somewhere Melanie couldn't hope to discover unless she followed him.

Tonight, she would be ready to do that.

But in the meantime, she had to consider all the other possibilities too. All the other things that could have happened to Alice.

After a quick pee and shower, she began a methodical search of the Tower Room, starting with the wardrobe in one corner and ending with the bed in the other, which she pulled out and deconstructed, taking off the mattress and even the slats under it.

Everything was remarkably spick and span, given the state of the rest of the house. Perhaps the police had cleaned the room after processing it. She found nothing of note – just a hair tie in a drawer and a woven red and orange friendship bracelet looped over a hook in the wardrobe. As Melanie ran it between her fingers and fastened it around her own wrist, she acknowledged the possibility that it hadn't even belonged to Alice. Maybe some previous occupant of the room had left it there.

But it was the sort of thing that would have been hers. Melanie could imagine it around the girl's delicate wrist – a reminder of a friend? A boyfriend?

She went to a window and looked down, to the roof several storeys below and to the unforgiving gravel below that. How new were these windows? They were the only ones in the house that had been replaced. Had Alice recklessly opened one of the old Victorian ones wide and tumbled out? Or had she and the Davidson children been messing around up here, and Alice had fallen against a window, it shattered, she fell...?

Had the family covered up what had happened, worried they'd be blamed, and quickly replaced the old windows with these ones?

She ran her hands over the join between the window and the sill. It didn't look as if it had been installed in the last few weeks. The silicone was slightly discoloured by dust and tiny bits of muck that had accumulated behind it.

At quarter to eight, Melanie made her way to the kitchen. Ken appeared half an hour later, parking his fat arse on an island stool, and groaned when she asked if he'd like a full English breakfast.

'Not feeling quite the thing,' he muttered. 'Can I just have coffee, please, Donna? Hot and strong.'

Caro was next to appear, seeming flustered and on edge as well as hungover as she drifted around the room. And then she virtually accused Donna of having lost her reading glasses.

'They were in a blue case.'

'Sorry – I haven't seen them.'

'You've moved everything around.'

Melanie felt like snapping: *Don't you mean 'Thanks so much, Donna, for clearing up our horrendous mess'?* Instead, she took a breath. 'I put all the kitchen equipment into the cupboards and other detritus into the drawers in the island or on the table. There wasn't a spectacle case.'

'If you find it, tell me.' And with that, she was gone, hardly having acknowledged Ken's presence.

Melanie supposed she should do something about the kids.

'Does Isabel get herself up and dressed, or does she need help?' she asked Ken, before it occurred to her that this might be something an experienced au pair would know without having to ask. But Melanie had no experience of seven-year-olds and their capabilities. 'I find it's always best to check,' she added. 'Kids vary so much in hitting milestones.'

Ken blinked.

He didn't know either? She was his daughter, for God's sake!

'She'll probably be fine,' he said, the sheepish expression on his face admitting, *Yes, I know, I'm hopeless.*

Melanie headed upstairs. At least there was no doubt about which room was Isabel's – the door had a china plaque on it with red roses twining around her name. Inside, the little girl was sitting on the edge of the bed. The room was gloomy and fusty.

'Good morning, Isabel!' Melanie pulled back the curtains and threw up one of the windows to let in a gust of sharp sea air.

Isabel was still wearing the grubby white onesie.

'Good morning!' Melanie repeated.

'Good morning,' Isabel whispered. She held out a hair slide and dragged another from her greasy hair. 'Can you do my hair and put these in for me?'

'How about a nice refreshing bath and hair wash first?'

It took a long time to get Isabel ready. Melanie was all fingers and thumbs plaiting her hair and arranging the slides to Isabel's satisfaction. 'That's not how Alice does it,' she kept grumbling. 'She starts the plait further up' or 'She puts the clips where the hair boofs out.'

Did Alice have younger cousins? Melanie wondered. Was she practised, as Melanie was not, in styling little girls' hair? When she'd finished, it was a weird feeling knowing that, thanks to Isabel's directions, Melanie had just replicated how Alice would have done it. She imagined Alice's gentle, clever fingers accomplishing in two minutes what had taken Melanie a quarter of an hour to achieve.

Back down in the kitchen, Isabel instructed her on how to make porridge with fruit just the way she and Tess liked it. Tess appeared, silent as usual, and began to shovel the food into her mouth.

'You must both be missing Alice,' Melanie tried as she poured them some milk.

Isabel nodded, her eyes filling with tears. Tess said nothing.

'One morning she was just *gone!*' Isabel blurted. 'I went to the Princess Room because usually she comes to mine to get me ready, but she didn't, so I went to find her.' She gulped a breath. 'And she wasn't there. Or in the kitchen. Then people found her clothes on the beach. But I think maybe Alice is playing a game.' The hope in the child's eyes was heartbreaking. 'She's just *pretending* she went for a swim.

Alice wouldn't. Not in the sea. When Mum said she'd better not swim in the sea because she wasn't good enough at it, Alice said, "Don't worry, I won't. The pool's scary enough for me." When she was little, she fell into a lake, and that put her off. But we were coaching her. To make her swim better. But only in the pool.'

This confirmed what the Snyders had said, that Alice would never have gone swimming in the sea, particularly not on her own. She was a weak swimmer and was well aware of the fact.

'She's not playing a game,' said Tess. She was staring at Melanie. There was something very unsettling about Tess, the watchfulness of her, the way she looked at Melanie as if she were the person she hated most in the world.

Unbelievably, Tess had already finished the whole bowl of porridge. She picked up the glass of milk, drained it as if performing an important task against the clock, and got up from the table.

'So, what plans do you two have for today?' said Melanie.

'None of your business,' said Tess, and left the room.

Isabel grimaced. 'Sorry about that. Tess is searching the woods. She knows places the police and people might not have looked. She's already done the birchwood, and now she's starting on the plantation by the road. Can we look for Alice too? Can we look for clues?'

Melanie nodded. This would be good cover for her own search of the place. 'That's a great idea.' Was it, though? Would Isabel's parents feel this was morbid and inappropriate? 'Brush your teeth first,' she said, as a nod to being a responsible childminder.

7

ALICE - 1 JULY

The dream was back. Alice was at the cottage door this time, and when she pounded on it, an angry voice from inside said, 'What are *you* doing here? *Go away!*'

But the next morning, the dream was gone, the sun was out, and Alice and Isabel were able to get outside and have some fun. Alice felt like she was seven years old again herself as they invented a whole world for their game, in which they were a pair of crime-busting sisters lying concealed in the long grass, ready to creep up on a gang who'd stolen the Scottish crown jewels from Edinburgh Castle.

Unwittingly, Christina and her mean girl friends were that gang. The four of them had been swanning around the house earlier, giving Alice orders and imitating her accent. Now, they were relaxing around the pool, which was hidden away from the house behind a belt of trees. There was a pool house converted from what looked like an old stone barn, and a table with a parasol, and loungers. The girls were all sleeping in the sun, and Alice was debating whether she should break cover and tell them to top up on sunscreen when Ken appeared, lumbering towards them through the grass on all fours like a bear that had just come out of hibernation.

'Target sighted?' he whispered. 'Who's got the rifle?'

Isabel giggled. 'There's no *rifle*, Dad! We're not the bad people – *they* are.'

'That's no fun. Okay, but if we *were* the bad people, who would you take out first?'

'Selina,' said Isabel and Alice in the same breath, making all three of them choke back snorts of laughter.

Selina was the worst of the mean girls, a snooty miss who treated Alice like she was invisible. She was lying on a lounger, her narrow face slack, mouth open – an Instagram nightmare. Alice wished she had not a rifle but a long-range lens.

That was the thing about mean girls. If you weren't careful, they could turn you the same way, like the mean was a virus that infected anyone who got too near for too long. Apparently these were Christina's old friends from her private school, which she'd left a year ago after some sort of boy trouble. Now she attended the local regular school, but Caro said she hadn't made friends yet and still hung out with these girls. Other rich girls, Alice guessed.

She'd caught them all smoking pot in the library earlier. At least, Alice assumed it was pot. It smelt sweet, and the cigarettes weren't from a packet, they were the kind you rolled yourself, droopy and thin. Christina had blown smoke right at Alice when she'd asked what it was. But when Alice had told Ken, he'd just puffed out his cheeks and said, 'They're going to do it anyway – at least here we can keep an eye on them.'

'Retreat, retreat!' Ken suddenly hissed.

Christina had sat up on her lounger and taken off her sunglasses. And now she was scowling right at them. Isabel squealed, jumped to her feet and started running through the long grass to the trees. Suddenly Tess was there too, running alongside her sister. She must have been creeping up on Alice and Isabel as the two of them were creeping up on the pool house. The two girls disappeared into the wood.

Five seconds later, one of them screamed, long and high.

As Alice and Ken ran towards the sound, a deep laugh rang around the garden, and Gray appeared from the trees, a stag's head swinging from one hand. His eyes met Alice's, and he lifted the animal's head to cover his own face. The effect was disturbing, like one of those primitive gods that were half man, half beast.

Isabel ran at her daddy. Ken swept her up in his arms and glared at Gray.

'You've really frightened her!'

'Sorry, Izz,' said the half-man/half-beast airily, obviously not sorry at all.

'Hey, shall we go get a snack?' said Alice, rubbing Isabel's back.

'Your... biscuits?' asked Isabel between gulps of tears.

'Sure. They're oat and rye cookies,' Alice hastened to add, in case Ken thought she was feeding the kids junk. 'We can have them with some tomatoes.'

'I... want... *human meat*,' groaned Gray, animating the stag's head to nod in time with the words.

'Okey-dokey,' said Alice lightly. 'One human-burger coming up. I wonder what Tess would like.'

'Tess ran off,' choked Isabel.

Gray laughed ruefully. 'Not before aiming a few swift

kicks at my shins.'.

'Good for Tess,' growled Ken. 'Come on then, Izz.' He set Isabel on her feet and took her hand.

Isabel looked up at Alice. 'Can we have some cheese with the biscuits?'

Calcium was good for kids. 'Sure!'

Alice followed Ken and Isabel across the lawn, and Gray fell into step alongside her.

'In my defence,' he said, 'I've just spent two hours on the phone to a suit in Canary Wharf, trying to persuade him to part with his investors' dubiously earned cash. We're trying to get a glamping venture off the ground, so schmoozing the suits is the order of the day. But those guys –' He grimaced. 'Something had to give.'

'So you let off steam by scaring the living daylights out of your nieces?'

He lifted the stag's head to cover his face again. 'What can I say? I'm not good with kids.'

Alice bit back a smile. 'I hope your shins ache.'

'Oh, do you, indeed? Not a very Christian attitude, Ali.' He lowered the stag's head and grinned at her.

Alice was suddenly conscious of the fact that she wasn't wearing much in the way of clothing – the cut-offs Mom didn't know she possessed and the cute white halter-neck top she'd bought at the airport.

'God moves in a mysterious way,' she said, feeling herself flush a little. 'His wonders to perform.'

'Hmm. Whatever that little kick-boxer is channelling, I don't think it's divine.' Gray laughed and threw the stag's head up in the air. Its antlers looked a little like wings, Alice thought fancifully, as it flew up and then tumbled back to earth, bouncing a couple of times on the grass.

'Poor thing,' said Alice. 'As if it hasn't already suffered enough.'

'Alas, poor Randolf.' Gray retrieved the head and patted the top of it. 'One of Ken's kills. You wouldn't think it, would you, but my brother's a crack shot. Poor old Randolf was never an alpha stag. And he really lost condition after last year's rut.' He sliced a hand across his throat.

'Survival of the fittest, huh?'

'Indeed. But I wouldn't have thought you'd be a believer in evolution and its mechanisms, Ali.'

'It's a squeeze to fit it all into six thousand years, but I guess God could do it.'

For a beat he looked at her.

She chuckled. 'Sorry, couldn't resist. I'm a Christian, but I'm not stupid. That Old Testament stuff about the age of the Earth isn't meant to be taken *literally*. God and evolution aren't mutually exclusive.'

'Ha, you got me!' He pushed a hand through his mane of hair, and Alice found herself staring at the strong line of his tanned jaw. 'Gail was never this entertaining.'

'Gail?'

'Our old housekeeper. Never cracked a smile. Mind you, if you've got a face like a fish, that may be physiologically impossible. Imagine an angry halibut dressed in black Primark trousers and a mint-green polyester top and you've got the general idea.'

Alice spluttered. 'Oh, *mean!*'

As if on cue, a voice said, 'Alice?'

She turned to see Christina marching through the long grass. 'Can you bring us something to eat? And some cold drinks? With ice? We're all on the fizzy water, and there're only a couple of bottles left in the fridge.'

The pool house had its own little kitchen.

'Sure,' said Alice.

Christina was looking from Alice to Gray and opening her mouth again, but Gray pre-empted her with, 'What did your last slave die of?'

Christina gave him a disgusted sneer and turned on her heel.

'All the kids are spoilt brats,' Gray said, loudly enough for Christina to hear. 'Each in her own way. Caro and Ken let them away with murder.'

'And what's your excuse?'

'*I'm* not *spoilt!*' Gray stamped his foot, screwing up his face. 'And *I – want – cookies!*'

'Okay, okay!' Alice laughed. 'Don't have a meltdown, Graham!'

As she served cookies and juice to Ken, Gray and Isabel, Alice almost danced around that kitchen. She felt like she was fizzing inside, and could hardly attend to the conversation as the other three sat around the island talking about what rye actually was.

She knew it was wrong.

She knew that what she and Gray were doing was Flirtation with a capital *F*. Alice had a boyfriend. And Gray wasn't even a nice guy. Randolf's head, perched now on the dresser by the door, seemed to look at her reproachfully. It had been totally not cool, scaring the kids like that.

Mom and Daddy would hate Gray. They'd be horrified if they could see inside her head right now.

'I'd better get those snacks for Christina,' she muttered.

She put some cookies, cheese and tomatoes, a selection of other snacks and the waters on a tray and carried it out to the pool.

Christina pushed her huge sunglasses up off her nose and looked at the tray. 'Oh, Alice, *honey*. You Americans and your supersize appetites. There are only four of us. There must be, like, ten thousand calories here.'

'And mostly empty ones,' drawled Selina. 'A full-fat dip. And are those fucking *Doritos*?'

Alice winced at the swear word.

Christina burst out laughing. 'Potty mouth! Is that what you'd call it, Alice? I bet you've never said *fuck* in your life.'

As if that was something to be ashamed of! Alice hated to hear folks use the f-word. It was so aggressive and unnecessary. As Mom said, there were so many powerful words in the English language, nobody had to use that one.

'No, I have not, Christina.' But she could feel herself blushing. Christina was two years younger than Alice, and Alice was in a position of authority over her, but the girl made her feel like she'd just rolled into town on the last load of hay.

She had a sudden yearning for Skip, for her friends, Kimmy and Parker and Jasmine, who had their faults, sure, but were fundamentally good people. They'd have bent over backwards to make a stranger feel welcome. As Skip said, just because you were a teenager didn't mean you had to be a heel.

'Have you ever said *bugger*?' Christina took one of the sparkling waters from the tray and held it to her bony breastbone.

'*Bastard*?' suggested one of the other girls.

'*Bastard*'s not so bad. You could start with that,' said Christina helpfully. 'Go on, Alice. Say *bastard*.'

Alice had, of course, been around people who cursed, but none of her close friends did so. Not even Skip and his buddies, as far as she knew. They used words like 'heel' rather than anything stronger, at least in her presence, like the old-fashioned gentlemen they were. That was what Mom called Skip: *an old-fashioned gentleman.*

What if Skip could have seen her with Gray just now?

She took a breath. 'Does it make you uncomfortable that I don't swear?'

'Yes!' said Selina. 'You're triggering us!'

They all laughed.

'Run along, Pollyanna!' chortled Christina.

Alice bit back a retort. *Don't descend to their level,* Mom would say. But as she walked away, she felt like she could cry – which was pathetic. She needed to pull herself together in more ways than one.

She was going to have a really fun, interesting time at Scallan Lodge, and prove to Mom and Daddy that she could hold down a responsible job all the way across the Atlantic. Then maybe they would agree to her going travelling next summer, or maybe even deferring and taking a gap year before she started her history degree at IU Bloomington.

On the other hand, maybe they'd be so angry about Alice running off that they'd never let her go anywhere ever again.

She wouldn't have had to run off, though, if they hadn't been totally unreasonable in the first place. Pretty much *everyone* went backpacking in Europe the summer after they'd finished high school! But not Alice. Oh no. Daddy had sat her down and told her it wasn't happening; she couldn't go 'off to the other side of the world' with Kimmy, Parker and Jasmine. Alice didn't have the 'necessary maturity and worldly wisdom', even though she'd held down a summer job with the local veterinarian for three years straight despite being bitten more times than she could count and having to have stitches twice. Alice was way more mature than Kimmy Brown. Kimmy couldn't go to the orthodontist without wanting her mom there to literally hold her hand, but her parents had been *Go for it* and helped the girls research cheap, safe places to stay.

The argument that Alice wasn't mature enough was, of course a smokescreen for the real reason Daddy and Mom, but especially Mom, didn't want Alice anywhere near Scotland.

She had tagged along to the bus depot to see Kimmy, Parker and Jasmine off on their big adventure, pretending to be happy for them, and they'd all cried and hugged, and the girls had promised they'd do it again next year with Alice.

Alice had gone straight home and googled 'summer jobs Europe'.

She needed to get a job – she couldn't get her hands on enough ready cash to join the girls backpacking.

The au pair ad had jumped out at her. It had been quirky and amusing, saying things like 'If you don't mind being stuck in the middle of nowhere with a bunch of crackpots, this is the job for you'. It had seemed like fate that the location was the Scottish Highlands, just sixty miles from Inverness. Then Alice had had a big row with Daddy about not doing her yard chores. Alice had spoken back and told him it was exploitation and she was the only kid she knew who didn't get paid for doing chores, and Daddy had said other parents' poor choices weren't his problem, which was pretty much what he'd said about Kimmy, Jasmine and Parker going to Europe.

In between the crying jags, Alice had put together her application and emailed it off.

The Davidsons had got back to her immediately, and

she'd had a video conference with Caro that same night. Caro had liked Alice, and Alice had liked her, and Alice had said sure, she could start work on June 30, the first day of the Davidson kids' school vacation. She didn't need to wait to get a visa – she had dual American-British nationality because she'd been born in the UK. Her parents had lived in Edinburgh for a short time back then.

She had taken her passport and, shockingly, five hundred dollars from the church collection. Daddy, who was an accountant, was the church treasurer, and he kept the collection money locked in the top drawer of his desk until he could get it to the bank, but Alice knew where he hid the key.

Daddy must be so ashamed of her right now.

It wasn't just any kind of stealing – it was stealing from disabled orphans. She couldn't help imagining those little kids in wheelchairs pressing their noses against a window as the lady who should be bringing the toys and computers and books came sadly up the walk, shaking her head, empty-handed.

It wasn't even like that would happen.

Daddy would replace the money. Probably add a whole lot more out of guilt on Alice's behalf, even though, she guessed, he wouldn't tell anyone but Mom what she'd done.

Don't think about it.

She crossed the lawn to the conservatory door. She could carry on vacuuming the rooms on the ground floor, and then find Caro and ask what she wanted done about the bedrooms. They were private spaces, and maybe each person preferred to clean their own room.

She made her way to the smallest lounge room (there were three!), where she'd left the vacuum cleaner, and was just plugging it in when she saw Caro through the open door, coming out of the library.

'Caro!' Alice scooted into the hall. 'I was just going to ask you –'

'What on earth are you wearing?'

Alice blinked.

'Alice.' Caro sighed. 'I know the weather's taken a turn for the better, but such... *revealing* clothing isn't appropriate.'

Alice looked down at her little halter-neck top and shorts. She guessed the top was tight and virtually backless, and the shorts were short, but Christina and her friends were out there right this minute in *bikinis*!

The tears she'd been holding back overflowed.

She'd thought Caro was so cool, but she was just as judgy as anyone in Branchfield!

Caro sighed again. 'Go and change into something more... modest.'

'Your daughter's out there right now in a *teeny tiny bikini*!' Alice found herself sobbing.

'That's pool wear. If she started flaunting herself about the house dressed like that, I'd –'

'I'm not *flaunting* myself!'

'Alice. Go and change, and then take some time out. Come and see me when you've calmed down, and we'll have a conversation about what is and isn't acceptable behaviour.'

And now she sounded just like one of Alice's teachers!

In the Princess Room, she changed into jeans and a T-shirt and sneakers, and then she ran back down the stairs and along all those twisty-turny passages and down through the hallway and out of the house. She wasn't going to 'see' Caro! She was out of here for the rest of the morning, and Caro could see how she liked it, doing all Alice's work!

8

MELANIE - 3 AUGUST

Isabel hurried from the kitchen, intent on the clue hunt, and almost collided in the doorway with her eldest sister Christina, who snapped, 'Watch where you're going!' without looking up from her phone.

'I'll have half a grapefruit and some toast,' she told Melanie, sitting down at the table and pushing away Isabel's dirty porridge bowl. 'Get this mess cleared up – I don't want to look at it.' Her lip lifted in distaste. 'Just a thin scrape of butter on the toast. And God, I need *coffee*. A latte – with *skimmed* milk and no froth.'

'I'm afraid I have other things to do, Christina,' said Melanie sweetly. 'I have to supervise Isabel. I'm sure you'll manage to make your own breakfast.'

Christina looked up, her plump mouth falling open. 'Uh, it's your *job*?'

'Nope. I'm an au pair, not a slave.' Melanie came over to the table. 'And I would be neglecting my duties if I didn't at least attempt to reform you.'

'What?'

'Going to run to Mummy and Daddy and tell them what nasty M– Donna said? Well, newsflash – no one wants their child growing up an entitled bitch, and I think when I've explained how I aim to prevent that happening, they'll be one hundred per cent behind me. Oh, and after you've had your breakfast, you can load the dishwasher. Tablets are in the drawer under the draining board, in case you're not aware.'

Shit.

Donna would never have said any of that.

'I'm sorry,' she backtracked hurriedly. 'I'm just feeling a bit stressed trying to keep on top of everything. I'd really appreciate your help!' And she gave the scowling Christina a big smile before hurrying from the room.

Melanie and Isabel started their search in the library, a huge room lined with chaotic bookcases. The hearth in the imposing Victorian fireplace had ashes all over it, testament to the fact that fires could be needed any month of the year in Scotland.

'There are too many books.' Isabel's lip trembled. 'If Alice left a clue in one of them, we'll *never* find it.'

'What kind of books does Alice like to read?'

'She likes funny books with cute animals! *Don't Let the Pigeon Drive the Bus*! We both *love* it! And *Don't Let the Pigeon Stay Up Late* and *The Pigeon Wants a Puppy*! But they're up in my room. Will I get them? And she gave Tess a book called *My Side of the Mountain*. She said it was her favourite when she was Tess's age. It's probably in Tess's room.'

'We can check those later. What about grown-up books?'

'She likes adventure books. There was one about a lady who went to Africa in the olden days.' Isabel's face fell. 'I can't remember what it was called.'

'How about we go round the bookcases looking for any books you remember seeing her reading? You might recognise the covers?'

Isabel nodded. 'I might do.'

As they worked their way around the room, Melanie gently probed about the Davidson family. 'Does Christina have a holiday job?'

Isabel giggled. 'No. Christina says she's already saving this family a shitload of money by going to a school for losers where half the kids have scurvy. She says there's nothing to eat in the canteen that isn't either chips or made from animals' bums and...' She frowned. 'Go-mads? But she's just angry that Mum and Dad can't afford for her to stay at her old school where all her horrible friends are.'

Melanie left Isabel looking for 'Alice' books in the library and headed upstairs. Gray was on his way down, a rucksack slung over one shoulder, Ordnance Survey map in hand. He was dressed in toffee-coloured cargo pants and a cotton khaki jumper, the outdoorsy look elevated, as he would probably think of it, by a fringed red and black scarf.

Melanie stood back against the wall to let him past, but he stopped when he was level with her, not moving to the banister side as most people would have, but staying in the centre of the staircase and invading her personal space.

'Good *morning*,' he said, his voice purring on the words as if he'd just said something suggestive. 'And how did you sleep, in the end?'

'Oh, fine, thanks!' Donna blinked up at him.

'I'm off out – won't be back for lunch. Got a packed one in here.' He jiggled the rucksack and then, for just a beat, his whole body, as if they had been transported to the dance floor of some seedy nightclub and he was trying his moves on her.

Melanie averted her gaze. 'Well, enjoy your walk.'

Gray probably spent a lot of time outdoors. On an early morning walk, could he have come across Alice on the beach when no one else was about? Could he have assaulted her, and when she resisted...

What?

Dragged her into the sea? Or into that Range Rover?

For a horrible moment, she thought something must have shown in her expression, because Gray brought his face close to hers and said, in a stage whisper, 'Your secret is safe with me, Donna.'

She recoiled. '*What?*'

'That you have a penchant for clandestine late-night... *cleaning.*' He whispered the last word, his eyes full of laughter.

Donna played along. 'I'm like those guerrilla gardeners who plant up streets with flowers in the middle of the night – except I clean skirting boards.'

'People will come from all over Scallan Lodge to marvel and ask one another, in hushed tones, "Who is this worker of overnight wonders, who brings us hygienic and sanitary conditions?"'

He guffawed and carried on down the stairs, that mane of glossy locks bouncing on his broad shoulders, and Melanie felt it almost like a physical force trailing behind him, the magnetic power of the man's personality. It made Melanie shudder, but possibly only because of what she knew, or at least suspected. The way he had of laughing with you, in particular – it would be dangerously attractive to a very young, very inexperienced woman.

How could Alice fail to fall under his spell?

She took a breath, squared her shoulders and carried on upstairs.

After a few wrong turns, she found the 'north wing', which Caro had told her not to bother about. It consisted of a corridor off which were grubby rooms with peeling wallpaper and damp patches on the ceilings. Some of the rooms were empty, and others contained shabby furniture, old bikes, piles of magazines and other detritus. A steep staircase at the end of the corridor took her downstairs to more of the same.

She returned to the first floor and the part of the house that contained the family bedrooms. Christina's room was neat and tidy, and a cursory poke through drawers and the walk-in wardrobe turned up nothing but a half-empty packet of cigarettes. Tess's and Isabel's rooms she didn't bother to search. Along a corridor and up a couple of steps was what she supposed they'd call the master suite – the largest bedroom, a dressing room and a huge bathroom. It was messy, the bed rumpled. She imagined Caro and Ken passed out here last night.

The other doors she opened gave onto guest rooms, bathrooms, cupboards... One door was locked, which, by a process of elimination, she guessed must be the door of Gray's bedroom. Interesting. When Caro had shown Melanie around, she'd indicated the door next to the big 'drawing room' and told her not to bother with that room, Gray's study. 'He keeps it locked anyway.'

There was no way to get into his bedroom, but the study might be another matter. Melanie made her way outside and peered into the window next to the conservatory. It was a huge Victorian one, the top and bottom sections fastened, unfortunately, by a catch. If she had a knife, she could maybe insert it in the gap and wiggle the catch open...

Something moved.

Gray was in there?

No. Thank God. The movement was in the reflection of the garden.

She jumped away from the window and smiled at Caro, who was coming across the grass towards her.

'What are you doing, Donna?'

She thought quickly. 'There's a butterfly trapped in that room.'

Caro peered through the glass, cupping her hands around her face to get a better look inside. 'That's Gray's study. Wherever he is, it won't be long before he's back – he spends ninety per cent of his time holed up in there. Not that I'm complaining.' She gave Melanie a look. 'Leave a note on the door telling him to open the window so it can get out.'

'Okay. Oh, I was going to ask you – the windows in my room don't seem to open. At least, I can't find the key to the locks on them. Are they new? All the others –' She indicated the study window. 'They're the old-fashioned Victorian kind.'

'We decided to replace the windows in the Tower Room for safety reasons. It's so high up, and with young children in the house... We shouldn't really have done it – the house is listed, and there are all sorts of restrictions as to what you can do. But no one ever checks up. We went for toughened glass, and we keep the windows locked at all times – I hope you don't mind? They're vented to all the up-to-date standards, so you needn't worry about poor airflow or anything.'

'No, that's fine. Well, I'd better go and see what Isabel's up to.'

'I was going to ask you – Ken, Tess, Isabel and I are heading out to a barbeque this afternoon, so would you mind keeping an eye on Christina and her friends? Make sure they don't get up to mischief? They tend to hang out around the pool.' She sighed. 'Christina's fragile at the moment, and those friends of hers... Alice said they were "toxic", and I must say she had a point.'

'It sounds like Alice had a wise head on young shoulders.'

Had.

Melanie was thinking of Alice in the past tense, she realised with a sudden, strange buzzing sensation in her head, as if she were about to pass out.

Caro grimaced. 'Oh, not really – she was a silly, naïve young girl.'

Well, of course she was silly and naïve. She was only *eighteen years old*!

'I don't know what I was thinking hiring her in the first place. If I'd been thinking straight... If I hadn't... Turns out she was a runaway. Her parents didn't even know where she was.'

Melanie nodded numbly. 'A terrible shock for them.' And as Caro frowned at her, she added hastily, 'I googled Alice after you said she'd gone missing.' Well, Donna would have done, wouldn't she? It was only natural.

'Poor things.' Caro shook her head. 'Alice really wasn't au pair material. She would just drop her work and go off out – sometimes with the littlies, sometimes not. We regularly have paying guests for the shooting and fishing, and Alice couldn't cope with them. I'm afraid she wasn't at all reliable. In fact, I would say she was... unstable. Possibly she had issues of some sort. I don't know, I'm not a psychiatrist.'

Was this victim blaming?

Or had Alice Snyder really been as troubled as Caro was implying?

Could she have deliberately put herself in danger in the sea?

'You, on the other hand, are obviously a well-balanced individual.' Caro was frowning at her. 'You've never wanted to branch out into something better paid?'

Melanie had filled Donna's CV with au pair and nanny jobs, one after the other, ever since she'd left school at sixteen.

'Oh, no,' she gushed. 'It suits me down to the ground. I've been to some wonderful places. Looked after some great kids. I love my job!'

Too much?

Caro's expression was sceptical. 'I can't think of anything worse than looking after other people's kids! My own are bad enough. Some days, five minutes with the little buggers and I'm ready to slit my wrists! Or theirs!'

She was joking, of course, but even so, Melanie had to repress a grimace.

'Maybe I won't want to do this forever,' she agreed slowly. 'I have thought about going to teacher training college, becoming a primary teacher.'

Caro frowned. Had she noticed that Melanie actually seemed a bit clueless around children? Had Tess blabbed about Melanie offering her a coffee? ('I'm not allowed!') Had Isabel mentioned that Melanie had tried to take her hand to help her downstairs? ('I'm not *three years old*!')

But, 'A laudable ambition,' was all Caro said.

As Melanie was preparing lunch with Isabel's 'help', Tess suddenly appeared and plonked herself down at the table.

Isabel immediately abandoned the tomatoes she'd been arranging on a plate and went to sit opposite her sister.

'Me and Donna have been looking for clues in the house and the sheds and the garages and the pool house and the boiler room and *everywhere*!'

Tess nodded, giving Melanie an appraising look. 'Good. Did you find anything?'

Isabel slumped, leaning her chin on her hands. 'No. Did you?'

Tess shook her head.

'You really think Alice could be – what, hiding in the woods?' Melanie set a plate of sandwiches down on the table in front of the girls.

'Of course not.' Tess grabbed a sandwich, but then let it drop onto her plate. 'I'm looking for her body.'

Isabel wailed, 'Don't *say* that!'

'Well, she's bound to be dead, isn't she?'

Melanie reached out a hand and rubbed Isabel's arm. 'Now, we don't know anything yet. Let's not jump to conclusions.' She sat down, and the little girl left her chair to climb onto Melanie's lap, turning her face into her fleece.

Melanie jiggled her, murmuring empty reassurances. 'You girls are very fond of Alice, aren't you?'

'We *love* her!' Isabel sobbed. 'Alice is the *best*!' She wriggled off Melanie's lap. 'I forgot the books! I'm going to get them from our rooms and see if Alice wrote anything in them.'

When she'd gone, Melanie turned to Tess, who was sitting glaring at the sandwich she wasn't eating. Very gently, she asked, 'What makes you think Alice is dead?'

Tess hunched her thin shoulders.

Melanie touched her back.

Tess suddenly turned on her. 'I know what you're thinking!' Her green eyes were fierce. 'Alice was only here for twenty-three days, so how could we really care about her? But some people – you can know them for years and years and not care about them at all, and other people – other people...' She gulped.

'You just click,' said Melanie quietly.

Tess nodded angrily. 'But she's dead now.'

'Why do you think that?'

At first, Melanie thought Tess wasn't going to answer. Then: 'Alice was scared.' It was hardly more than a whisper, but it was like a punch to Melanie's stomach.

'Scared? Of what?'

'I don't know. She wouldn't say.' Tess suddenly pushed her chair back, the legs squealing on the flagstone floor.

'Do you think it was –'

'I don't know, do I?' Tess's face contorted. 'I *don't know!*'

MELANIE HAD no intention of babysitting the awful Christina and her no doubt equally awful friends. When Ken, Caro and the younger girls had left for their barbeque, she decided to take the opportunity to get into Gray's study. If anyone caught her, she could always say she was worried about the mythical butterfly.

She selected a range of knives from the kitchen and returned to the window.

The larger knives were no good – she couldn't angle them up between the frames of the two sections of the window. Too inflexible.

In the end, an ordinary butter knife did the job. It was small and bendy enough to wiggle up and under the 'leg' of the catch. By jiggling the knife at the same time as pushing up on the lower frame of the window, Melanie managed to slip the catch open.

The window was stiff, though, and required all her strength to open, her arm and shoulder muscles protesting as she pushed it up. But at last there was a Melanie-sized gap between the sill and the bottom of the window, and she limboed through it.

Gray evidently never opened the window. The air in the study was foetid, slightly sweet, cloying. There were two dirty coffee cups on the desk and a mouldy banana on a plate. Unlike in the rest of the house, everything in here was new – sectional bookcases, filing cabinet, office-style desk and chair. On one wall there were framed photographs taken, presumably, at various events held by Bring It On. Randoms and minor celebrities, even a few household names, were featured cosying up to Gray and beaming at the camera against the backdrop of a floodlit marquee or an old paddleboat or a grand room with a party in full swing. As Melanie looked along the rows of pictures, she realised that, in addition to their wealth, the people in them all had one thing in common.

They were all female.

From fresh-faced teenagers to elderly *grand dames*, the women seemed more than happy to pose with Gray, their eyes dancing, mouths relaxed in genuine, beaming smiles.

They were having fun.

For the first time, a shiver of doubt ran through her. Gray Davidson was obnoxious and self-centred and vain – but the charges against him had been dropped, after all. Was he just a highly promiscuous man who, by the law of averages, was sometimes going to flirt or sleep with a woman with issues, a woman who would cry rape when discarded?

There was a big photograph of Gray on his own, obviously professionally done. He was posing up a storm, literally, against a backdrop of thunderclouds, hair streaming out behind him as he looked into the middle distance, eyes narrowed as if contemplating the profundities of the universe itself.

All this confirmed what Melanie had felt about Gray from the start – he was a complete narcissist. There were no photos of his family, not even Ken or Caro with clients. No drawings or home-made wonky containers or fluffy hamsters like Melanie's boyfriend, Grant, had in the room he laughingly called his study. Grant's nieces and nephews were always making him stuff, and he was touchingly proud of their very dubious artistic talents.

The thought of Grant had guilt nipping at her.

When she'd decided to take the au pair job at Scallan Lodge, she hadn't confided in him because he'd have been horrified by the danger she was walking into. He'd have tried to stop her or tried to come with her or in some other way queered her pitch. She hadn't lied to him – she'd just said she had to go away for a while, and he hadn't pressed her. The romantic side of their relationship was still very new, and they were being careful to respect each other's independence.

But what would he say if he could see her now?

She started with the box files on the bookcases, but they just contained financial stuff, contact lists, government publications detailing various rules and regulations. The filing cabinet was locked.

She turned her attention to the laptop on the desk, opening it and turning it on.

As it was booting up, a high-pitched voice drifted in at the open window.

'Oh my God, look at the state of this one.'

Melanie ducked down behind the desk, but she needn't have worried. Crawling to the window and peeping over the sill, she saw that the gaggle of teenage girls coming out of the conservatory were intent on the screen of a phone.

'I know,' said Christina brightly, trying to grab the phone from the thin girl in possession of it. 'She's in my class. I followed her because she followed me – she only has, like, three hundred followers, and I felt bad for her.'

The girl held the phone out of Christina's reach. 'The *really* tragic thing is that she must have thought, "Yeah, I look so hot in this! My muffin top squidging over my Tesco jeans is going to get me at least eight likes from all my discerning followers!"'

One of the other girls screeched. 'And look at the comments! Do you think they're ironic?'

None of them even seemed to notice that the study window was open and a selection of knives were lying right there on the ground next to it. They walked away along the path through the trees that led to the pool. Melanie didn't know what made her look up, but when she did, she saw a boy perched amongst the foliage of a sycamore tree. He had a pale, soft-looking face and gingerish hair and was staring not at the girls but straight at Melanie.

And then his face was gone.

Shit.

Had he seen her crawl in through the window?

Would he tell Christina?

If Christina challenged her, she'd just have to go with the butterfly story.

She returned to the desk and the laptop, but, as she'd expected, it was password-protected, and she didn't know Gray well enough to be able to guess what his password might be. She tried a few variations of BringItOn, but nothing worked.

If he was some sort of sexual predator, he'd be careful, wouldn't he? He wasn't going to leave any incriminating evidence lying around or easily accessible on a computer.

Gray had an alibi – he was supposedly in London at the time of Alice's disappearance – but it would be easy enough to set something up to satisfy the police, who were not, after all, seriously looking at any alternative explanations for Alice's tragic accidental drowning.

She stood and looked again at the photographs – all those women, stuck up on the wall like a stamp collection.

Melanie knew, deep in her gut, that this man was dangerous.

Tonight, if he left the house again, she had to be ready to follow him.

She left the way she'd come in, shutting the window and attempting to flick the catch back in place with the butter knife, but she couldn't manage it. She would have to just leave it unlocked and hope that Gray wouldn't notice.

9

ALICE - 3 JULY

'Now let's have Alice on her own,' said Gray, hustling Tess and Isabel aside with all the bossiness of a professional photographer. 'Run along, girls.'

Tess glared at him. 'I didn't want my photo taken in the first place.'

It was a perfect day for photographs, the sky blue and cloudless, light dancing on the ocean. The sand was so fine it was almost like warm liquid, sifting between Alice's bare toes as she tramped across it to the place Gray indicated.

'Just the sea, the sky and the babe,' he said, flicking his hair off his face and lifting the expensive-looking camera with its big lens.

Alice and the kids had only been on the beach ten minutes when he'd appeared, eating up the sand with that long-legged stride, hair swinging, eyes sparkling. He'd had a camera case slung over one shoulder.

'I need human interest!' he'd informed them airily. 'I suppose you lot will do.'

He seemed to be taking ages, fiddling with the settings on the camera, and Alice turned away to check on Isabel and Tess. They were both hunched over a rock pool, Tess no doubt explaining to Isabel about the creatures in it. That would keep Isabel interested for about five seconds.

'Ali?'

She turned back to Gray and the camera.

'Relax! Act natural!'

Being told to do that always made Alice tense up as she tried to work out how the heck you looked natural when posing for a picture.

'Let's lose the baggy sweatshirt,' Gray suggested. 'It's as if you've purposely gone out and selected the only garment in the shop that doesn't suit you.'

'Well, thank you!'

'That was a backhanded compliment.'

Alice grinned. 'Good to know.' But she pulled off the hoodie and let Gray take it from her.

He tossed it onto the sand. 'Begone, vile raiment!'

Alice laughed, although she wanted to pick it up and pull it back on. The breeze off the sea was a little chilly.

He set the camera down on a rock and came over to her. 'Hmm. What's underneath isn't much better, is it?'

Alice looked down at herself. She was wearing a white T-shirt and an orange skirt that came to her knees. Ever since Caro had got on her case about her clothing, she'd been careful to cover up.

'You have very photogenic arms,' he said.

'*Arms?*' Alice snorted.

'Have you *never* been *complimented* on your *arms*?' Gray closed a hand around one of her elbows, gently, almost reverently, and pushed up the short sleeve of her T-shirt, tucking it into her bra strap. Then he ran his fingers down the whole length of her arm, his touch feather-light, sending shivers through Alice's whole body.

'The human form,' he said softly. 'In all its glory.'

Could arms blush? Alice was sure hers were right now.

'No photograph can really do it justice.' He smiled, contemplating her. And now he was pulling at the waistband of her skirt, rolling it so that the material folded over and over again. His knuckles kept touching her stomach, making the soft skin there kind of jump with the tickliness of it. When he was done, the skirt's hem brushed the middle of her thighs instead of her knees.

'That's better.' He stepped back, eyes narrowed, as she imagined an artist would look at his model. That was all this was, then? She was just an object for his photography?

He picked up the camera again and fiddled with it. She wished he would put it down, come back to her, touch her again –

Skip was suddenly in her head. *He* touched her like he was ticking off bullet points in a *How to Get to Second Base* manual. Schoolboy fumblings, as Kimmy had described her own boyfriend's moves.

Gray had probably slept with a lot of girls. Women.

He would know exactly what –

Oh my goodness! What was she thinking?

Alice wasn't going to sleep with *anyone* until she was at least engaged, let alone some guy she'd only just met!

Gray started clicking off shots, telling her to back up, get her feet in the water, put her *beautiful arms* above her head.

'Botticelli,' he murmured, coming closer, squatting on the sand and angling the camera up at her, then stepping away again for a different shot, tossing his hair out of his eyes. She loved his glossy hair, the way it flowed, rippled, slipped –

'You know the painting I mean?' he continued. '*The Birth of Venus*. Late 1400s.' He came right up to her again, and she dropped her arms, folding them under her chest. What her body was feeling, where her brain was going – it was all *so wrong* in so many ways! She needed him not to touch her, and he seemed to sense this, just giving her a quirk of a smile. 'Venus rising from the waves. She was born fully formed as a woman – a *naked* woman, naturally. The painting depicts her standing on a giant clamshell, being blown to the shore by Zephyr. Waiting on land to cover her nakedness with a cloak is the Hora of Spring.'

'Goodness,' said Alice.

'You should google it. You look a little like her. It's always been one of my favourite depictions of a woman in art. She's modest, is young Venus, covering her breasts and sex with her hands, but at the same time she's not ashamed of her body. Her expression is entirely serene.' And now he did touch her, just a light brush of a finger against her wrist, the braided bracelet against her hand, but it made Alice shiver again. 'Let's try to recreate it, shall we? Don't worry, I'm not suggesting you strip off! But if you could stand like this...'

He put one hand to his chest and the other between his legs. 'She had a handful of her own long hair in her left hand, to completely cover *this* area.' He squeezed his crotch. 'If you sort of bunch up your skirt, we'll get the same effect.'

He was always wrong-footing her, she thought wildly, as she inched her right hand up to her left breast. She felt off-balance with him, as if he were teaching her a scary new skill, like roller-skating or riding a bike. But he was the kind of guy who would suddenly let you go, and you'd find yourself flying down a hill with no brakes.

'I'm not sure I...' Alice dropped her hand from her breast. 'I think – it's – I'd better go check on the girls.' And before Gray could do or say anything in response, she'd snatched up her hoodie, pulled it on and run off down the beach.

10

MELANIE - 3 AUGUST

All that evening, Melanie expected Christina to confront her, tell her what her friend had seen, ask her what the hell she thought she was doing breaking into Uncle Gray's study. But Christina said nothing. She was her usual sulky self, just appearing briefly to take a plate of pasta up to her room, hardly making eye contact with anyone.

Was the boy Christina's friend? The girls hadn't seemed to be aware of him, up in that tree. Melanie had assumed he was messing around, waiting in ambush maybe, but what if he hadn't been part of the group at all? What had he been doing here? The nearest neighbour was three miles away.

When Melanie had loaded the dishwasher and listened to Isabel reading *The Pigeon Wants a Puppy*, she returned to the Tower Room. Caro's explanation for flouting the listed building rules and replacing the windows – did it add up? There were other high windows in the house, secured only by catches and perfectly accessible to the kids. Surely it would have been a lot simpler, cheaper and safer just to lock the door at the bottom of the stairs?

She made her way down the stairs to the little hallway. There was no natural light, and only two bare bulbs, one in the stairwell and one in the hall. The walls were painted white, no doubt in an attempt to brighten up the rather grim space, but this only succeeded in making it feel cold and unwelcoming. And all the big pieces of heavy Victorian furniture didn't help.

The hallway door was one of those thick old pine ones, panelled and also painted white. There was a lock, but no key.

The floorboards were uncarpeted. Not waxed, not polished. Scuffed and a bit grubby. Amongst all the other marks were some lighter ones, faint but, once you had seen them, obvious. Scrape marks from here to the carved feet of the chest of drawers that sat against the wall opposite the loo.

Melanie squatted and peered at the marks. Had they been caused by the feet scraping along the floor? She went to the chest of drawers and tried to pull it out away from the wall, but it was too heavy. The drawers would have to come out. When she'd done that, she managed to drag the still heavy piece of furniture across the floor to the door and then back again.

Yes.

The marks she'd just made were in a slightly different place from the original ones, but otherwise pretty much identical. But there were more of the old scrape marks. This chest of drawers had been pulled over to the door and back again not once but twice or more.

Had Alice used it, in the absence of a key, to barricade herself in?

11

ALICE - 7 JULY

Alice, Tess and Isabel were on a mission to identify every plant they saw, using the book Tess had received last Christmas. Often they didn't need the book, though – Tess was a little encyclopaedia, reeling off names. The white pompoms, Alice discovered, were called cotton-grass. But some plants were new to Tess, and these she described in a little notebook, with a sketchy drawing.

'So I can remember them later,' she explained.

They were walking slowly along the track that went west from the house. Alice was beginning to get her bearings. The main track from the public road went first to the house and then turned west through these scrubby fields, running parallel to the coast. If you started out from the house in the other direction, along a much less well-defined grassy track to the east, you soon came to the beach. Where you were much more likely to encounter Gray.

'Here's a new one, I think.' Alice pointed to a flower in the verge. 'It's pretty!'

Each flower had five petals somewhere between blue and purple.

'I think that's meadow cranesbill,' said Tess, consulting the book. 'See, the seed heads are like beaks! That's how it gets its name.'

'They are a little like birds.' Alice squatted to look at the nearest example, then straightened, turning a slow three-sixty, her arms – her *beautiful* arms! – flung out like she was Maria in *The Sound of Music*. 'Oh, it's just so wonderful here! I knew I would be right at home in Scotland! I feel like bursting into song!' She laughed at Tess's face. 'Don't worry. I won't.'

'I want you to burst into song!' protested Isabel. 'What does it mean?'

Alice demonstrated with a warbling rendition of the first two lines of 'The Hills Are Alive' – which were all she could remember. All three of them started to laugh, and then they couldn't stop, as first Isabel and then Tess joined in, in the most ridiculous singing voices they could produce.

After what had happened with Gray at the beach a few days ago, she had kind of been avoiding him, spending all the time she could with Tess and Isabel. Being silly with the kids felt so good! She wished she could magically wind back the clock – eighteen, seventeen, all the way back to Tess's age, or even Isabel's. When life was so much less complicated and so much easier.

Next, they played follow my leader. Alice thought maybe Tess would find this game too babyish, but no, she seemed to enjoy it. At the point where the track widened before passing a stone building, Isabel, who was in front, skipped towards it, and Alice, who was next in line, skipped after her. It was a bigger building than you first realised, U-shaped with a cobbled yard in the middle.

'This used to be the stables,' Isabel explained, running around the yard. 'They kept horses and carts and carriages here in the olden days.'

'Quite a way from the house,' said Alice, running after her. 'We must have come quarter of a mile at least. But I guess the rich folks in the big house wouldn't want smells from the stables offending their aristocratic noses.'

'From the horse poo!' Isabel laughed as she put her arms out and walked, toe to heel, along a sort of dipped channel in a series of long, flat stones that ran around the yard, set into the cobbles, and leading to drains in the corners.

It was at this point that Alice realised Tess wasn't there.

'Tess?' she called, opening the nearest door and peering inside. This must have been the stables, a long building with stalls along one side. '*Tess?*'

But she was nowhere to be seen.

Alice grabbed Isabel's hand and returned to the track. 'Tess? Come out, come out, wherever you are!' She made her voice light and cheery.

The track wound its way around another field and down into a wooded little valley. Alice kept on calling Tess's name, but the dense, dimly lit trees and vegetation seemed to swallow it up.

'She'll be fine,' Isabel kept telling her. 'Tess is just weird.'

'What's that?' Alice pointed to a tumbledown building amongst the trees, its stone walls and its roof covered in ivy, its windows missing. At the door there were little yellow flowers like in the garden of the cottage from Alice's dream.

'The old mill,' said Isabel. 'It's creepy.'

Alice didn't want to go inside. 'Tess?' she called. 'Are you in there?'

There was a movement at the door – but it wasn't Tess. Two teenage girls, maybe Alice's own age, appeared, and a stocky, sandy-haired boy behind them. Another boy came around the corner of the building.

Alice blinked. Who were these people? What were they doing way out here?

'Is Tess wearing cargo pants and a green T-shirt?' the taller girl asked. She was homely but nice-looking, with smiley eyes.

'Yes, she is! You've seen her?'

'She's down by the burn. The stream.' The girl pointed.

'Oh, thank the Lord! Well, thank *you*!' Alice wanted to ask them where they were from and what they were doing, but she didn't want to seem like she was accusing them of trespass or something. They were obviously nice folks. She smiled and headed for the path she could see leading down through the vegetation.

Tess was standing staring at the water of a little creek burbling by.

'Tess, honey! Thank goodness! Why did you take off like that, without a word?'

Tess shrugged.

'You gave me a scare.' Alice went to stand next to her. 'Are you okay?'

A nod.

But Tess wasn't okay.

Alice knew it.

'Why did you take off?' she persisted gently.

'I like it here,' Tess said at last, her voice harsh, defiant.

'Okay. Yeah, it's peaceful. And I like the sound of the

water. Let's stay here a little while.' At least the creek was so shallow there was no danger of Tess or Isabel getting into trouble in it.

Alice could hear Isabel nearby, talking to those kids. 'I'm gonna go check on your sister, okay? Don't move, Tess. I mean it.'

'Problems?' the sandy-haired boy asked when Alice rejoined them all. They were sitting outside the ruin on a low wall, a couple of rucksacks at their feet. Isabel was drinking from a bottle of soda.

'Is it okay?' the homely girl said at once. 'She said she was thirsty, so...'

'Sure. Thank you, that's very kind.'

'Thank you,' parroted Isabel, coming up for breath.

'You want some?' The sandy-haired boy offered Alice another bottle. 'Unopened and not previously slurped from,' he added.

Alice suddenly really wanted some of that orange soda, but she didn't like to take these nice folks' picnic. They might have walked a long way and be a lot thirstier than she was. 'Thanks, but I'm fine.'

'I'm Murray,' he said. 'This is Shona.' The homely girl smiled. 'And Katie and David.'

Katie was small and plump, and David had spectacles that reminded Alice a little of Harry Potter.

'I'm Isabel!' Isabel beamed. 'And Alice is Alice!'

Everyone laughed.

'Nice to meet you all,' said Alice. 'Where have you walked from?'

'We live in Balnabo,' said Katie. 'A village on the shore of the sea loch. About four miles that way.' She waved vaguely. 'You're American?'

'Yeah, I've come a little farther than that. From Indiana.'

'Alice is our au pair! She's staying in the Princess Room. We live in Scallan Lodge. My mum and dad own this whole place.' Isabel waved the soda bottle around.

'So you're Christina's sister?' said Katie, with a look at Shona.

The atmosphere had suddenly gone strange. All the group were looking at each other, Alice realised, passing something unspoken amongst themselves. And not anything good.

'Unfortunately, yes,' said Isabel. 'I'm going to see if Tess is okay.'

'All right, but don't you two go any farther.' Alice put on her stern face.

'Hey, Isabel, wait for us,' said Shona, with a smile at Alice as if to say *Relax for five minutes – we've got this.*

As Isabel skipped off down the path with Shona, Katie and David, Murray held out the bottle of soda to Alice again. 'You know you want to,' he said. 'Go on. We have plenty.'

'If you're sure. Thank you!'

'Christina Davidson, eh?' He made a face. 'I hope you don't have to *au pair* her too?'

'Uh, kind of? My duties are many and various.' Alice was quite pleased with that turn of phrase. 'But I'm enjoying it!' An image of Gray flashed into her head, Gray clutching the bulge in the front of his jeans, and she felt herself flushing all over again.

Murray was looking at her closely. 'Really? Christina Davidson was a couple of years below us at school – we've all just finished sixth year at Gairloch High, and Christina only moved there from her private school at the start of the summer term, but it's a testament to her notoriety that we all knew her, or were aware of her, anyway.'

Alice took a delicious slug of soda. 'Her notoriety?'

'Christina isn't just your average bitch – she's outstanding in her field. She once told a teacher she needed to leave the room because of the smell of *unwashed bodies*.'

Alice snorted. 'That sounds like Christina!'

'The whole family is weird,' said Murray, his voice oddly careful. He wasn't looking at her now, he was looking down, picking at the strap of the rucksack.

A little silence developed. It was strange, but Alice felt like she'd known Murray a lot longer than just a few minutes. It wasn't an awkward silence at all.

'Yep,' Alice said in the end. 'But I like them! Especially Isabel and Tess. They're great kids. Christina – I think she maybe had a difficult childhood, when her mom was a single parent, and she's kinda desperate to belong, you know?'

'Belong to what – the top ten Instagram narcissists?'

She laughed. 'But don't you think those people who put themselves all over social media – it's because they're insecure and want to feel... loved, I guess? And it's something they can be in control of, a little. If you have a problem with someone – simple, you block them. It would be kinda nice to be able to do that in the real world sometimes.'

'Hmm. So you're a fan of social media?'

'I think it works for some folks? But I don't do it much. My parents didn't let me have any accounts until I was sixteen, and then when I got some, I couldn't stand all the...'

'Crap?' Murray suggested.

'Yeah.'

Murray rummaged in the rucksack again and produced a cereal bar. 'Like half of this?'

Alice nodded happily. 'Thanks! See, there are definitely advantages to meeting people in the real world!'

As they ate, she studied him surreptitiously. He was wearing baggy shorts and hiking boots. His calf muscles were enormous, but his upper body was a little soft around the edges. He probably didn't work out like Skip did. Like Gray probably did –

'It's a summer job, is it?' he said. 'The au pairing?'

'Uh-huh. I really wanted to come to Scotland. I've always wanted to visit, from when I was a little kid. I was worried I wouldn't feel anything, any connection...' She wanted to tell him more about that, but really, she had only just met him, and he didn't want to hear her whole life story. 'But I do.' She was blushing again, she just knew it. 'I love it here,' she finished in a sort of embarrassed mumble, like it was possible this boy could see inside her head.

'You'll only be working for the Davidsons for, what, a few weeks?'

'Just the summer holidays,' she confirmed. 'They need an au pair on a more permanent basis, but hiring me gives them time to find someone.'

'You won't be tempted to stay on, then.'

'Uh, I hadn't really thought about it. I've told my folks I'll be back in the fall, but I guess if I really like it here, I might be able to persuade them I need to take a gap year...'

'No!' He immediately grimaced an apology. 'I mean, it would be great to have you around for a whole year, but – they're bad news, the Davidsons. That house –'

The sounds of high voices approached up the path.

'Really,' said Murray quickly. 'You shouldn't even stay there for the summer. You should leave. You shouldn't stay in that place a moment longer than you have to.'

'What do you –'

'Trust me on this,' he muttered as Isabel ran across to them and jumped on Alice, telling her they'd seen a dipper, the cutest bird in the *world*, and Alice had to come and see it *right now.*

12

MELANIE - 4 AUGUST

All night, Melanie stationed herself at the laundry window, waiting for Gray to leave in one of the vehicles. She was determined that he wouldn't sneak out without her noticing this time, and, with the help of a mix of strong coffee, pacing and stretching, managed to stay awake through all the long hours of darkness.

But she might as well not have bothered. None of the vehicles out there moved an inch.

At six o'clock, she gave it up and made her way stiffly back to the Tower Room in the harsh morning light, wondering if she could snatch an hour's sleep. She felt spaced out and unequal to the demands of the new day.

Just an hour...

But when she opened the drawer in which she kept the long T-shirts she used as nightwear, she froze, staring down at her clothes. Everything was almost back as she'd left it, but not quite. She was a bit anal about arranging everything just so, with the folds all facing the front. Now, one of the piles of T-shirts was reversed.

She opened another drawer. The rolled-up pants were neat enough, but the bra straps weren't folded exactly the way she had left them, and some socks were out of alignment. In the wardrobe, there was only her case. At first she thought it hadn't been disturbed, but then she noticed that the zip wasn't pulled all the way around.

Someone had definitely been in here.

They must have seen or heard her making her way downstairs last night, and taken the chance to rummage through her things. They'd evidently been in too much of a hurry to put it all back properly. Or maybe they just hadn't noticed how organised everything was.

Had it been Caro? Was she suspicious of 'Donna' and had decided to have a quick snoop?

Or Gray? Instead of leaving the house as he'd done the night before, had he taken advantage of Melanie's absence from the Tower Room to paw through her stuff? Just because he could?

Had Alice noticed the same thing? Had she blocked the door to stop whoever was snooping around getting in while she was asleep? Or was there another reason why she'd pulled that heavy piece of furniture across the floor to barricade herself in?

Tess had said she was scared of something.

Whoever had been in the room, Melanie could still feel them here. She could almost smell their breath, the alien odour of their skin, the difference they'd made to the stagnant air that was contained in this room where the windows were never opened.

She believed Tess.

She believed that Alice had been scared.

There was danger here.

She felt it, and not only in the Tower Room. It was in all the silences, the somehow *expectant* silences, in the high, grand spaces of the house as she made her way through them. She kept looking behind her, but of course there was nobody there – only the shadows that moved, disconcertingly, as the clouds outside scudded across the sun.

The breezy, bright day out there seemed to belong to another world, a world from which the grim edifice that was Scallan Lodge stood apart. Last night, she'd felt it, all through the dead small hours as she'd waited in vain for Gray to appear – the weight of this place, pressing on her in the dark. And now her body felt strange, as if it didn't belong to her, as if she were moving through the house like a ghost.

That was probably sleep deprivation.

But she sensed, all up and down her spine, that she was running out of time.

She had to find out what had happened to Alice, and fast.

After she'd bathed Isabel, and the two of them were crossing the landing to the stairs – Melanie remembering *not* to take the little girl's hand – she glanced out of a window and saw him again. The boy she'd seen yesterday in the sycamore tree was down there in the garden, standing just in front of the trees.

Was he some sort of peeping Tom?

'Who's that?' she asked Isabel, pointing.

'Oh!' Isabel smiled, and waved frantically from the window. 'That's Alice's friend Murray! *Murray! Murray!*' She tapped on the glass.

The boy jumped, looked up, backed hurriedly into the trees, then stopped and waved uncertainly before diving into cover.

'And who is he?'

'He lives in Balnabo. He's nice. Alice is in *luuuuve* with him!' Isabel giggled, before her face fell.

'I'm going to talk to Murray for a second.'

'Me too!'

'No – I need to ask him about Alice, and he's more likely to tell me things if it's just the two of us.'

Isabel nodded. 'Okay. I'll start breakfast.'

Was that safe for a seven-year-old? Heating pans, chopping fruit?

'You can get yourself some milk, but wait until I'm there before doing anything else.'

The grass was wet with the rain that had fallen in the night, sopping into Melanie's trousers and trainers as she made her way to the spot where the boy had been.

'Murray?' she called softly. 'Murray, are you here?'

Nothing.

She waded through brambles and nettles into the trees, and jumped her height when a pheasant flew up right at her feet, making the harsh gobbling noise that always sounded like it was chastising whoever had had the temerity to disturb it. Watching its flight, she saw, in the distance, near the cove, someone walking along the dunes. Someone with broad shoulders, narrow hips and long, bouncy dark hair.

Gray, a rucksack on his back.

So rather than taking a vehicle, he'd sneaked out last night on foot?

No – he was heading away from the house, not returning to it.

Shit.

He was already out of sight. Even if she jeopardised her job by abandoning breakfast and Isabel completely and going after him, by the time she got to the beach, he'd be long gone. But maybe she should try.

She was heading across the overgrown back lawn when Christina's voice called, 'Where are you going?' The girl was standing at the conservatory door, her face for once free of make-up, hair pulled back in a messy bun. She was still in her pyjamas, nursing a mug of something. 'If you expect me to pull my finger out to the extent of getting Isabel her breakfast, you can think again.'

Cursing inwardly, Melanie waded back through the grass. 'No, that *would* be asking a bit much, given Isabel's exacting requirements. Three strawberries, one small handful of blueberries...'

'And don't get me started on the consistency of the porridge.' Christina was frowning. 'Why are you out here?'

'There was a boy in the trees. Isabel said he's a friend of Alice's. Murray. I just wondered...' She shrugged. 'If he could maybe throw some light on what happened to her.'

'What do you mean *throw some light*? She's dead. The silly cow got herself drowned.' Christina turned away abruptly, but not before Melanie had seen the tightening of her face.

'Why is this Murray hanging around?' Melanie followed her into the conservatory, which smelt of wet earth and jasmine.

'How should I know?'

'Is he your friend too? Is he... your boyfriend?'

'Ugh, *no!*' Christina was looking towards the dunes. 'But it must take him, like, over an hour to get here from his house, so I suppose there must be some attraction. Maybe he's the kind of sick puppy who gets a kick out of being at the scene of – where she was last alive.'

Had she been about to say *the scene of the crime*?

Melanie just came straight out and said it:

'What do you know about Alice going missing?'

Christina's eyes narrowed. 'I don't know anything. Why are you so interested, anyway, Donna?'

Melanie shrugged. 'I'm sleeping in the room she slept in. Everything I do, there are reminders of her. Isabel and Tess won't stop talking about her.'

'Oh yeah, everyone loved Alice.'

'But not you.'

Christina subsided onto one of the wicker chairs and set the mug down on the table next to it. 'I gave her such a hard time,' she said slowly. 'Selina and Olivia and Milly, they were *awful* to her. We – *bullied* her, I suppose. But she was still nice to me. She said... she said my friends were toxic and I would be better off without them. It was like, even when she was being bullied, she wasn't thinking about herself. But I've known them *forever*! And they're good to me. They give me clothes and take me places with their families. Mum and Dad say we're not going on any more holidays this year, and I can't have any new clothes until Christmas.'

So the girl was floundering. She wasn't handling the consequences of the family's financial decline, her loss of status in the eyes of her rich-kid friends.

'Well, fast fashion isn't the thing any more, is it?' Melanie sat down on a chair opposite. 'I thought your generation rejected conspicuous consumption of the planet's resources?'

Christina gave a hollow laugh. 'You haven't met Selina.'

'No, but I did overhear you all bitching about a girl in your class. Maybe Alice is right and you need to take the opportunity of being at a new school to make some new friends.'

'Like Murray Campbell and those other dorks?'

Melanie stood. 'If you see Murray, can you try to talk to him? Find out if he does know anything about Alice?'

Christina sighed. But then she nodded. 'Okay.'

13

ALICE - 10 JULY

When Alice came downstairs in the morning, she found Caro, Ken and Gray already up and arguing in the kitchen.

'I don't believe this!' Caro fumed. She looked like she'd been crying. 'I don't believe you've done this!' She was glaring at Gray, the set of her features reminding Alice a little of Christina. 'And you!' She turned on Ken. 'Couldn't you have made some excuse? No. *No*, Ken, it's not happening. Call them back and say it's not convenient.'

Gray just shrugged.

'We can't do that,' said Ken quietly. 'We can't afford to put their backs up. If that's what they want, that's what they'll have to get.'

'They may not even –' Gray began.

'Oh – Alice,' said Caro, as Alice coughed and came in at the door. 'I'm sorry, sweetheart, but – we have some unexpected guests arriving today. Paying guests. A shooting party. For the deer stalking, you know. We accommodate them here, give them the whole hunting-lodge experience.' Her voice was tight, as if she was having trouble controlling it. 'It's going to mean much more work for us all, I'm afraid.'

'Is it a lot of folks?'

Caro sighed. 'Only two, but – well, you'll see.'

She sure did.

They were named Tim Gilbey and Edward Norcott, and Alice's first assumption that they were a gay couple was soon challenged when Tim grabbed her ass. At least, she thought that was what happened. It was over so quickly that she wasn't quite sure. Tim, a jowly guy with slicked-back grey hair and a big red nose, was braying with laughter at his own joke and explaining it to Edward as the two of them walked past Alice in the hallway. That was when Alice felt his hand on her behind.

Or had he just brushed past her?

He continued on his way, ignoring her and talking with Edward and Ken.

Maybe she made a mistake?

As Alice and Caro served dinner, Edward said, 'She must join us,' in the offhand way he had, like he was someone who was used to barking orders. He didn't even look at Alice, and at first Alice didn't get that he meant her. But Caro laid another place and said, 'Do you mind?' Alice had already eaten with Isabel and Tess and didn't want anything more. But she had to sit there next to Tim and put up with him patting her back and asking her questions – How old was she? She was lovely and slim – what dress size was she? Did she have a boyfriend? If she was such a good God-fearing Christian girl, did she believe in 'hanky-panky' before marriage?

'No, I don't,' Alice said firmly. The nerve of the guy!

To change the subject, she asked Caro and Ken about the

windows in her room. 'I can't get them to open,' she said. 'The locks seem to be missing the key?'

'It'll be somewhere,' said Ken vaguely. 'That's the problem with this bloody place – you put something away and then when you want it again, there're literally hundreds of places it could be.'

'We'll have a look,' said Caro.

'That would be good. It gets kinda hot in there, and it would be nice to have a cool breeze.'

'I'm sure it gets *hot*,' said Tim with a smirk.

Caro exchanged a look with Alice, but neither she nor Ken said a word, which Alice found a little disappointing. But Tim was their guest, after all. Their *paying* guest.

And then Edward started talking about the shooting they would do tomorrow. He was what Alice knew her daddy would have called a Big I Am. He was an ordinary-looking guy, but you could tell he was important, at least in his own eyes. He had a way of looking at Alice, as if he had the power to look right inside her.

'I'm determined to bag an eighteen pointer,' he said.

'A red deer stag with eighteen points on its antlers,' explained Tim, opening his mouth wide as he laughed.

Edward joined in, the sound more like a hacking cough than a laugh. What in the world was so funny about killing animals for kicks?

14

MELANIE - 4 AUGUST

'I meant to tell you,' said Caro as the two of them stood at the sink, Donna washing up the breakfast dishes, Caro running herself a glass of water. 'You remember I mentioned we sometimes have paying guests? We've two coming tomorrow, Hooray Henry types who can be a little, well, demanding. It's important to keep them onside.'

Melanie's heart sank. 'You want me to blitz the house?'

'No, no. They don't care about that sort of thing. It's more their stomachs we have to worry about. They like their food and their drink. And one in particular can get a little... rambunctious.'

'In what way?'

Caro sighed. 'Throwing food around, sexist comments, generally behaving like an overgrown schoolboy.'

Melanie went cold. 'Were they here when Alice disappeared?'

'What? No. God, no, Donna. They *were* here when Alice was, but they left a few days before she went missing. And anyway, they're perfectly harmless, just a little irritating.' She suddenly grabbed Melanie's wrist. 'Where did you get that?'

Melanie didn't pull away. She made her arm passive in Caro's grip.

The friendship bracelet.

The images she couldn't get out of her head came rushing back: Alice, pulling the heavy chest of drawers across the door as a barricade against... what?

Tess's pale little face, the words wrenched out of her: *Alice was scared.*

'I found it in my room,' said Melanie. And then she left a silence.

'It was Alice's,' Caro said at last. 'One of her friends from home made it for her.' Her grip on Melanie's wrist tightened and then released. 'You shouldn't be wearing that. I should return it to her parents.'

'I'm sorry. I had no idea.' Melanie stared at the braiding of the bracelet, imagining that far-off world of Branchfield, Indiana, and a group of girls, totally unlike Selina and the gang, sitting on one of those long American porches braiding bracelets for one another.

'Donna? Donna! Can you take it off, please?'

'Okay, okay!' Melanie wrenched off the bracelet and shoved it at Caro.

'Whoa!' said Caro, standing back a pace. 'Calm down, Donna.'

'I'm sorry.' Melanie took a long breath. 'It's just – Alice. It's really getting to me. The girls are so upset about her, and – it's just so awful, a young girl like that. The police definitely think she drowned?'

Caro was turning the bracelet over in her hands, as if she might find answers in the intricacies of the braiding. 'That's their thinking, yes, although of course they've been following up other lines of enquiry.'

'What do *you* think happened?'

Caro closed her fist on the bracelet, pushed it into the pocket of her jeans and took a swig of water. 'I'm hoping against hope that she might have just taken off – left her clothes on the beach to mess with everyone. The police found hardly any money in her purse, and no one can be sure that some of her clothes aren't missing. She could have taken the necessities and gone.'

'But how likely is that? By all accounts, Alice was a lovely girl. Very considerate of the feelings of others. Why would she do that? Why would she want to cause her parents, and everyone here, such heartache?'

'Oh, Alice was no angel, believe me! After she went missing, we found out that she'd run away from home without telling her parents anything except that she was going to the UK for a summer job. They hadn't spoken to her since – she didn't answer any of their calls, just sent the odd text message to let them know she was okay. As if that was going to make them worry any less! My God! If it was one of mine... Alice wasn't *considerate*, Donna. Not at all. In fact, I was on the point of firing her when she disappeared.'

Melanie swallowed. 'Why?'

'She was neglecting her duties. She couldn't cope with the paying guests. And she was spending too much time with the local boys.'

'Murray Campbell?'

Caro set the glass down on the draining board with a clonk. 'I've no idea of their names. Christina tends to steer clear of that lot, thank goodness. But the police have spoken to them. They came forward, after Alice went missing, with a variety of ridiculous accusations.'

'Like what?'

'That we were in some way to blame. I did wonder if that was deflection, if Alice met those boys on the beach and something happened.' She shook her head. 'But I think it far more likely that she's gone off with one of them.'

'Gone where?'

'Maybe it's wishful thinking, but I keep imagining them on one of the islands. Coll, Tiree, Colonsay... Working in one of the hotels under assumed names. There's a lot of casual work at this time of year, and I don't imagine there's too much checking of references and so on. Talking of which – I've been meaning to ask you about one of the referees you put on your CV.'

Well, that was an abrupt – and unwelcome – change of subject.

Melanie wiped her hands on a dish towel and turned to meet Caro's gaze, making her expression mildly enquiring, as if to say *Ready to answer any questions you might have, but how tedious.*

Her referees were two of Melanie's dodgy old mates, one of whom still provided the criminal element of the Highlands and Islands with false documents and was on her CV under the identity of Roger Howden, former employer of nanny extraordinaire Donna MacKenzie. The other, Nicola Edwards, was using her own name but posing as a lecturer on Donna's childminding course.

'Due diligence, I tried calling her twice, but it just went to voicemail. So I checked with the college, and they have no record of a Nicola Edwards on the staff.'

Oh no!

Why would Caro start checking up on Donna *after* they'd employed her?

They must be suspicious.

There was nothing she could do but brazen it out. 'She might be listed under her married name – she got married just after I left, I think.'

'And her married name is?'

'Sorry, I don't know.'

'Why wouldn't she give you her current name to use on your CV?'

'She uses both now, I think.'

'I'll try calling her again,' said Caro.

No no no!

Nic was sharp, but how could she talk her way out of this?

Caro got out her phone and tapped in the call.

Melanie held her breath as Caro stood there, hand on hip, waiting.

And waiting.

Eventually, she gave up. 'I'll try again later. I'm sure it's as you say, but you understand, with kids involved, we have to dot every *i*?'

'Of course.' Melanie turned back to the sink. 'I'm sure Nicola won't mind.'

As soon as she got the chance, she needed to call Nic.

15

ALICE - 12 JULY

lice was dusting the pictures in a corridor when Tim appeared, strolling towards her with a wide-legged, swaggering walk, like a cowboy in an old movie.

Oh no.

But Alice gave him a polite smile.

'What have we here, then?' he said.

'Excuse me?'

He pointed at the picture she was dusting. 'A local scene?'

The painting was a watercolour of a fishing boat in a bay.

'I don't know,' said Alice, moving away from him to the next picture.

'Ah, this is more like it.'

It was a painting of a woman in an old-fashioned bonnet. He reached a hand over Alice's shoulder and pointed to the corner of the painting. 'I can't quite make out the signature, Alice. Can you?'

Now he was pressing right up against her.

'You're lovely,' he breathed in her ear. 'You're a beautiful girl.' He smelt meaty and gross.

She jabbed her elbow into his chest and tried to wriggle away, but he didn't move, pressing himself even closer. She felt his hand squeeze her left buttock.

'Get – *off*!' Alice hissed.

'What's going on?' Ken, thank the Lord!

He was striding towards them – almost running, his face grim.

Tim moved away. 'Alice no like Tim,' he said in a squeaky baby voice, pushing out his lower lip. 'Alice no nice to Tim.' His sad little-boy eyes made her skin itch, like he was still touching her.

She expected Ken to slap him down, but he just said, 'Um, Alice. I think Tess needs your help in the kitchen.'

But Tess wasn't in the kitchen.

Just Gray, standing at the island slicing strawberries. 'Tess and Isabel are demanding strawberry milkshakes the way you make them. I'm not sure what exactly that entails, but apparently it involves chopping a few for the top and blending the rest.'

Alice got the milk from the fridge and the ice cream from the freezer. Her hands were shaking a little. 'It's pretty easy. You just hull the strawberries and whizz them up with milk and ice cream.'

She went to the sink and ran water over her wrists, the way Mom always did when she was feeling out of sorts. The cool water on your skin was soothing.

'Hey,' said a soft voice behind her. 'Are you okay?'

One second she was running water over her wrists, and the next she was in his arms. Sobbing her heart out! But it felt *so good* just to be held in his strong, hard arms. Her face was pressed against his chest, and between sobs she breathed in his musky scent. Now his hands were in her hair, and suddenly she felt a sharp pain all across the back of her scalp as her head was yanked back. He'd just tugged on her hair, and *hard*! And now he was pressing his mouth down onto her lips, and –

No!

This was too much!

'*No!*' she sobbed against his lips.

Immediately, he let her go, and she actually felt the warmth of his body leave her as he stepped back, hands up. 'I'm sorry. God, Alice, I'm sorry. I keep forgetting that you're just a kid.'

'I'm eighteen years old!' Alice needed to offer him another reason for this rejection. 'Tim just grabbed my ass!'

He took a deep breath. 'And I just compounded the offence by pawing you too –'

'Oh, no,' she whispered. 'Tim – that was way different.'

He smiled, and gently, so gently, ran his fingers through the tears on her cheeks. 'I'm glad to hear it.' He picked up a box of tissues from the island and handed it to her. His expression had darkened, his eyes suddenly flashing. 'That bastard,' he breathed.

'It may have been an accident,' said Alice, wiping her face with a tissue. She didn't want Gray confronting Tim and maybe doing something stupid.

That made him smile. 'I see. Easy mistake to make. He probably meant to grope his *own* arse.'

She laughed shakily. 'He may have overbalanced, and...'

'Okay, I'm using that. I overbalanced, and my lips somehow landed on yours.'

'Oh, stop!' She smiled up at him. 'Thank you for – well, making me feel a whole lot better.'

'If he touches you again, come to me. I'll sort him out.'

'No – please, don't. But... Thank you.'

'What are friends for, if not to have one another's backs? We're friends, aren't we?'

Alice nodded.

He was fiddling with his friendship bracelet, taking it off. And now he was fastening it around Alice's wrist.

'Oh!' she exclaimed. 'No, I can't!'

'You don't like it?'

It was still warm from his own wrist, and as she moved her arm, it moved slightly against her skin, sending little shockwaves of electricity through her.

'I love it,' she whispered.

For the next couple of days, Alice steered clear of Edward and Tim, often taking the girls outside or up to the Princess Room, which meant she was also less likely to see Gray. Which was a good thing! But she kept fingering the soft bracelet on her wrist. Was it so very wrong, what was happening between her and Gray?

Of course it was *wrong*! She had a *boyfriend*!

And Gray was right – the age difference was an issue. The disparity in experience.

'Isn't that Uncle Gray's?' Tess asked suddenly, staring at the bracelet.

They were in the Princess Room, taking it in turns to scan the ocean with Tess's binoculars.

Alice was saved from responding by Isabel, whose turn it was with the binoculars, suddenly squealing and waving.

'It's Murray!' she whooped. 'He's got binoculars too! *Look!*'

He was on the beach, waving back at them.

'Give Alice the binoculars,' said Tess. 'It's not *you* he's interested in.'

Alice trained the binoculars on the distant figure. Murray immediately started cavorting, doing a silly walk and trying to stand on his hands, which, given his sturdy build, was never going to end well. Soon Alice was laughing along with the girls.

It was like God had known exactly how she was feeling and had put Murray there to say, *Look, not all guys are creeps or wronged boyfriends or dangerously attractive pirates! Some guys can just be friends!*

Now Murray was beckoning, and Alice gave him a thumbs up.

'Come on, then.' She set the binoculars down on the windowsill. 'Look, there's Shona and Katie too. Let's go get a picnic so we don't eat all their food!'

16

MELANIE - 4 AUGUST

Melanie couldn't find her phone. She knew she'd left it in her room, in the drawer of the bedside cabinet on the right, the side she slept on. Whoever had been in her room must have taken it. It had face recognition, so at least they wouldn't be able to get into it and realise that it belonged to Melanie Macfarlane, not Donna MacKenzie. That Melanie was a community nurse, not a nanny or an au pair.

Why had they taken it? Because they were suspicious of Donna?

That pointed to Caro.

It was vital to contact Nic immediately, before Caro called her back. And she hadn't brought a laptop or a tablet.

She found Christina in her room, lying on the bed and looking at her phone, as Melanie had hoped.

'Hi!' she said breezily.

'Ever heard of knocking?'

'Sorry, but the door was open. You haven't seen my phone, have you?'

Christina shook her head.

'Can I borrow yours for a sec? I need to send an email.' It would have to be email – she didn't have a hope in hell of remembering Nic's mobile number.

Christina looked from Melanie to her phone and back again. Then she sighed. 'Here.'

Melanie logged in to her webmail account and sent a quick message to Nic to tell her what had happened, that Nic needed to find out the names of staff at the college where Donna had supposedly been a student. Hopefully there'd be a Nicola – it was, after all, a common name for women in their forties. If not, Nic could say she went by her middle name or something. Either way, she'd be forearmed with the genuine name of a staff member when Caro called her. She also told Nic that her mobile phone seemed to have been taken by someone in the house, so Nic shouldn't call or text it.

She was about to send the message when it occurred to her that Nic could also be useful in another way. She asked Christina for the landline number at Scallan and added a PS:

Could you get me another phone and a couple of trackers? One for a vehicle, one that would go in a rucksack? Let me know when you have them and I'll meet you in town. You'll have to call me on the landline. It's 0141 4960435.

She logged out, closed the browser and handed the phone back to Christina. 'Thanks!'

'Mm.' Christina turned over on the bed, nose in her

phone again, as if the two minutes it had been out of her possession meant that intensive bonding was now required.

'You said before that Murray is "weird". What did you mean?'

A long silence. Then: 'He's too dorky to have had anything to do with it, if that's what you're thinking.'

Melanie's heart stopped. 'To do with what?'

A charged silence.

'Alice disappearing,' Christina said at last, her voice hardly above a whisper.

Melanie dropped her voice too. 'Christina, do you know something about what happened?'

'No. Of course not.'

'But you have an idea…?'

Christina rolled over on the bed to fix Melanie with a glare. 'Stop hassling me, Donna! Why are you so interested, anyway? You're obsessed with Alice! You never even met her, but you're more bothered than anyone about her going missing. It's like you're – a journalist or something, rootling around trying to get people talking about it. *Are* you a journalist? Are you not really an au pair at all?'

Shit.

'Of course I'm not a journalist! Why would a journalist be interested in Alice?'

Christina laughed harshly. 'Yeah. Loads of people get drowned in the sea every summer, don't they? Why would anyone be interested in just one more?'

THE NEXT DAY, as Melanie performed her various tasks, she had a good look for her phone. It was possible one of the kids had taken it. She searched their bedrooms, but it wasn't there.

She was doing the ironing when Tim Gilbey came swaggering into the laundry room and parked his considerable arse on the table. 'And what do you like to do for fun, Donna?'

The paying guests, aka deer murderers, were repulsive – and, Melanie felt, would bear scrutiny, even though Caro had said they weren't here when Alice disappeared. They had met Alice, after all. One of them could easily have taken a shine to her and come back later, lurked around until she left the house alone...

They were just the kind of arrogant, entitled pricks who saw women as commodities. They'd been throwing their weight around all day, and despite the fact that the Davidsons no doubt needed their money, Melanie had heard raised voices in the kitchen earlier, the normally affable Ken shouting, 'Just because you want something *right now* doesn't mean it's possible!'

Melanie gave Tim a withering look. 'Laundry,' she said, sweeping the iron across the front of a shirt.

'I can see the attraction.' He rootled around in the pile next to him and picked out a pair of women's pants, twirling them around his stubby finger.

And now he was down off the table and looming over her. 'Want a hand with that?'

The hand wandered to her breast, and she whacked the hot iron into his face.

'APPARENTLY THE DOCTOR has assured Tim there'll be no permanent scarring,' said Caro, coming into the conservatory, where Melanie was sweeping the floor. 'And he's not pressing charges.'

'No pun intended,' said Melanie.

'What?' Caro barely seemed to be listening. She took a drag on her cigarette and stared out of the glass.

'Well, it's his lucky day.' Melanie wielded the broom vigorously, brushing the debris towards the door. 'Because I won't be *pressing charges* either.'

'*What?*'

'For the sexual assault.'

Caro sighed. 'Well, they'll be gone tomorrow, thank God.'

'I know you said they'd left by the time Alice went missing, but could they have come back?'

Caro stubbed out the cigarette and dropped it into a pot. 'No.' She folded her arms as if she was cold. 'They're not my favourite people, they're cavemen to be honest, but they would never... No, Donna. No.' Was she trying to convince Melanie or herself?

When Caro had gone, Melanie abandoned the broom and stepped outside. She walked slowly around the side of the house and across the lawn to the gates, as if her feet were taking her, of their own accord, away from this place.

What happened to you here?

She wished she could go back in time, grab Alice, spirit her away from Scallan Lodge. She turned and looked up at the house, at the Tower Room, and for a mad moment thought she could see Alice up there looking back at her.

The gravel popped as a car approached from the gate.

Melanie stepped off the drive onto the grass, glancing into the car as she did so.

She froze at the same time as the passenger door flew open and a woman staggered from the moving car.

She was tall, a good few inches taller than Melanie, and wearing a green and white floral summer dress and practical lace-up shoes. Her hair was scraped back into a ponytail from a pale, gaunt, ill-looking face. The man who followed her out of the car was also tall, distinguished-looking, with neat grey hair.

The Snyders.

Tonya and Warren.

She recognised them from the press, from the appeals they'd made when Alice first disappeared.

Tonya grabbed Melanie's arm. 'You're *Melanie Macfarlane!*'

Oh shit!

How did Tonya Snyder know that?

There were people, lots of people, from Melanie's old life that she really didn't want finding her and ruining the new leaf she'd turned over, so she'd been careful to keep herself off the internet. She was pretty sure there were no details about her on there, no photographs. She'd told her friends a story about a stalker to explain why she couldn't be featured in any of their social media accounts, and when her manager had wanted a group photo for the Kinspelve Medical Centre website, Melanie had given the same reason for ducking out of it.

So how did Tonya Snyder know who she was?

'What are you doing here? *Did you do this?*' Tonya grasped Melanie's shoulders and shook her.

Warren, his face pale and set, said, 'Are you involved?'

Melanie couldn't speak. Through the material of her T-shirt, Tonya's nails were digging into the flesh of her shoulders.

'What – have – you – *done?*' Tonya looked suddenly wild,

this eminently respectable church-going woman, her lips pulled back from her teeth in a snarl.

Melanie was breathing fast, gulping air. She still couldn't speak.

'Tonya,' said Warren, and put a hand on her arm.

Tonya released Melanie's shoulders abruptly.

Melanie had to pull herself together. Someone could look out from the house at any second and see them. She had to defuse this. Fast.

She swallowed down the emotion. 'They could be watching. Can we please act as if we're having a normal conversation?' She forced her trembling lips into a smile.

Warren, after a beat, nodded and fixed a smile to his own face, but Tonya continued to stare at Melanie as if she were a monster.

'I decided to come here,' Melanie said through the smile, 'after I found out that Alice had disappeared. After I spoke to you on the phone.' That awful, awful phone call. It would have been hard enough in any circumstances, but Melanie had still been reeling from the news of Alice's disappearance. 'When you said you'd been here, that you'd spoken to the Davidsons and were suspicious of them, that you thought they could have something to do with it... They cared so little about Alice that they were already advertising for a new au pair... I decided to apply for the job. To see what I could find out.'

Tonya's eyes widened. 'And – they *gave you the job*?'

'I'm here under a pseudonym. Donna MacKenzie. They don't know who I am. Obviously. Please – don't tell them. I think you might be right and someone here, probably Gray, is involved. Odd things have been happening, and there are scrape marks on the floor by the door to the Tower Room, where I think Alice might have dragged furniture across to block the door...'

An *umph* sound came from Warren, like Melanie had just hit him.

Tonya's face had gone very still.

'I need to stay here if I'm going to find out what happened. It might not be Gray. There are paying guests who are also creepy as hell.'

Caro was coming across the lawn towards them.

'*Please*,' Melanie whispered. And she found herself saying, although she knew immediately that it was the wrong thing, 'She's my daughter too.'

17

MELANIE - 5 AUGUST

Tonya's eyes flashed. 'You gave up the right to call her that the *second* you gave her up.'

'*I didn't give her up!*' Melanie shot back.

'*She was taken from you for a reason!*'

Tonya was staring at Melanie as if she could see right through her, right through the veneer she'd built up over the years, all the way inside to the feral teenager she had once been, that wild little creature who had somehow given Alice life.

The Davidsons evidently hadn't noticed Melanie's resemblance to Alice, because it wasn't strong, but Tonya had immediately, as soon as she'd clapped eyes on Melanie. Melanie knew, from poring over Alice's social media accounts, that there was a resemblance between them, mainly in body shape but also, a little, facially. Tonya had recognised not Melanie herself but Alice. A mother knew every inch of her child's face and body, every nuance of expression, every little quirk in the way she held herself, turned her head, moved her body as she walked.

There was no time. Caro was almost upon them, looking from Melanie to the Snyders and back. It was too late to explain, to stop the train wreck.

For a long moment, no one said a word. Then Tonya opened her mouth, and Melanie knew that it was over, that she would never, ever have another chance to save her child. If she was still alive. If one of them had taken her.

Alice.

But before Tonya could speak, Caro said, 'I'm sorry, but I'm not sure how much more we can tell you about what happened.'

Tonya shook her head. 'You know more than you're saying. More than you've told the police. We know you do.'

Here was where Tonya or Warren would tell Caro that their suspicions had solidified in the light of discoveries – such as the scrape marks on the floor – made by Melanie, Alice's birth mother, here under false pretences to ferret out the truth.

But Tonya wasn't even looking at Melanie. It was as if Melanie wasn't even there.

'We don't know anything,' Caro said wearily. There was another cigarette dangling from her left hand, and the smell of it, the acrid waft of smoke on the summer air, made Melanie want to gag.

'*Yes you do!*' Warren Snyder suddenly shouted. 'What have you done to her? What have you done to Alice?' He was right in Caro's face.

She staggered back.

'Whoa, whoa!' called Ken, lumbering across the lawn, Gray trailing him.

'*You!*' Warren was running, past Ken, grabbing Gray by the collar. 'You fucking *monster*! What have you done?

Where's Alice?' He sobbed on her name, his face contorting, and Melanie felt her own face start to collapse.

She was conscious of Caro narrowing her eyes at her before turning away and going after Warren, who was now grappling with Gray.

Gray was trying to pull free. 'She ran away from *you*, Mr Snyder. Why was that? Maybe if you're looking for someone to blame, you should look closer to home!'

Warren punched him.

Gray went down.

He fell, hard, onto his back, his long hair whipping forwards, his head smacking the ground. For a moment he just lay there. Then, with a wordless sound, he turned onto his side, pushed some strands of hair off his face and put a hand to his nose. Melanie watched with a sort of detached satisfaction as rivulets of blood poured through his fingers, over the back of his hand and onto the grass. He started to cough, wetly, but his gaze all the while was on Warren, who stood looming over him, as if just waiting for him to get up so he could hit him again.

Everyone else seemed to be frozen for one, two, three seconds.

Then Caro moved.

'Oh my God! Oh my God!' she twittered, crouching at Gray's side. 'Are you okay?'

Gray grabbed the tissue she offered but never took his eyes from Warren.

Warren stared back at him, his face twisted in a strange expression that was full of hatred and contempt but also something else, something so much worse.

Despair.

If this man is involved, Warren might as well have cried out loud, *there's no hope.*

Tonya hurried over to Warren, putting herself between him and Gray.

'No,' she said gently, touching her husband's stricken face. 'This isn't the way.'

Ken was heading for the house. 'I'm calling the police!' he shouted.

'Call them!' Warren yelled back. 'Get those fucking idiots out here! We're not leaving until we have some answers!'

WHEN THE POLICE ARRIVED, the tall, dark and handsome detective inspector who introduced himself as John Macneil suggested that they 'talk inside'. The Snyders had been sitting in their car, and Gray by this point had gone to get cleaned up while Caro, Ken and Melanie stood awkwardly together in the porch. As they all trooped into the hall, Tim Gilbey and Edward Norcott appeared, Tim's face like a slab of raw meat. They completely failed to read the room, Tim starting on about being 'attacked with a hot iron' again and Edward saying Donna should be dismissed, but when Ken said, 'The police are here to talk to us and Alice's parents about her disappearance,' he shut up, and the two of them slunk off to the library.

Caro suggested the conservatory. Did she, subconsciously, want to keep the Snyders out, and this was a compromise of sorts? Not quite inside the house?

But it suited Melanie.

She hurried along the passage to the kitchen, threw some biscuits on a plate and boiled the kettle. When she appeared with the tray, on which she'd set the big teapot, milk jug, sugar and mugs as well as the plate of biscuits, Caro looked relieved.

'Oh, Donna, what a good idea.'

Whatever conversation had been going on stopped as she and the DI's sidekick, a rangy youngster called DC Smith, handed round the tea and biscuits. But when Melanie left the conservatory, instead of carrying on through the 'drawing room', as Caro called it, and back to the kitchen where she belonged, she walked towards the door to the hall until she was out of sight of everyone and then doubled back round the edges of the room to stand outside the open glass doors to the conservatory.

'You need to look at *his* alibi again.' Warren's forceful voice carried easily to Melanie.

'I wasn't even in Scotland.' In contrast, Gray sounded very calm, very smooth. 'And I've plenty of witnesses to that effect.'

'He's got a history of sexual assault,' said Warren, as if Gray hadn't spoken. 'You need to check out his alibi. He'll have got friends lying for him.'

'The people my brother was meeting are potential investors, not friends,' Ken said wearily. 'At least, they *were* potential investors in a glamping business we're trying to get off the ground. They could have no reason whatsoever to lie for him. The relationship is purely business – and not even that any more. They've pulled out, unsurprisingly, after being quizzed by the Met regarding Gray's movements.'

'Rest assured we are looking into all lines of enquiry,' said DI Macneil. He was young, fortunately – probably not much older than Melanie herself – and so was unlikely to have been based at Inverness Police Station during the period, about fifteen years ago, when Melanie had been regularly brought in there. She didn't recognise him, anyway. 'The fact that we've drawn blanks so far – I'm afraid you must prepare yourselves for the increasing likelihood that Alice got into trouble in the sea, as it has appeared from the outset.'

'You don't think she could have taken off again?' That was Caro.

Tonya snorted. 'Of course she didn't! DI Macneil, these people obviously know more than they're letting on. There's something not right here. Alice was *frightened*. By *someone in this house*. The new au pair – when we asked her about Alice, about anything she might have picked up, she said there are scrapes on the floorboards behind the door to the Tower Room, where heavy furniture has been pulled across the floor. Alice was trying to stop someone getting into her room!'

A silence.

Melanie winced.

What were the Davidsons going to make of Melanie noticing the scrapes and saying nothing, then blurting it all out to the Snyders?

'Right,' said DI Macneil. 'Well, we'll need to see these marks and possibly get the forensics team back.'

'How on earth were they missed the first time round?' demanded Warren Snyder.

'I don't know,' said the DI grimly. 'They shouldn't have been. In fact, it's rather unlikely that they were. Could the new au pair have damaged the floor herself somehow and be blaming Alice?'

'Possibly,' said Caro.

Melanie burst into the room. 'Of course I didn't damage the floor myself! Why would I be dragging furniture around?

But *someone* has been!' Melanie, of course, *had* dragged the chest of drawers across the floor and back to see if she could replicate the marks, but there was no way they could know that.

'Donna!' rapped out Caro.

'Come and see!' Melanie glared at the two policemen.

Everyone trooped behind Melanie in a grim procession through the hall, up the stairs and along the twisting corridors to the tower stairwell. Melanie pointed to the marks on the floor.

'Ah!' Gray looked shame-faced. 'I'm afraid that was me! We did a deep clean after the forensics people had done their stuff. I pulled all the furniture out of position, here and in the Tower Room, so I could hoover behind everything.'

'Why drag this big chest of drawers all the way across to the door?' Melanie demanded.

'I needed to move the dresser and the sideboard – and to make room for them, I had to drag this beast what seemed like miles at the time, I can tell you!'

'When I first mentioned the scrape marks,' said Tonya slowly, 'when we were sitting in the conservatory, why didn't you say anything?'

Gray lifted his broad shoulders. 'I didn't think. I'm afraid everything that happened around that time – it's all a bit of a blur.'

'How convenient,' said Tonya acidly. She was standing by the door, one hand resting on the panel above the doorknob.

Melanie had done that too – put her hand somewhere Alice would have touched. Alice, when she was here. *Right here.* As the thought bloomed and unfurled, pushed its way to the front of her brain, she fought it back down, made it fold itself up again deep inside the recesses of her consciousness. She had to hold it together, and the only way to do that was not to think about Alice actually *being here*, actually *doing things*, if she could help it. Not to think of her dragging that chest of drawers to the door because –

Because *what*?

Who had Alice been so afraid of?

Tim Gilbey? Edward Norcott?

Gray?

Ken, even? That boy Murray?

As they all trailed back downstairs, Melanie found Gray right behind her. He hissed into her ear: 'You need to get over this *obsession* you seem to have with Alice.'

Melanie whipped round to face him. 'That sounds like a threat.'

He said nothing, and her stomach plummeted.

It was him, then.

This meant it was him?

Everything seemed to go still, and suddenly her fear was gone, as if this confirmation had been all she'd needed to channel her coursing adrenaline away from the urge for flight and into the other response.

Fight.

She held his gaze until he smiled and turned away.

Outside, the Snyders were being browbeaten by DI Macneil.

Melanie slipped into the shadows of the massive stone porch.

'We're perfectly happy for you to hand out missing-person posters and ask around about Alice,' said the DI. 'But please – leave the investigation to us.'

'Because you're doing such a great job,' sneered Warren.

'I understand you've been doorstepping Melanie Macfarlane's neighbours in Perthshire.'

'They told us she'd gone to look after her dying father,' said Tonya, 'but no one could tell us his address. We need to talk to her.' She flicked a look back at the house, to Melanie. 'We know Alice recently accessed her adoptive mother's details on the register. We thought it possible she could have gone to find her.'

'The Perthshire police have already spoken to Melanie Macfarlane. She assured them that Alice hadn't been in touch, and seemed genuinely shocked to find out she was missing. You agreed to give her your phone number, didn't you? Did she not get in touch?'

'She did, yes, but we'd like to talk to her again.' This time, the look Tonya shot Melanie, while DI Macneil continued to assure them that they were exploring every possible avenue of enquiry, was desperate.

'You know where we are,' Tonya cut in. 'At Lochside Chalets. Chalet number six. Please keep us updated on every development, no matter how small. *Please.*'

As they got into their car, Melanie waited, and when Tonya looked at her again, she nodded.

18

ALICE - 16 JULY

'They're dreadful,' said Alice as she finished recounting what had happened, whacking with a stick at the portrait of Tim she'd drawn for Murray in the sand. She'd tried to do Edward, but couldn't remember a single one of his features, like he sort of faded away from her memory when he wasn't right there in front of her.

Murray stomped on Tim's right eye. 'Bastard,' he said in disgust. 'You need to get out of that place, Alice.'

She shrugged. 'They'll be gone in a couple of days.'

'I have to tell you something.'

A scream carried on the breeze. Isabel was sliding down the dunes on Alice's jacket, and Tess was chasing after her.

'This sounds serious!'

'Well, yeah. It is.'

'So spill!'

Murray folded his arms over his fleece and looked past Alice up the beach. 'One night after we'd finished our final exams, at the end of May, a few of us were camping out here. We had sleeping bags and tents and lit a fire on the sand. There was a lot of drinking going on, and we were all freaking each other out telling ghost stories and making stuff up about serial killers and the like.' He flicked a look at her. 'The talk inevitably turned to Scallan Lodge and the rumours about strange goings-on there. At about midnight, when we were all fleein' – drunk out of our skulls – we decided to try to get into the place and have a nose around. We waited until all the lights were out, and then we broke in.'

Alice must have been gaping at him, because he grimaced.

'I know. Pretty bad. I hasten to add that that's not the sort of thing any of us are in the habit of doing. We were demob happy is all the defence I can muster. Katie found a window that wasn't quite closed. I think it was the utility room or something. David wriggled in – he's the skinniest – and opened the back door for the rest of us. We then proceeded to sneak about the place, although the amount of giggling and *shh*-ing we were doing, we weren't exactly as quiet as mice.

'Anyway. Katie's sister Erin – she's a couple of years younger than the rest of us; she's in Christina's class – she got separated from the group and found herself in a corridor, in the pitch dark. A door opened, and a torch shone right in her eyes. A man backed her into a corner and told her to take her clothes off and not make a sound. She was so scared, she did it. She thought he was going to rape her. But he just shone the torch up and down her body, muttered something like "No, I don't think so," and told her to get out.'

'Oh my goodness!'

'She came running through the hall naked, right into Katie's arms, gibbering incoherently. I gave her my sweater, and we somehow got her out of there and back home. That was weeks ago. Erin still hardly leaves the house, and she's terrified that Katie could be in danger from *the torch man*, as she calls him, if she comes anywhere near Scallan – so Katie has to tell Erin we're going elsewhere if we come out here.'

'That poor girl! Has she had counselling? What did the police do about it?'

Murray grimaced. 'Erin and Katie haven't even told their parents. We couldn't tell anyone, given that we'd broken into the house, and there was only a drunk girl's word that anything had happened.'

'But even so, don't you think you *should* tell the police? I bet it was Tim!'

'What does Tim sound like? Is he Scottish?'

Alice shook her head. 'He's from London.'

'Unlikely, then. Erin said she thought the guy had a Scottish accent, although he was kind of whispering, so it was hard to say.' He kicked sand over Tim's face. 'She thinks it was Gray Davidson.'

'*What?*'

Murray narrowed his eyes at her. 'Is it so hard to believe it could have been?'

'Well – yes, it is!'

But, hugely inappropriately, Alice found herself imagining the scene. A dark corridor. Gray, lurking in the shadows. Growling at the terrified girl to strip. And then the light of his torch, moving slowly over her bare skin –

'Gray wouldn't have done that!' she almost shouted.

'Okay, okay! If you say so.' Murray pursed his lips.

'I think I know him a little better than you do.' She pushed her right hand up the long sleeve of her T-shirt and ran her fingers over the soft woven cotton of the friendship bracelet. Since Tess had noticed it, she'd started wearing it further up her arm, out of sight.

'Oh, I'm sure you do,' said Murray.

'What's that meant to mean?'

'Nothing.'

In the tense silence, Alice felt the weight of disappointment settle on her shoulders. Murray was just another guy who was interested in her in *that* way, then. She should probably be flattered, she guessed.

'Gray Davidson's got – quite a reputation,' Murray said in the end. 'Maybe you don't know about the sexual assault charges?'

Alice could only stare at him.

Murray nodded grimly, as if in response to an unasked question. 'He was accused, a couple of years ago, of sexually assaulting a woman at an event their company staged. And one of their staff too, late at night, *in the pitch dark*, in their London office. He got off. The charges were dropped. But –'

Alice's heart was pounding. 'Well, the fact that the charges were dropped surely means it was nothing? That the women made it up?' She twisted the bracelet on her arm.

Murray made an exasperated noise. 'You need to leave that place, Alice. The sooner the better. And in the meantime, you need to be very, *very* careful around Gray Davidson.'

CARO WAS LYING on the couch in the small lounge room. Alice hesitated. Was she asleep?

But then: 'What?' Caro muttered, pushing herself up. Her hair was wild, her eyes heavy.

Alice came into the room. 'Caro, I need to talk to you.'

'So talk.'

Alice had already told Caro what Tim had done, and she hadn't seemed too bothered about it, saying only that Alice had to be 'more careful' around 'those sorts of men'. But Alice had been thinking. Tim, not Gray, must have been the 'torch man' who had made that poor girl strip naked and scared her out of her wits, no matter what Murray thought.

'I'm not comfortable with having any sort of contact with Tim.' Alice took a breath. 'While he's here, I think I need to go elsewhere.'

Caro sighed. 'Tim's a prick. But you don't have to worry about him. Or Edward, come to that. They've gone. They left early.'

'They have?'

Gray! Gray must have confronted Tim about what he'd done to Alice, threatened him, maybe, and Tim, like the coward he was, had hightailed it out of here.

Caro nodded and subsided back onto the couch. She looked dreadful, as if she'd just received devastating news.

'Is everything all right?'

Caro didn't respond at first. Then she said, 'We have to put up with them, and people like them, for the money. We don't really have a choice. I'm sorry, Alice. This place costs an arm and a leg just to keep wind and watertight. And the start-up costs for our wonderful shiny-new glamping business… It's all a bit of a nightmare at the moment. We need all the ready cash we can get.'

Alice, naïvely perhaps, had assumed that anyone living in such a grand house must be very wealthy. She knew they'd wound up their old business, but had assumed they still had plenty of money.

'I hope I haven't caused a problem? They didn't ask for their money back, did they?'

'No.' Caro closed her eyes. 'No, Alice, it's fine.'

19

MELANIE - 28 JULY (5 DAYS BEFORE ARRIVING AT SCALLAN LODGE)

Melanie Macfarlane was singing along to the radio as she drove around the last couple of bends in the narrow single-track road that led to her cottage. She loved her job as a community nurse, but the navy polyester uniform had been designed by sadists. It was sticky and uncomfortable, and no one could find a size that fitted them properly. Melanie had settled on the ten as the least bad option, but the top was too tight at her bum and far too baggy around the shoulders and arms. She couldn't wait to get changed into her walking gear, call Grant and get out into the hills.

She grinned at the thought of him.

When she'd first joined the local mountain rescue team six years ago, Grant Phimister had mentored her and had been a big factor in her sticking it out, his cheery, weather-beaten face somehow making it all bearable even when she was soaked to the skin and her muscles were screaming at her to stop, lie down, not climb another step.

They'd been friends ever since, but had recently become something more.

'Friends with benefits,' Melanie's best pal Laura had chuckled when Melanie told her what had happened in the bothy at Ben Alder. The bothy had no electricity, just candles and firelight, and she and Grant had snuggled under a blanket together, watching the orange flames in the primitive little grate while rain fizzed down the chimney and pelted at the windows. It had seemed so natural, the hug, the kiss, as if they'd both agreed beforehand that this would happen. And what had followed... Melanie had never dreamt that sex could be like that. For the first time, she had fully understood why it was called *making love*.

What she had with Grant was so much more than *friends with benefits*.

And Melanie was still on cloud nine.

So when she saw the police car parked outside her cottage, the endorphins told her it was nothing – probably something to do with the rescue last week on Schiehallion, involving a school party who'd been woefully unprepared for the sudden change in the weather and ended up stumbling about in low cloud without compasses. Maybe they needed Melanie to make a statement about that. She hoped they threw the book at whoever was responsible. Those kids could have died.

Melanie parked alongside the police car and got out, slinging her bag over her shoulder.

There were two uniformed officers in the car, male and female.

'Melanie Macfarlane?' said the sturdily built woman, tugging at her jacket as she got out of the car. Melanie obviously wasn't the only one with uniform issues.

'That's me.' She smiled.

'I'm PC Greig, and this is PC Bain. Can we go inside?'

'Yes, of course. Is this about the rescue on Schiehallion?'

They looked at each other. 'No. It's a personal matter.'

And still, she didn't have any concerns. Police turning up like this would put the fear of God in most people, Melanie guessed, wondering if they were here to break bad news about the loss of a family member. But Melanie didn't have anyone left to lose.

Or so she'd thought, until they told her, sitting there on her new grey couch, side by side, the man looking uncomfortable, the woman sympathetic.

'Alice,' Melanie repeated stupidly.

PC Greig nodded. 'Her parents – her adoptive parents... They've been having a few issues with her. They refused to let her go backpacking in Europe, and one day, she just took off. Stole some money, left a note saying she had a job in the UK and would be back in the autumn. And it seems that the Davidsons, the family who employed her as their au pair, also had some problems with Alice. One theory is that she's punishing everyone by letting them think she might have drowned.'

Melanie nodded numbly. That made sense.

That made sense, didn't it?

'Yes,' she got out in the end.

PC Greig's eyes were heavy with pity. 'Her parents say she accessed your details on the adoption register a few weeks before leaving home. I understand you've kept those up to date? This address, Fern Cottage, is listed there, with your phone number and email?'

'Yes,' said Melanie.

'One possibility we're pursuing,' said the man, 'is that

Alice might have left some clothes on the beach to freak out her employers, and run off to find you.'

'Melanie...' It was probably against protocol, but PC Grieg leant across the coffee table and took Melanie's cold hand in her warm one. 'Have you heard from Alice?'

'No.'

'Okay. Okay, my love.'

Melanie gripped the woman's hand like a lifeline. 'And this happened four days ago? If she's in the sea... It's too late now, isn't it? She can't – she can't still be –'

'*If* she's in the sea,' said PC Grieg. 'That's just an *if* at the moment. Her parents, her adoptive parents, the Snyders, are adamant Alice wouldn't have gone swimming. She's not confident in the water.'

The man put a piece of paper on the coffee table. Turned it to face Melanie. 'These are the mobile numbers for Tonya and Warren Snyder. They'd like you to get in touch. And obviously, if you do hear from Alice, you must let us know immediately.'

Melanie nodded.

'You must have been very young when you had to give her up,' said PC Greig, squeezing her hand.

'I was sixteen.' Melanie sat back, pulling her hand away.

When they'd gone, she stared for what seemed like hours at those telephone numbers, but when she looked at her watch, she saw only minutes had passed. Mechanically, she opened her bag and got out her phone.

Her call was answered on the second ring.

'Hello? Tonya Snyder speaking?' The voice, although definitely American, wasn't what Melanie had expected. It was clipped, the vowels flat.

Melanie took a breath. 'Hello. This is Melanie Macfarlane. The police gave me your –'

'Is she there? Is she with you?'

'No. I'm sorry.'

'Has she been in touch?'

'No.'

'*Tell me the truth!*' screamed Tonya, her voice cracking, and then a man said, 'We're on speaker now. This is Warren Snyder.'

'I'm telling the truth,' Melanie said numbly.

'You'd better be!' Tonya's hostile voice seemed very far away. 'You *bitch!*'

'Tonya!' said Warren. There was a short hiatus, and then his muffled voice, evidently speaking to his wife some distance from the phone, said, 'We need to find out what she knows.'

'I don't know anything,' said Melanie. 'I only wish –' She had to stop and breathe before she could get out, 'You have to believe me.' The hand holding the phone to her ear had started to shake. Hearing them, the panic in Tonya's voice, the damped-down emotion in Warren's, had made it all real.

This was happening.

Alice was missing, presumed dead.

After a short silence: 'I believe you,' said Warren heavily. 'But we were so hoping...'

There was no time for this. 'You told the police you don't think Alice would have gone swimming in the sea?' Melanie said briskly.

'No!' Warren's voice was louder, as if he had brought the phone closer to his mouth. 'She absolutely would not have done so. Alice has always disliked swimming. It still scares her, to go out of her depth.'

In Melanie's mind's eye, she saw a toddler in water wings, crying and grabbing at the nearest adult. An older girl, being admonished by her PE teacher, told to join the other kids in the pool right now and stop being so daft. But the toddler and the girl had no face, just a blank.

She didn't know what Alice had looked like then. She'd only seen photos of her as a teenager, on her social media and in the press after her disappearance.

'There's something about that family, the Davidsons,' Warren was saying now. 'Neither of us liked them. We feel there's something... off about them.'

'*It's your fault!*' Tonya suddenly yelled. 'The whole reason she wanted to come to the UK was to find you! That's why we *didn't want her to!*' Her voice broke. 'If it weren't for you, we'd have let her go backpacking with her friends, and she'd never have run off to stay with random people we know nothing about!'

Melanie couldn't follow this, but it wasn't relevant. She made her voice calm. 'Warren, you said there was something *off* about the Davidsons. In what way?'

She heard him sigh. 'It's hard to put into words. Their reactions to things we said, the way they were looking at us, at each other...'

'They're already advertising for another au pair!' Tonya choked. '*Four days* after Alice goes missing! That shows how much they care. *Oh, too bad, she's gone – well, easy come, easy go!*'

MELANIE STILL KNEW PEOPLE.

Bad people.

Well, Nic wasn't *bad*, not really, but she'd been in and out of prison ever since Melanie had first known her. When Alice had been taken away and Melanie had gone off the rails good and proper and lost her council flat, she'd lived in a squat where Nic ruled the roost. Nic had taken Melanie under her wing, shown her the best places in Inverness and Aberdeen to shoplift, explained how not to get caught, shared her booze and cigarettes.

An hour after the conversation with the Snyders, Melanie called Nic and told her what had happened.

'I need to apply for that job. I need to go to Scallan Lodge as their new au pair and find out what happened to Alice.'

'Oh, Mel.' Nic sighed. 'What's the point? The Snyders are in denial, sounds like, and that's only natural, but don't you get sucked into their sad little fantasy that Alice is somehow still alive and – what? Where the fuck do you think she could be?'

'That's what I have to find out. I know she's probably dead, I know there's probably no mystery and everything is just as it seems. But I have to be *sure*, Nic.'

Nic sucked her teeth. 'Yeah. I suppose I get that. Okay, then. What do you need me for? Want me to do you a glowing reference?'

Next on the list was Kenny Balfour, a fence Melanie still kept in sporadic touch with. He agreed to be her other referee, although for a hefty fee. He also arranged for fake documents – a passport and driving licence.

And that was Melanie all set up as Donna MacKenzie, a nanny and au pair with a spotless record of relevant training and employment.

20

MELANIE - 6 AUGUST

Melanie needed those trackers. And a new phone.

What was taking Nic so long?

Her attempts to follow Gray when he left the house with a map and rucksack, as if off for a hike, were failing miserably. The first time, she'd been waylaid by Ken, and by the time she'd shaken him off, her quarry had disappeared. And now, Gray was heading off across the marshy fields behind the old stable buildings, where it was too exposed to follow him without being seen.

She stood at the corner of the stable, trying to decide what to do. Should she wait until he was out of sight and then follow him? Or perhaps try walking along the coast and then cutting up to where she projected his route would take him?

Just at that moment, as if he had read her mind, he stopped and turned. She froze, hoping he wouldn't see her. But now he was moving his arm in an exaggerated wave. Plastering a smile to her face, she lifted a hand in response.

Well, there was no point trying to tail him now.

Back at Scallan Lodge, she went straight into one of the downstairs loos and locked herself in. There were grey splotches all over everything, floating around each other. She slid down the door to the floor, breathing hard, and looked up at the small Victorian window with its rippled glass, up at the grubby brown-painted ceiling. Even this little toilet had a bad feel to it, like the setting of a scene in a horror film.

Gray was onto her.

Was he?

Should she go to the police? But what evidence did she have against him?

She could feel it all accelerating beyond her control, the dark gathering around her thick and fast, but she had to keep going. She had to try not to think about Alice too much, about what Gray might have –

No.

No no no.

Her brain, thank God, wouldn't let her go there. It was as if there were blocks on certain neural pathways, the ones that would take her to places she couldn't bear to go, as if whenever her thoughts tried to get through, they were diverted off elsewhere. But the barriers were crumbling.

She was in a race against time, not only against the shadows gathering around her, but against the shadows within, the darkness in her own fragile mind that was reaching out to claim her.

Tim Gilbey and Edward Norcott were leaving. After dinner, they went upstairs to pack – Caro was driving them to the airport – and Melanie made a start on stacking the dishwasher. She had just dropped in a handful of cutlery and was turning back to the worktop when she sensed someone invading her personal space behind her.

'Well, Donna, I'm off!' It was Tim Gilbey, his nose and left cheek still fiery and scabbing up a little where his skin had connected with the hot iron.

'Bye, then,' she said, picking up a plate.

'Oh, but I'll be back *very soon*.'

He took a step closer. She could smell him, woody antiperspirant overlying BO. She didn't look at him as she scraped the plate into the food waste bin.

His hand closed over the rim of the plate, and he brought his face right up to hers, so close that his features blurred. But she stopped herself from flinching and pulling her head away. Made herself hold his gaze as he said, 'We've unfinished business, you and I.'

'Oh yes,' she said. 'We certainly do.'

And it was he who pulled away.

Melanie turned her back on him and put the plate into the rack with a clatter.

When she looked round, he'd gone.

21

ALICE - 17 JULY

Alice was avoiding Gray now in earnest. Which wasn't fair. She didn't believe he'd assaulted those women – the charges had been dropped, and that didn't happen these days unless the police were pretty confident a guy was innocent. And she was sure Tim, not Gray, was the 'torch man'.

It was her own thoughts and feelings about Gray that were the issue. How could she have listened to that awful story about Erin and thought that *she* would have liked Gray to run a torch over *her* naked body?

She didn't like the person she was becoming when she was around Gray.

When he came into the kitchen, Alice made an excuse to leave it. When he offered to help her dust the library, she said, 'Oh, thank you *so much* – if you could dust in here, that frees me up to supervise the girls outside.'

But then he followed her. Right round the house to the Frog Fountain, as they called it, where Isabel and Tess were checking for trapped amphibians.

Gray clapped his hands together. 'What are we playing?'

'We're not *playing*,' said Tess in disgust, hands on hips. 'Why are you always hanging around us now?'

'You probably have work you should be doing,' Isabel added, as if to soften the blow.

'Well, the more the merrier!' Alice made herself smile at Gray.

Tess scowled. 'It's not *merrier* with *him*.'

Gray's smile was slipping.

'How about a game of hide-and-seek?' Alice suggested.

'Yeah, hide-and-seek!' Isabel scrambled out of the dry fountain. 'Come on!' She grabbed Alice with one hand and Tess with the other. 'Uncle Gray, you have to count to a hundred!'

'Make that *two* hundred!' shouted Tess. Then whispered to Alice and Isabel: 'We can shake him off now!'

'No, we mustn't,' said Alice weakly, although this had been her intention too.

She should be teaching Tess to be kinder. Alice had the uncomfortable feeling that Tess wasn't shy, she just found most people beneath her contempt. She soon melted away, as she was apt to do, leaving Alice and Isabel to find a hiding place for themselves. They ran along the track that ended up at the old mill, but they both decided the mill itself would be too spooky to hide in.

'How about here?' Alice suggested as they came to the stables.

'Okay!'

The cobbled yard had nothing in it and was no use for hiding. The building in which the horses would have been stabled had wooden partitions, but Isabel rejected Alice's idea that they could duck down behind one of them. 'Too easy for Uncle Gray to find us.'

They explored the other buildings around the courtyard. A storeroom with lots of packing crates had possibilities, but 'too many spiders,' said Isabel, pointing to all the cobwebs in the corners. Next door was another room with boxes and crates in it, this one with a wooden floor rather than a cobbled one. Isabel's feet drummed on it as she ran back and forth. Then she stopped.

'There's a trapdoor!' She squatted near the back wall. 'I never noticed it before! I think these boxes used to be over here.'

There was a long, flat metal bar set into the wood, extending across the trapdoor and fitting over a loop on the floor with a padlock on it. Isabel grabbed the padlock, and it came open.

'Be careful,' said Alice as Isabel pulled at the metal bar. 'Don't get your fingers pinched.'

'Can you open it?' Isabel's little face was pleading.

'Okay, but it might be dangerous. There might be a big hole underneath. Stand well back.'

Alice took hold of the metal bar and pulled it up.

The square trapdoor opened to reveal steps going down into the darkness. A damp, musty, stale-air smell rose up, overlaid with bleach. The underside of the trapdoor, weirdly, was lined with a sort of thick grey plastic sheeting.

'Ugh,' said Isabel, peering past Alice. 'Is it a dungeon?'

'It's just a cellar.'

'There's a light switch.' Isabel pointed to a white plastic switch on the floor next to the steps.

That was also a bit weird. There didn't seem to be lights fitted anywhere else in the stables.

'Can we go down?' But Isabel didn't sound too sure.

'I don't think I want to hide down there. Do you?'

Isabel shook her head. 'But we could have a look. There might be bones. It could be a plague pit.'

Tess and Isabel liked to watch TV programmes about archaeology, particularly if skeletons were involved, preferably with indications of violence: skulls shattered by blunt force trauma, leg bones with sword cuts or, better still, signs of butchery indicating cannibalism.

'Don't get your hopes up,' said Alice.

'If it was a plague pit, we couldn't get the plague from it, could we?'

'No. The plague bacteria or whatever would be dead by now. But it's not old enough to be that anyways. Okay, wait up, Isabel. I'll go first.' Alice backed down the steps, flicking on the light as she went.

'*Awwww*,' said Isabel, her voice heavy with disappointment as she saw what was down there.

Nothing.

The cellar was completely free of bones. That was obvious at once. It had a concrete floor that had recently been cleaned. Alice backed slowly, helping Isabel's feet find the steps above her. There was a wooden rail down the open side of the steps, but it was flimsy.

'Careful,' Alice kept saying.

'What is this place for?' said Isabel once they were down. She ran her hands along the stone walls. 'It stinks of cleaning.'

'Yeah, bleach.' Alice wrinkled her nose too.

'Aha!' came a loud voice from above their heads.

Alice jumped.

Isabel screamed.

Gray laughed, and his pirate face appeared at the trapdoor opening.

'Found you!' he exclaimed in triumph, flicking back his hair as he turned to descend the steps.

Isabel glared at him. 'You can't have counted to two hundred already!'

'I'm a quick counter. Onetwothreefourfive...'

'What *is* this place?' Isabel interrupted.

Gray crouched to her level. 'Guess.'

'That's silly.' Isabel backed away from him. 'It's not like it's going to be anything interesting.'

'Very true, Izz.' He straightened, quirking an eyebrow at Alice. 'I'm afraid it's just a storage space for some of the supplies we'll need for the glamping business. Things that don't mind the damp and the rats. Plastic bottles of things like shower cleaner, disinfectant...'

'Rats?' Isabel began clambering back up the steps.

Alice quickly followed, very conscious of Gray behind her. *Quick, quick*, she wanted to snap at Isabel when she stopped at the top, blocking Alice's way.

'Look at that.' Isabel pointed to the grey plastic on the underside of the trapdoor. There were scratches and gouges on its edges. 'Did rats do it?'

'Maybe,' said Alice.

But it looked more like someone had been trying to prise the trapdoor open.

'Come on, Isabel. Let's get out of here.'

Alice practically pushed the girl up the last few steps and out to the courtyard and the sun, leaving Gray to secure the trapdoor.

'I don't like that place,' said Isabel.

'Me either,' said Alice.

'It's *neither*,' Isabel corrected her, with a little smile. 'Can we do cooking now? Can we run so Uncle Gray won't know where we are?'

'Oh, Isabel... that's not nice.'

But when Isabel took off across the courtyard, the sound of her sneakers hitting the cobbles reverberating around the enclosed space, Alice ran after her, wanting nothing more, in that moment, than to put distance between herself and Isabel, and Gray and that cellar.

22

MELANIE - 6 AUGUST

She was prepared to wait up all night if she had to. She made a thermos of coffee and stationed herself in the laundry room with the window open and the light off. There was no moon, and she couldn't see a thing, but the parking area was right in front of her. She'd hear Gray crossing the gravel.

Three hours later, something woke her from a deep sleep.

She lifted her head from the windowsill and rubbed her face.

A car door clonked softly.

She groped her way to the back door and opened it slowly just as the popping of gravel under tyres and a slight shifting of the darkness told her that one of the vehicles was on the move. She walked blindly forward, across the grass, until her foot hit the gravel surface.

A faint shooshing on the track told her that the vehicle was far enough away that she could risk getting out the tiny torch she'd found in a kitchen drawer and use it to make her way to her own car.

Would the sound of the engine wake people in the house?

She had to risk it. When she fired it up, it seemed horribly loud, reverberating around in the dark. She flicked on her side lights. Gray knew the layout of the driveway and track well enough, evidently, to navigate it with minimal cues, but Melanie needed some light. The house would shield her, for now, from his view.

She eased the car around the side gable. Now taillights were visible some distance beyond the gateposts. She tried to imprint what she could see on her mind and switched off her own lights.

But all too soon, the ground under her wheels softened – she had veered off onto the lawn. She needed to wait until those taillights disappeared before continuing. She couldn't remember where the forest began, but once he was swallowed up by it, he wouldn't be able to see her behind him.

When the red dots of light had gone, she turned her sidelights back on and eased between the gateposts and on up the track. With so little illumination, it was a constant strain to keep the wheels on the track, but she began to get the hang of it and moved up from second to third gear.

And then she realised something.

She must be beyond the place, now, where the taillights had disappeared, but there were no trees here. Up ahead, a smaller track dipped down to the right off the main one. He must have veered off onto that, turning sideways-on to where Melanie had been watching, so it had looked to her like the taillights were being concealed by trees. And then, as he'd descended the offshoot track, she would no longer have been able to see his lights at all.

She turned onto the offshoot. It was overgrown, the grass in the middle swishing against the underside of her car. And the surface was terrible, full of potholes. The car bucked and tipped as if in protest.

No lights were visible ahead. The track twisted down into trees, getting rougher all the time, and Melanie wondered if she should pull up and get out, continue on foot. But the track could go on for miles.

Her hands were slick on the steering wheel.

The track was becoming more and more overgrown, gorse bushes encroaching on either side scratching at the car like fingernails. What was along here? A hut of some sort?

Abruptly, the track widened into a little clearing hemmed in by trees. Heart pumping, Melanie flicked her headlights on to full beam. But there was nothing here. Just trees and gorse and weeds. No other vehicle.

And she definitely hadn't passed one on the way.

The track hadn't divided at any point, and it stopped right here.

So where the hell was he?

She turned around and drove slowly back the way she'd come, up onto the main track and then down to the house, flicking her sidelights off whenever she could. As she did so, she realised what must have happened, and a shiver went through her.

He must have seen her lights as she drove round the side of the house, when she'd delayed for a second or two before switching them off. He had seen the lights and switched off his own, to make it look as if he'd turned off the main track. Which meant he knew someone had followed him.

As she eased in through the gates and onto the gravel drive, the house loomed ahead of her in the dark, more a felt presence than a visible one.

Had Alice died here?

How likely, after all, was it that Gray was going to her? There could be any number of reasons why he was sneaking out of the house, both through the day and at night. If he was keeping Alice somewhere, why did he walk there during the day but drive at night? It didn't make any sense.

What did make sense was that Alice was dead, and had been ever since she'd first disappeared.

Had they been filled with terror, her last moments? Had she screamed, struggled? Had there been pain? And then release.

Release into nothing.

Melanie could feel those barriers in her brain fissuring, but with a supreme effort of will, she concentrated on what she had to do now. Drive back to the parking area, flicking on her sidelights occasionally so she could see her way. Get out of the car and walk to the back door, using the dim light from her phone. Return to the utility room and wait.

This time, she didn't sleep. She sat at the window staring into the dark and making herself think of trivial things – what she would have for breakfast. What she would cook for lunch. What activity she could suggest for Isabel and Tess, although she knew what they would insist on doing.

Look for clues.

They had loved Alice. Those girls had loved her, in the short time they'd had together, and from them Melanie was catching the echoes of the joy Alice had brought into their lives; lives that were not, perhaps, very happy. Not in this family.

Until Alice.

Alice loved to sing. She had taught the girls not the latest hits but sweet American folk songs. There was one called 'Come Follow Me'. Melanie had heard Tess sing it under her breath a few times and asked her what it was. Tess and Isabel had then demonstrated how it should be done. Alice had taught them to sing it in a round, with each voice chiming in:

Come follow, follow, follow me
Where shall I follow, follow thee
To the greenwood, to the redwood, to the redwood,
redwood tree
Where shall I follow, follow, follow
Come follow, follow, follow me.

Alice loved to bake 'cookies' and had shown Tess and Isabel how. Her favourites were cinnamon chocolate chip.

Alice loved to snuggle with the girls under blankets while they ate the cookies and watched, of all things, documentaries on archaeology.

Alice loved 'kitties' but was allergic to their dander, which had been a problem when she'd helped out at the local vet's surgery. She'd hoped she might grow out of it, as her doctor had said she might, and some day be able to have a cat of her own.

Don't think about that.

What was in the pile of ironing to be done tomorrow, on the table behind her? A red T-shirt. A white one. Caro's white shirts. Caro only seemed to wear white shirts, each one different. The linen ones were a nightmare to iron, and creased again in a second unless you hung them up straight away and carried them upstairs on their hangers.

Outside, the gravel crackled.

She could just make out the shape of the vehicle, drawing up next to Caro's. She heard the door open and close. And then light, torchlight, in which she could see a man's bulky figure.

It was Ken.

Ken?

He shone the torch at his feet and then across the parking area to the other vehicles. Eerily uplit, his face was pale and jowly, like a scary clown's. He walked to the Audi, Gray's car, and put his hand on the bonnet. He ran his hand across the bodywork, then moved to Caro's 4x4 and did the same. Then to Melanie's little Fiat.

Shit.

He would be able to feel the warmth from the engine.

The torch went off.

Melanie found herself ducking down under the window, although she knew he couldn't see her in the dark.

He'd gone to Gray's car first. He'd seen lights following him and assumed it was his brother. Why? Could Ken be having an affair, and had been off for an assignation with someone? If so, Melanie wouldn't put it past Gray to blackmail him over it – nor, presumably, would Ken.

But now Ken knew it was Melanie who'd been following him.

What would he make of that?

23

ALICE - 18 JULY

'You did really well!' Isabel assured Alice as they got out of the pool. She and Tess were 'coaching' Alice, encouraging her to swim lengths and even put her head underwater a couple of times. Alice hated the feel of it, though, water in her nose and mouth.

She wrapped a towel around herself as soon as she was out of the pool. She was wearing her navy one-piece, but even so. She didn't want another reprimand from Caro. And Gray was there, perched on one of the loungers. He was trying to talk to Tess, who was briskly towelling her hair dry – he wasn't even looking at Alice. But she'd felt his eyes on her all the time she was in the water. As he looked at her now, it was like his gaze was a physical thing, like she could feel it on her body. The friendship bracelet, she realised suddenly, was exposed on her arm. She really should take it off, but he might be offended, she guessed.

Part of the reason she'd come out here to the pool had been to get away from him. But he'd followed them, so Alice had cut short the coaching session as soon as she could without hurting Tess's and Isabel's feelings. They were so serious about improving her swimming – it was the sweetest thing, that they were worried about her lack of ability. Tess in particular was a really good swimmer and had been showing off a bit, executing perfect dives at the deep end – and every time, Alice had held her breath. What if she hit her head on the bottom? What if Alice couldn't swim down and get her?

When Gray had turned up, at first she'd been relieved that another adult was available in case of problems, but soon she was wishing him anywhere but here.

She hurried into the pool house after Isabel.

Christina was in there too, brushing her hair at the mirror. 'I just saw some of your little weirdo friends at the beach.'

Alice had told Christina she'd met Murray and the others, and Christina had said more or less what Murray had about the Davidsons: *They're weird. Don't let them latch onto you.* At the time, Alice had shut that conversation down. But now, she asked, 'What have you got against them?'

Christina caught her fall of light brown hair up in a scrunchy. 'They're weird, and they're also just *nasty*. You know how when you're at a new school, all the oddballs flock around you because they're, like, *desperate* for *anyone* to be their friend, and a newbie is fresh meat and doesn't know what they're like? They did that to me. And when I made it clear that I didn't want to be part of their sad little club, sitting around arguing about who was the best captain of the starship *Enterprise*, they kind of turned on me. Slagged me off to everyone so I couldn't make any other friends.' She flicked a look at Alice. 'I suppose they've told you I'm a terrible person?'

'No,' lied Alice, pulling the towel more securely around herself. 'But they told me I should leave Scallan Lodge.'

Christina's hands on her hair went still. 'Because of me?'

'No.'

Christina waited, but Alice could hardly relay Murray's suspicions about Gray to his niece. She settled on, 'They said there've been some strange things going on here.'

'Like what?' Christina turned away from the mirror to face Alice. Maybe it was because of the lack of make-up, but she looked very young, suddenly, her big blue eyes reminding Alice of Isabel.

'I don't know,' Alice lied again.

'They're probably just trying to cause trouble for me and my family. *Strange things going on!*' Christina snorted and turned back to the mirror. 'We could sue them for slander.' She opened the make-up bag on the shelf under the mirror and took out a tube of foundation. But instead of applying it, she just stared at her own face, then flicked a look in the glass at Alice.

Were Murray and his friends just trying to cause trouble? All that stuff about Katie's sister and the 'torch man' – had it really happened, or were they messing with her?

She needed to talk to them.

'They were at the beach just now?'

'Yes. But, Alice – forget it. They're not worth it.'

As Alice jogged along the track towards the beach, she felt her spirits start to lift. She was most relaxed away from the house, she realised, when she was out on her own or with Tess and Isabel. Away from Gray. But there was also something oppressive now about Scallan Lodge – probably Tim and Edward had coloured her subconscious feelings about it, and maybe about Gray too.

At first she thought there was no one on the beach. And then she saw the cutely rounded little shape of Katie, sitting reading a book in the shade of one of the dunes.

'Hi!' Alice plonked herself down on the sand. 'I'm playing hooky – left Christina to mind her little sisters for once.'

'Enjoy it while you can.' Katie set aside her book and turned to face Alice. She had small, clever, piercing grey eyes.

Alice grinned. 'I mean to enjoy every second! I love it here – the peace and quiet, the scenery...' She waved a hand around them. 'It all feels so... so far away from trouble, like nothing bad ever happens here.' She had intended this to be a lead-in to talking about the 'torch man', but found herself babbling on: 'My ancestors come from Scotland. From the Highlands.'

'Oh. I'd have thought Snyder was maybe a German name.'

'It's Dutch, originally. But I'm adopted. I was with my birth mother in Inverness until I was three months old; then my parents adopted me. They were living in Edinburgh at the time, but they moved back to the US when I was two.'

Katie was one of those good listeners who reacted to what you were saying. Sympathy, interest and curiosity chased each other across her face. 'Wow – so are you going to look for your birth family while you're here?'

Alice shrugged. 'Maybe. I haven't decided. I got my birth mother's details from the adoption register. But I don't know.' The cottage from the dream flashed into her head. Fern Cottage, it was called. Alice had examined that cute little house and its flower-filled garden from every possible angle on Google Streetview, and she supposed it had lodged so firmly in her mind that her subconscious kept worrying at it.

She shivered.

In the dream last night, she'd actually come face to face with her birth mother for the first time. Alice didn't know what Melanie Macfarlane looked like – she hadn't been able to find her anywhere on the internet, which in itself was a bit worrying – but the dream had conjured up a scary-faced woman with scowling eyebrows. She'd been on the phone as she'd come out of the front door and walked down the path towards Alice. She hadn't looked up. Alice had said, 'Hello!' but the woman had carried on speaking to whoever was on the phone and walked right on by, as if Alice weren't there. 'Are you Melanie?' Alice had gone after her. 'I'm Alice.' The woman had got into her car and driven off, leaving Alice standing there.

'Have you always known you were adopted?' asked Katie.

Alice nodded. 'It was never a big deal.'

Well, it hadn't been until a few months ago, when Alice had started asking questions, and Mom had told her some things. Like Melanie Macfarlane had been just sixteen when she'd had Alice. Like she had convictions for theft, being drunk and disorderly, and assault. Like the social workers had decided Alice needed to be taken away from her mother. When Alice had asked why, Mom had got this terrible look on her face, and eventually she'd admitted, 'They were worried she might do something to you.'

Alice's insides had churned. 'What do you mean, *do* something?'

'Something to harm you.' Mom had spoken harshly,

almost as if it were Alice's fault. But then she had pulled Alice into a tight hug, and soon they were both sobbing, although neither one of them was a crier.

Later, it had occurred to Alice to wonder if the reason her parents were stricter than anyone else's was because they were terrified that Alice could have bad genes. Maybe she needed a firmer hand than other people's biological kids.

She could feel herself tearing up again now.

'But you want to meet your birth mother?' Katie said gently.

'No. No, I really don't think I do.'

It was weird, but being so far away from Mom and Daddy was bringing home to Alice just how lucky she was to have them, how much they loved her and wanted the best for her. They weren't the kind of folks to deny their adopted child the chance to know her birth mother out of jealousy or some such. There had to be a good reason why they'd go so far as to veto a trip to Europe just in case Alice made contact with Melanie Macfarlane. Alice was sure that was the real reason they'd stopped her going backpacking with her friends, rather than a supposed lack of maturity on her part.

'Well, you've got time to decide. You're staying for the whole summer, Murray was saying?' It was almost as if Katie was expecting her to contradict that assumption.

'Yeah, that was the plan. But... Well, Murray told me what happened to your sister. Erin? And now I'm not so sure about staying.'

A wave of homesickness washed over her. She wanted her mom and dad! She wanted Skip! She wanted her own friends that she'd known since they were all five years old! Although Kimmy, Parker and Jasmine weren't in Branchfield right now, of course. And after all the fuss there must have been when Daddy and Mom read that note, it would be so humiliating to go back now with her tail between her legs.

Katie was looking past her towards Scallan House. 'Yeah, Erin's still not right. I wanted to go to the police. But Erin – she's a bit notorious for making things up. When she was little, she was always pretending she had a stomach ache so she wouldn't have to go to school or the dentist, and even now, when it suits her, she'll lie without even thinking about it.'

'So you think she's lying about the torch man?'

Katie shook her head. 'Oh, no. I'm sure it happened. You should have seen the state she was in. Completely hysterical. But anyone who wasn't actually there – they're not going to believe her. Even Mum and Dad would probably think she was just attention-seeking. And Erin wouldn't make a statement anyway. She says she just wants to forget it ever happened.'

'I think it might have been one of the paying guests who did it – Tim Gilbey, he's called. He kind of assaulted me too. He pushed himself against me and grabbed my behind.'

'Oh, Alice! *Ugh!*'

'I haven't said anything to the police either. I know what Erin means about just wanting to forget about it. But maybe we should both make statements against him.'

'But Erin doesn't know who the man with the torch was – and in fact, I'm pretty sure it was Gray Davidson.'

Alice sighed. 'So Murray's been peddling that theory to you too.'

'We've discussed it, of course, but it's not just Murray – we all think it must have been Gray. Everyone knows he's dodgy. I was once out for a cycle along the road here, the road that passes the gates to Scallan Lodge, and I met Gray

Davidson in his car. He had to pull into a passing place. And there was this young girl in the passenger seat. I mean, *really* young. Maybe fifteen.'

Oh, for crying out loud! This was how these sorts of rumours started. 'Well, Christina's sixteen. Isn't it likely it was one of her friends, and Gray was running her home?'

Katie shrugged. 'Maybe.'

'Did this girl look frightened?'

'No...'

'She didn't try to get out of the car, or signal to you?'

'No. If she had, obviously I'd have done something. Called the police. In hindsight, after what happened to Erin, I wish I had.'

In other words, Katie hadn't been concerned enough at the time to do anything about it, which suggested there wasn't much to be concerned about in the first place. Now, though, she was seeing red flags all over the place.

Alice was beginning to think Christina maybe had a point. She'd seen it happen in Branchfield. Folks took against someone, like Katie, Murray and the rest seemed to have taken against Christina, and the next thing, there were whispers all around town about the person's whole family.

'Gray Davidson's a very attractive guy,' Alice said slowly, carefully. 'If he was interested in a woman, he wouldn't have to... well, *force* her to do anything. Women are probably throwing themselves at him all the time! He probably rejected those women, and they made the allegations to get back at him.'

'Yeah, Murray said you'd fallen under his spell.'

'And you've charged and convicted him!' Alice was getting mad. 'All of you!' She stood. 'The poor guy was *cleared* of any wrongdoing, wasn't he?'

'The women withdrew their accusations. It's not quite the same thing. I know he's attractive and charismatic and all that, but a lot of psychos are, Alice. Don't get sucked in.'

'Have you even *met* Gray? Talked to him?'

'No, but...'

And that said it all.

24

MELANIE - 8 AUGUST

Melanie lay in bed, holding Frog against her chest and watching the early morning light come and go with the clouds passing the windows. Alice had lain here like this, although probably not for long. She was the kind of girl who was up and at 'em, as the Snyders would no doubt say, as soon as she woke.

Alice's eyes would have gazed about her, taking it all in.

Those eyes. The way they had fixed on Melanie, held her, possessed her.

Told her *I trust you*.

And now she was failing her baby all over again.

As usual, Ken was the first of the Davidsons to appear for breakfast, and as Melanie bustled about getting his fry-up, she rehearsed what she would say when he confronted her about last night. But Ken just sat there at the table, reading a document on his laptop and pretty much ignoring Melanie, other than to smile at her and say, 'This looks amazing,' when she set the plateful down in front of him.

Then Isabel appeared with Caro, who drifted to the window, leaving Melanie to see to her daughter's breakfast. Isabel chose cornflakes for a change, and as Melanie poured them into a bowl, she became aware of Isabel standing next to her, staring up at her face.

'You have a princess nose,' she said. 'Just like Alice's. It's all nice and cute.'

Melanie laughed, maybe a little too loudly, and walked away to the fridge. 'I don't think there's anything particularly cute about *my* nose. Do you want ordinary milk or oat milk with your cornflakes? And some fruit?'

Isabel was soon distracted from the dangerous territory of Melanie's facial features by the important issue of how many strawberries were 'right' to have with cornflakes. When the bowl was finished to her satisfaction, Isabel added another spoon and said she was going to find Tess and share it with her. Caro soon drifted away too, leaving only Melanie and Ken in the room.

She decided to take the bull by the horns.

'Last night, I couldn't sleep and went for a walk outside,' she said. 'And a car passed me with no lights on! I thought maybe someone was sleep-driving or something – is that a thing?' Donna giggled. 'I tried to follow them in my car, but I lost them. I hope there wasn't an accident.'

Flimsy.

Ken blinked at her. 'How odd.'

'I know! It was weird!'

'Lucky you had your car keys on you.'

'Oh, well, I keep them in my jacket pocket. And it wasn't

really *lucky*, because I wasn't able to catch up with them and do anything about it. I hope they're okay.'

'Possibly it was poachers.'

'Oh – really? Oh dear! Just as well I didn't catch up with them, then!'

'Just as well.'

Her heart was racing as she turned away to the sink. What was Ken up to? And why had he gone to Gray's car first to check if the engine was warm? Could *Ken* possibly be holding Alice prisoner, somewhere nearby, and was worried that Gray was onto him? But she didn't get any sort of creepy vibe off this man.

Just what was going on in this family?

'Murray wants to talk to you,' said Tess when she appeared in the kitchen. 'He's waiting on the beach.'

'How do you know that? Tess – have you been down to the beach on your own?'

A shrug. 'I often go there.' She opened the fridge. 'You'd better go and see him.'

Melanie headed for the beach along the track between gorse bushes, their blooms bright yellow under the blue sky and filling the air with the scent of coconut. The gorse gave way to the marram grass of the dunes, and underfoot the track became sandy before opening out onto the beach.

A bulky figure was standing looking at the sea – a stocky, sandy-haired boy in long khaki shorts and a white T-shirt that was rather tight across his barrel chest.

Murray.

Finally.

'Hi,' she said when they were within talking distance. 'You're Murray?'

He stared at her, wide-eyed. 'And you're the new au pair.'

'I've been wanting to talk to you,' said Melanie. 'About Alice –'

'They've done something to her!' he blurted, his gaze jumping from Melanie's face to something behind her – the house? – and back again. 'The Davidsons. Well, Gray, probably. You know he's been in trouble before over sexual assaults? He's done something to Alice.' His voice wobbled.

'You can't know that.'

'*You* know it too! I saw you breaking into his study. What did you find?'

'Nothing,' said Melanie. 'Everything was locked up, and I couldn't get onto the computer.' For some reason, she immediately trusted this boy.

'I've tried to follow him, but it's not as easy as it looks in films. The police should be doing this. The police should be watching the house, tracking his movements –'

'Is that what you've been doing?'

He nodded. 'Trying to. But it's such a massive house, it's impossible to cover all the exits, even when I can persuade one of my friends to help out. And the couple of times I've seen him leave, I haven't been able to stay on his tail. I've been to the police, I've tried to get them to take an interest in Gray, but apparently he has a watertight alibi. They're not interested. They even had the cheek to say they hoped I wasn't *harassing* him.'

'Alibis can be set up,' said Melanie.

'Exactly! I *know* it's him! And if he's keeping Alice somewhere...' He frowned at her. 'I should be telling you to get out of there, as I told Alice. But – if you're careful, maybe you'll be able to find stuff out.'

'I'm trying to.'

He narrowed his eyes suddenly. 'Cop car!' He pointed over her shoulder. 'At least, it's not a *cop* car, but I'm pretty sure that's DI Macneil's Alfa Romeo. Heading for Scallan Lodge.'

MELANIE RAN the distance from the beach to the house like an Olympic sprinter.

Was there news?

Had the police found her?

Had she been wrong all along about Gray, and Caro had been right? Was Alice off working in a hotel somewhere – maybe she'd cut and dyed her hair, but someone had eventually recognised her from the appeals?

DC Smith was standing smoking by the back door. He hurriedly dropped his cigarette and stood on it as Melanie ran up to him.

'Have you found her?' she gasped.

He frowned at her – and yes, yes, she knew she was making a spectacle of herself, and it was probably suspicious, but she didn't care.

'*Alice?*' she almost shouted.

He shook his head as Murray lumbered up, sweat pouring off him.

'You haven't found her?' Melanie persisted.

'No. The DI's just letting the Davidsons know that there's been a development.' He frowned at Murray.

'This is one of Alice's friends,' Melanie said impatiently. 'What development?'

'Yes, I know who he is. I thought the DI had had a word with you about harassing the Davidsons?'

'I haven't been *harassing* them!' Murray sounded as angry as she felt. 'Just tell us! What's happened?'

'It seems Alice's birth mother has gone AWOL. She told her employer that she had to go and nurse her dying father, but it turns out that Melanie Macfarlane never even knew who her father was. Her mother was a prostitute, and the dad could have been anyone.' He shrugged. 'Then Melanie herself got pregnant by some random and had Alice when she was sixteen. Baby was taken off her. She's maybe always wanted the kid back.'

Melanie couldn't think of a single thing to say, but Murray cut in with, 'So, what – the birth mother kidnapped her? That's your theory?' He snorted.

'No,' said the DC with terrible patience. 'The *theory* is that Alice *may* have tracked down her birth mother, and the two of them have gone off somewhere together. Melanie Macfarlane may not be the most responsible person in the world.'

Shit.

Was there a photograph of Melanie somewhere in a police file? She'd been convicted of various minor offences as a teenager. It would only take DC Smith or DI Macneil glancing at a mugshot to ruin everything.

'Sounds pretty unlikely,' said Murray.

The policeman gave him a look, as if to say *I couldn't care less what you think.*

'You need to be monitoring Gray Davidson,' Murray went on. 'He's behaving suspiciously, going out with a rucksack and so on. He could be going to Alice. You need to carry out surveillance on him.'

DC Smith smiled. 'Someone's been watching too many cop dramas. You think we have the resources to "carry out surveillance" on random people who weren't even here when the person went missing? You need to give yourself a reality check, son.'

MELANIE STOOD UNDER THE SHOWER, letting the water wash over her head. Maybe she was worrying unnecessarily? If there were photos of her in files or databases, surely the police officers on Alice's case would have seen them already? If they had done so, Melanie aged thirty-four must look different enough from her scrawny, peroxide-haired teenage self for them not to have made the connection.

She gave the shower a quick clean and stepped out, wrapped a towel around herself and opened the door to disperse the steam. The extractor fan didn't seem very efficient, and the little windowless space was like a sauna.

She towelled herself dry and pulled on clean clothes, bundling the dirty ones into the linen basket by the sink. As she straightened, she screamed, her subconscious registering before her conscious mind what she was seeing in the mirror.

A man's face.

She wheeled round.

Gray was smiling at her.

She yanked the door shut and locked it.

'Sorry!' came his voice, muffled by the thickness of the door.

How long had he been standing there?

'Piss off!' Melanie shouted. 'You *sick pervert!*'

'Well, that's a little harsh.' His voice was suddenly louder, as if he was standing right up against the door.

'*Go away!*'

'All right, Bathsheba!' A chuckle. 'Although I don't imagine you know your Bible like Alice did. I only came to tell you there's a phone call for you downstairs.'

Maybe it's Grant rushed through her, and suddenly she wanted nothing more than to hear his voice, that calm, reassuring, low buzz –

But it couldn't be Grant, because he didn't know where she was or what she was doing. It must be Nic. No one else had the landline number.

She opened the door and glared at Gray. 'Get out of my way.'

He took two exaggeratedly large steps backwards and put his hands out to the sides, as if to hold back a whole crowd of perverts intent on ogling Melanie in her shower.

Melanie scooted past him and hauled open the door to the rest of the house.

By the time she got to the landline in the hall, Nic, of course, had rung off. Never the most patient of people. Melanie redialled the last number that had called, and soon Nic's raspy voice was saying, 'Finally!'

'Hi, Sarah. Sorry I missed your call.'

'Oh, don't mention it, old bean!' Nic found it hilarious, the way Melanie spoke now.

'Although I was rather expecting to hear from you before now.'

'Aye, sorry about that. Sorry to have a *fucking life* outside of digging you out of the shit, Mel, and running your fucking errands.'

'You know what it's for.'

A sigh. 'I only picked up your email yesterday, all right? Like I said, I've been busy. But I've got you those items.'

'Great. Thanks, N – Sarah.'

'There was a text message from your wifey an' all, saying to call her. About the reference. Spoke to her earlier. Told her my married name's Nicola Black. Aye, and before you ask, there's a Nicola Black on the college staff. I did check. Put on my telephone voice too. Kept the effing and blindings to a minimum.'

Melanie couldn't help smiling. 'Well, there's probably some sort of diversity quota they have to meet...' Belatedly, she looked around the hall, but there seemed to be no one to overhear, so she dropped her voice and whispered, 'that specifies that for every hundred normal employees, they have to have one wee minger from Paisley.'

'Fuck off.'

'I'll email you about meeting up some time soon!' said Melanie brightly. That was best done by email, just in case anyone was around to overhear.

That afternoon, she borrowed Christina's phone again and sent a message to Nic suggesting tomorrow at three o'clock at a pub on Academy Street in Inverness. Then she googled Bathsheba. It seemed she was the wife of Uriah the Hittite, and she first appeared in the Bible naked on a roof:

> *And it came to pass in an eveningtide, that David arose from off his bed, and walked upon the roof of the king's house: and from the roof he saw a woman washing herself; and the woman was very beautiful to look upon. And David sent and enquired after the woman. And one said, Is not this Bathsheba, the daughter of Eliam, the wife of Uriah the Hittite? And David sent messengers, and*

took her; and she came in unto him, and he lay with her; for she was purified from her uncleanness: and she returned unto her house.

Further googling told her that Bathsheba had had the last laugh, ending up David's queen and conniving to put her son, Solomon, on the throne.

It had been happening throughout history, she supposed: men using women like objects. And women finding their own ways to fight back.

Tomorrow she'd have the trackers and would be able to follow Ken or Gray when they left the house. Meanwhile, she had to make herself safe.

In the hallway under the Tower Room, she removed the drawers from the chest of drawers and pulled the carcass across the floor to block the door at the bottom of the stairs, just as Alice had done. With the drawers and their contents back in place, the big lump of mahogany would be heavy enough to keep anyone from forcing the door open.

She wrapped herself in the duvet Alice had slept under and tried not to think about what that Bible verse might mean to Gray Davidson.

25

ALICE - 19 JULY

Alice knew Tess wanted to talk to her.

In a way that was completely out of character, she'd been following Alice around all day, helping with the chores and just hanging out. While Alice was ironing in the laundry room, Tess would be sorting the clothes into coloureds and whites. While Alice was cooking, Tess would be going through the contents of the fridge and deciding whether stuff was far enough past its date that it should go in the trash. Not that anything went in the actual trash here – or as little as possible, as Tess sternly pointed out when Alice casually threw a tub of mouldy coleslaw into the big enamel trash can by the door.

Tess retrieved it, emptied the contents into the little green pail under the sink that Alice had kind of been ignoring, washed the tub and took it to the plastic recycling box in the utility room.

When she came back, Alice said, 'How about a break and a snack? I think we've earned it, don't you?'

They had strawberry jam on Alice's home-made bread

and milkshakes. While Alice chattered on, Tess remained mainly silent, sitting opposite her at the table and tackling her bread and jam and her milkshake with her usual quiet efficiency, as if she were at a fuel stop and had to get it all onboard asap. But as she ate, she stared at Alice in a way Alice began to find a little trying.

'Well, spit it out!' she said at last.

Tess stopped mid-chew.

'Not literally,' Alice added, and that made Tess smile. Alice touched the back of her hand briefly. 'I get the feeling you've got something on your mind.'

'No. I don't.'

'Oh, okay. But if there was something you wanted to talk over, you know I'm always here to listen? I would try to help if I could.'

Alice changed the subject, and they ended up talking about Isabel and her obsession with the pigeon books.

'She's too old for them,' said Tess.

'Well, *I* like them, and I'm eighteen!'

Tess shrugged. Then she said, out of nowhere, 'Sometimes I hear things.'

Oh my goodness! She was hearing voices?

'At night, usually.'

'That sounds like you've been having some bad nightmares.'

Tess shook her head. 'I wasn't asleep. Uncle Gray says I'm... *uncanny*. The kind of person who could tap into another dimension.'

'Oh, honey! That's nonsense!'

'A few times, I've heard these banging noises, like a... a poltergeist. And this other time at night, I was woken up by someone screaming. I thought it was Mum or Christina. But when I went out into the corridor, everything was really quiet, and it was really cold, even though it was the middle of summer. I checked on Christina, and she was asleep. And so was Mum. Dad said it was probably a fox.' She wrinkled her nose in disgust.

'Well, could it have been?'

'No! It was a *woman* screaming.' Her gaze was fixed on Alice, as if Alice was the one person who could help. 'If there really is some sort of... supernatural thing in the house, and only I can hear it – what does that mean? Is it going to come and get me?'

Oh my *goodness*!

'Absolutely not!' Alice took her hand and squeezed it. 'Tess, you're a very smart girl. You don't believe in all that stuff, do you? Supernatural stuff?'

Tess's face went blank, closed up again, and Alice knew she'd made a big effort to open up about this, and now she was retreating back into her shell because Alice was failing her. Alice hadn't given her what she needed.

Which was *what*?

What should Alice say now?

She took a deep breath. 'The mind is a powerful thing. It can play tricks on us, especially late at night. Once when my friend Kimmy and I were having a sleepover at her house, we'd been telling each other scary stories in the dark, and then we heard these weird noises, like a werewolf or a vampire was scratching at the window trying to get in. We were so scared we couldn't even scream, we just grabbed each other. Then there was this loud *miaow* – it was one of the kitties, letting us know the cat flap was jammed.'

Tess shook her head. 'This wasn't an animal.'

'Okay. But there are lots of other explanations that don't involve monsters and spooks.'

'Like what?' Tess was looking away now, as if seeing something Alice couldn't.

'Well, now, if it wasn't a fox, it could have been...' Alice stopped. Of course. That must have been the night Murray and his friends broke in. It must have been Erin she'd heard screaming. In which case...

Somebody in this house really did corner her and make her take her clothes off.

'Was it when Tim and Edward were staying?'

Tess frowned, then shook her head. 'Why?'

So it had been Gray.

Had it?

Alice felt hot all over and then suddenly freezing cold. She couldn't help her shoulders giving a little shiver, and wrapped her arms around herself. She could feel the braid of the bracelet against her skin, and she shivered again.

'Alice?' Tess persisted. 'What's it got to do with Tim and Edward? It wasn't a *man* screaming.'

'It could have been a horror movie they were watching,' she said weakly. 'I think Edward likes them.' He probably did.

Tess shook her head. 'It wasn't a TV scream. It was *in the house*.' Her eyes were big and scared. 'It was someone or *something in the house*.'

'Oh, not this again,' said Christina's voice.

Alice turned. Christina, dressed in tiny shorts and a little top just like the ones Caro had told Alice to change out of, was frowning into the fridge. 'Are there any cherries left?'

'In the box at the back.'

'You're so disgustingly organised.'

When Alice turned back to Tess, she was gone.

'Tess doing her spooky kid stuff?' Christina took a handful of cherries and put them in a bowl. 'I thought she'd grown out of that. Although, let's face it, she's never going to be normal.'

'But is it possible that –' Alice grimaced. 'Katie said her sister had a really disturbing experience here.' She couldn't say they'd broken into the house, could she? 'She was kind of attacked by a guy near the house.'

'Are you talking about Erin?' Christina laughed. 'That girl's such a liar. You can't believe anything she says. Everyone who knows her knows that. I've heard those rumours, and they're a load of crap. If she was attacked in this house, why didn't they go to the police? *Because we broke in and we'd get in trouble.*' Christina mimicked a high, silly voice.

Alice supposed that it was the same here as in Branchfield or any other small place – nothing could happen without everyone for miles around knowing all about it.

Christina continued, 'Like the police are going to do anything about the drunken misbehaviour of a load of dorks who before that had never done anything worse than cross the road when the green man wasn't showing.'

What was it Daddy said when Alice blustered like that?

'The lady doth protest too much.'

Christina glared at her. 'Piss off, Alice. You don't know anything.'

But as Christina turned to go, Alice caught a look in her eye, a look that scared her, a look that mirrored the way Tess had stared at Alice just a few moments ago.

It was like they were each trying to say, in their own ways: *Help us.*

26

MELANIE - 9 AUGUST

Gray loped along maybe a hundred metres ahead of Melanie, the hood of his navy jacket pulled low over his eyes, head dipped against the driving rain coming in off the Atlantic. The weather at least was in her favour this time. When you were battling the elements, you were a lot less likely to be looking around you.

Melanie had thrown on a waterproof before hurrying out of the house after him, but she was just wearing boat shoes, which were already sodden. She was going to have blisters.

But who cared?

Her heart was pounding.

Maybe she wasn't going to need those trackers after all.

What if this was it?

What if he was going to Alice?

She couldn't help the scene of rescue playing over and over in her head. Alice, cowering in a corner, maybe chained to a wall. Melanie dropping to her knees and gathering her into her arms –

No.

She mustn't hope too much. Something superstitious in her was afraid that if she imagined it, it wouldn't happen.

Gray was heading up the track away from the house. Melanie's jacket was dull green and hopefully merged with her surroundings, and she was keeping to the edge of the track where the vegetation in the verge was in its high-summer glory, the rose bay willow herb a riot of purple flowers, grasses tall, their feathery heads waving around as the wind and rain battered them, up above her head in places and, together with the brambles and nettles and campion, good cover. In this driving rain, even if Gray did look round, he probably wouldn't spot her.

Soon he had vanished into the trees.

When she got to them, he had disappeared around the next bend. She jumped as something flapped in the treetops above her, but it was just a couple of fat wood pigeons, their wings beating against the branches of the pine trees as they got airborne with some difficulty.

She hurried on.

At the bend, there was still no sign of him. The empty track stretched out, dipping down and then up again, but the next bend was too far ahead for him to have reached it already.

He must have gone into the trees.

Was there a path?

She started to scan the edges of the track on either side, looking for a gap in the vegetation. Eventually she found a path of sorts, trampled grass and bare peaty soil, winding away into the trees. But she'd only gone a few metres when she realised it must be an animal track. The branches of the trees were attacking her upper body, allowing no space for a human to get through unless they crouched.

She turned and started making her way back through the dripping trees.

One of them moved.

'BOO!'

He had jumped out at her from behind a tree and was filling the path, blocking out the light, looming over her.

She screamed.

Gray laughed. 'And where are you off to?' His hair was straggly with the rain, his eyes amused.

She was frozen. She couldn't think what to say or do.

'Not exactly weather for a walk, is it, Bathsheba?'

It was as if the trees themselves were against her, pressing in on her, on the two of them, from all sides, cutting them off from the rest of the world. Too thickly planted to run through. She couldn't get away from him.

Well, so what?

When she'd lived in the squat, Melanie had dealt with men a lot scarier than Gray Davidson. She channelled Donna, simpering up at him.

'Who's Bathsheba?'

'A temptress.'

'A what?'

'A very naughty lady indeed.' He took a step closer to her. In the gently falling rain, the scents of summer were magnified, carried on the humid air, the scents of peat and pine and green leaves. But underneath, she could smell *him*, musky and rank as a goat.

'What did she do?' Donna blinked rapidly, seductively, or so Melanie hoped.

'She knew King David was watching her, but still she stripped off on the roof of her house. Took a long bath, right in front of him. Bewitched him with her *charms*.'

Melanie kneed him in the balls as hard as she could.

'*Ahhh!*' He doubled up, hands clutching his crotch.

She shoved him, and he toppled over into the wet brambles.

Melanie ran.

27

ALICE - 20 JULY

Alice woke with a determination to spend time with Christina and find out what was troubling her. Books were often a good way to get a conversation started. Maybe there was something appropriately angsty in the library that the two of them could get talking about. She had her hand on the library door, about to go in and have a look around the shelves, when raised voices inside the room stopped her.

'It's too late.' It was Ken's voice. 'There's nothing we can do about it now.'

'*I know that!*' Caro was almost shouting. 'But you need to keep your *fucking brother* under control. Keep him away from her, at least.'

'And how do you propose I do that? Let's face it – neither of us can *control* him. We need to keep *her* away from *him*.'

'How?' Caro groaned. 'We can't be watching her every minute of the day. Oh God!'

'We have to try.' Ken sounded very tired. 'I know it won't be easy.'

Oh my goodness!

They were talking like Gray was some kind of wild animal!

Alice backed away from the door.

And then she was running, up the stairs and along the corridors, and up the final set of stairs to the Tower Room. She threw herself onto the bed and pulled the covers up around her.

What business was it of theirs anyway, what she and Gray did or did not do?

They were both adults.

They were both consenting adults.

And Alice had decided that she just didn't believe the story about Erin and the incident with the torch. The girl was flaky. The screaming Tess had heard at night must have been something else – a movie or a TV or Netflix drama.

It just wasn't fair, the way everyone had it in for Gray! He wasn't out of control. When he'd kissed her, that time in the kitchen, and she'd pulled away, he had immediately backed off and apologised.

He'd been an absolute gentleman.

Even if a tiny, wicked part of Alice wished he hadn't been.

28

MELANIE - 9 AUGUST

Back at the house, Melanie locked herself in the shower room and tried to calm down. What was Gray going to do now? Would he try to get her sacked?

She looked at her flushed face in the mirror. It was vital she got a tracker onto that rucksack. He could be keeping Alice anywhere in those woods, in a hut or a cabin, maybe. She could ask Tess whether there were any buildings in that area. But getting a tracker on him was key.

Under the mirror, there was a wide glass shelf on which Melanie had arranged a hairbrush, nail brush, tweezers, and a mug with her toothbrush in it. She always rather anally separated out the various items so they weren't touching, but now the hairbrush was touching the end of the tweezers. And the mug was empty.

Someone had been in here messing with her things again.

But why?

She stood staring stupidly for a moment at the empty mug.

DNA.

Cheek cells and hair follicles.

Did the police suspect that Donna MacKenzie was Melanie Macfarlane, Alice's AWOL birth mother, and so had taken her toothbrush and hair samples to obtain DNA? Presumably they already had Alice's for comparison.

No. They'd need a warrant to do that, and they'd need to tell her what they were doing. They couldn't just sneak in here and take things without going through the proper procedures.

Which meant it hadn't been the police.

The Davidsons knew Alice was adopted – it had been mentioned in the press, and the police had been here updating them on progress in tracking down her birth mother. And both Caro and Ken had been in the kitchen when Isabel had remarked on the similarity of Melanie's nose to Alice's. Either of them could subsequently have mentioned this to Gray.

One of the family must suspect that Donna could be Melanie Macfarlane. If they had Alice's hair or toothbrush, it would be a simple matter to send the samples off to one of those online DNA testing places and get the results back in a matter of days.

But the very fact that they'd taken samples for DNA testing meant they couldn't be sure of her identity.

Yet.

She was on borrowed time. And there was a real risk that the trackers wouldn't work, or remain undetected. Murray was right – only the police could supply the sort of resources needed to find out what Gray was up to. She needed to persuade them to look properly at Gray before her cover was blown and she lost all credibility.

Or worse.

AFTER PICKING up the trackers and a new phone from Nic at the pub on Academy Street, Melanie drove to the police station on Burnett Road. It had always reminded her of a supermarket, which was apt, as she'd often been brought here from Tesco or M&S after being caught shoplifting. Would there be officers on duty who remembered her?

She looked very different now. She was a respectable community nurse – currently masquerading as an au pair, but still. Her hair was well conditioned and her natural colour. She'd removed all the piercings from her face just after turning twenty, and she'd been young enough that the holes had closed up.

But she kept her head down as she entered the lobby and approached the desk.

'I need to speak to DI Macneil, please,' she said, pretending to fiddle with something in her bag, and only making eye contact with the uniformed woman at the desk once. 'It's Donna Mackenzie. About the missing girl, Alice Snyder.'

The woman said, 'Just one moment,' and looked back at the computer.

Folk being hypnotised by screens could be a good thing, Melanie reflected, if you were an ex-con needing to avoid scrutiny.

'He's in a meeting until two thirty. I'll leave him a message. If you come back then, he may be able to see you.'

'Okay, thanks.' She scuttled away.

When she was eventually shown into an interview room at three o'clock, DI Macneil kept her waiting another half hour. She wasn't on the clock – she'd told Caro she had an abscess at the back of her mouth and the only dentist she'd found who could give her an emergency appointment was in Dundee.

DI Macneil eventually came striding into the room and took a seat opposite Melanie at the table, the metal chair legs screeching on the vinyl floor as he made himself comfortable. 'So, Ms Mackenzie, what can I do for you?'

'I wanted to let you know that Gray Davidson has been – behaving inappropriately towards me. Spying on me in the shower room. Threatening me. Well, kind of.' She told him about the Bathsheba comments and about how he'd menaced her in the woods. 'I think he must have something to do with Alice Snyder's disappearance. He goes out with a rucksack – it's possible he might be keeping her somewhere around there. I can show you on a map where he was walking. You need to search that whole area again. He might have been holding her somewhere else, then moved her nearer to Scallan Lodge once you'd completed the search.'

DI Macneil's expression gave nothing away. He was a very handsome man, with chiselled features and dark-lashed brown eyes.

'I know he has an alibi,' she went on, 'that he was supposedly hundreds of miles away. But it's surely possible he could have driven back up here overnight, and none of the people he was with would have been any the wiser.'

'Alice was last seen at around ten o'clock on the night of 8 July. She had disappeared by seven thirty on the morning of 9 July, when little Isabel went to her room and found her missing.'

'Well, that's possible, isn't it? What's the drive time here from London? At night, when the roads are quiet –'

'Gray Davidson was partying with his potential investors at a nightclub in – well, I won't say where, but there are plenty of witnesses, not to mention CCTV footage, to attest to the fact that he was there until four in the morning. And they were round the table at nine the next day discussing the glamping business that the Davidsons are trying to get off the ground. The building in which the meeting was held also has CCTV in the lobby and outside. That confirms that he was there.'

'Are you sure?'

He puffed out a breath. 'Human beings are fallible, corruptible, but CCTV doesn't lie. Gray Davidson was hundreds of miles away when Alice Snyder went missing. There's absolutely no doubt about that. We'll look into your allegations against him, but we certainly won't be using resources to carry out another search of those woods on the basis that someone who's been eliminated from the enquiry was out there for a stroll.'

For a long time, Melanie sat in her car with the key in her hand. The theory she had been building had just crumbled to dust. Gray couldn't possibly have taken Alice. He wasn't holding her captive somewhere, just waiting for Melanie to swoop in to the rescue.

So what had happened to her?

What had happened to Alice?

Had Ken taken her after all?

'Where are you?' she whispered. 'Where are you, my wee darling?'

29

ALICE - 20 JULY

Alice knocked on the study door.

'Come!' said an imperious voice.

She cracked open the door.

It was a square, bright room. Gray sat behind a big darkwood desk, his hair tucked behind his ears. He looked so incongruous here, a pirate dealing with the paperwork involved in all that swashbuckling and murdering, that Alice couldn't help but smile. Looking up, he returned her smile with a grin.

'Do you have five minutes?' she said.

'Certainly. What's up?'

Alice came into the room. 'Ken and Caro – I just heard them talking about us.'

Gray frowned. '*Us?*'

'They don't approve. They were talking about needing to keep us apart...'

He whooped. 'Romeo, Romeo, wherefore art thou, Romeo!' He got up from behind the desk and struck a pose.

'The star-crossed lovers!' And then, suddenly, he was serious. 'Is there an "us", Alice?'

She swallowed. He was too close.

Gently, he took hold of her shoulders, and then his mouth was on hers, pushing her lips open, his tongue, hot and insistent, wrapping around hers. She tasted the saltiness of him, and now his hands were stroking her back, up and down and around, sending sensation zinging through her.

She shouldn't be doing this!

His hands were back on her shoulders, and then one of them was up the skirt of her dress, between her legs, and the zinging was suddenly concentrated *there*. She grasped his wrist and pulled that hand away, but he was still gripping her shoulder with the other.

He released her mouth and laughed.

'Come on, Ali! Drop the outraged innocence! I've wanted to do this, and *you've* wanted me to do it, ever since we first laid eyes on each other!'

'I – no!' Alice got out. 'I thought I did. But I *don't*!' She grabbed his other hand and tried to prise it off her shoulder, but he only gripped tighter. 'I'm not ready for this! And – if I was, I'd be doing it with my boyfriend, not someone like *you*!'

He laughed again. 'Someone like me? What *do* you mean, Alice?'

He thrust his hand back between her legs. She tried to pull away, but he wouldn't let her. She tugged at his arms, pushed at his chest, but he was stronger. She begged him, '*No!*' but he just laughed. She dug her nails into his wrist –

He let go of her abruptly, with a curse, just as Alice realised there was someone else there.

Ken.

'You *fucker*!' Ken shouted, as he literally threw Gray across the room.

Gray landed in a heap by the window. But he was still laughing. 'Not, regretfully, literally. Her virtue is quite intact.'

Then Caro's arms were around her, and Alice was out of the room, walking mechanically at Caro's side along the passage and through the hall and outside. In the big open porch, Caro let her go, took a couple of paces away from her and brought out the inevitable cigarette. Alice subsided onto the shallow stone step. It was drizzling, and everywhere she looked, there was impenetrable whiteness. Low cloud obscured the tops of the trees and mist inched towards them across the lawn.

A noise behind her made her whip her head round, but it was only Caro flicking a cigarette lighter. Her mind's eye had conjured a picture of Gray sneaking up behind her. Which was ridiculous. He would hardly do that with Caro standing right there.

Caro took a long drag on the cigarette. 'Did anything happen with Gray?'

Alice got up to stand with her back against one of the stone pillars. 'If you mean have we slept together, no.'

'Alice.' Caro shut her eyes for a moment, smoke wisping from her nostrils. 'Gray is thirty-six years old. A relationship really isn't appropriate.'

'I know that. I don't want a *relationship* with him!'

Caro sighed. 'Well, in that case, you have to stop leading him on. Every woman has to learn how to give out signals to men when we want them to back off.'

'I told him no and I was trying to push him away! What more of a signal could I give?' Through the thin material of her dress, the stone pillar at her back was hard and cold, but she pressed her shoulders against it, glad of its support, its solidity. Her whole body felt weird, insubstantial, like it wasn't somehow quite *there*.

'Before that, Alice, long before that, you shouldn't have given him the wrong idea.'

Alice nodded. That was true. She had been *so stupid*!

'You need to keep away from Gray altogether.'

A shudder went right through her, and she took a step away from the cold pillar. 'Those assault allegations...'

'Who told you about that?'

'Some local people. They weren't just allegations, were they? Those women weren't lying. He really did assault them.' She wrapped her arms around herself, squeezing her shoulders where Gray had gripped her, feeling them tremble under her hands. How could she have got it so wrong? How could she have been *attracted* to Gray Davidson? He had just tried to – tried to –

'Cost us an arm and a leg to buy those women off, and even then, the business still went belly up.' Caro grimaced. 'No smoke without fire, apparently.'

It took a second for Alice's punch-drunk brain to understand what Caro was saying. 'But – but that's *terrible*!'

'They took the payout. It was their choice, Alice. No one put a gun to their heads.'

'But he *assaulted* them!'

Caro smiled. 'Ker-*ching*!'

Alice couldn't believe what she was hearing. She couldn't believe Caro was *smiling*, although it was a grim smile with no real humour in it.

Alice was suddenly very, very angry. 'I'm going to tell the police what you just said.'

Caro waved the cigarette in the air, as if to say, *Go ahead*.

And Alice imagined what would happen if she did go to the police. Nothing at all. Caro would deny having said anything, and what could the police do anyway, if those women had been paid to keep quiet?

'I heard you telling Ken that Gray's out of control. I thought you were being ridiculous, but it's true, isn't it? He *is* out of control! He – he did something to a local girl.'

'*Did something?*' Caro's tone was faintly mocking.

'He made her strip. In the dark, in this house.'

Caro raised her eyebrows.

'And – he shone a torch over her body.' Spoken out loud, it did sound totally weird, totally unlikely. She got why Erin wouldn't go to the police. Imagine saying that in one of those bleak interview rooms, with cops staring at you.

'And now I suppose she's angling for a payout too.' Caro shrugged. 'She's missed the boat there. That well is dry.'

Alice took a step towards her on trembling legs. 'She's not *angling for a payout*! She's *traumatised*! She hardly leaves her house! She hasn't even told her parents what happened!'

Caro flung back her head and laughed, the harsh sound bouncing off the high granite walls of the house behind them. 'Another silly little girl caught in his web.' Caro dropped the cigarette and mashed her heel down on it. 'You need to let him know in no uncertain terms that you're off-limits.' She waved a hand at Alice. 'Stop dressing so provocatively. That material's so thin it's practically see-through.'

Alice could feel cold sweat beading around her hairline. She looked down at the floral-print summer dress she was wearing. She'd thought it was fine. Knee-length with a highish scoop neck that showed zero cleavage.

'And stop giggling and fluttering your eyelashes at him. You do it with Gray, and you did it with Tim and Edward.'

'That's not true!'

'It may not be a conscious thing. Flirting often isn't, especially at your age. But it's more than that. You flatter their egos, you listen to them when they drone on about their boring little obsessions like it's the most fascinating thing you've ever heard. You're too *nice*.' She sighed. 'Men aren't like us. What I said about Gray being out of control... All I meant was that men like him, all men, in fact, find it a lot harder than we do to control their... *urges*.'

Alice shook her head numbly. 'But surely men should be just as able to control themselves as women are?'

'Oh, the idealism of the young!' Caro barked another mirthless laugh. 'Testosterone. It's a bloody nightmare. You know how stags go demented in the rut? Either fighting or fucking anything that moves? That's all down to a spike in testosterone in the autumn. But humans don't have a breeding season. The males of our species are awash with the stuff all year round, the bastards.'

A wave of hysteria rose in Alice as an image came into her head of Gray and Tim trotting around Scallan Lodge, pawing the ground and bellowing.

But all the laughter went out of her as Caro went on, 'They can't help themselves. Even Ken... The way he ogles you sometimes... It's pathetic. But it's no wonder, really. I mean, look at you.'

Alice stared at Caro, trying to muster her thoughts. 'That's not fair,' she said slowly. 'This isn't about me and how I look or what I choose to wear. I told Gray no, and he kept on... He *assaulted* me!' She swallowed. 'I think I want to leave.'

'Oh, *Alice*! Yes, all right, he should have stopped immediately when you told him you'd changed your mind, but sexual urges – they can't just switch them off in a heartbeat. It wasn't *assault*! He thought you were up for it because *that's what you made him think*!'

Alice felt a huge blush spreading over her face.

It was true.

She *had* 'led him on', as Caro put it.

And now…

'He scares me,' she whispered. 'I don't want to be around him.'

Caro puffed in exasperation. 'Now you've made your feelings clear, he isn't going to get himself… well, *worked up*, shall we say, when he's with you. But it will help if you consider more carefully what you wear and stop flirting with him. Simply staying away from him might be the best idea.'

'How can I do that, when he lives right here in the same house?'

Caro took a squashed packet of cigarettes out of her back pocket and fished out a fresh one. 'I'll have a word with him. Don't worry. And don't freak out – whatever you might have heard about Gray, he's not some kind of maniac who's going to press his attentions on someone he knows doesn't want them.'

But that was just what he'd done to her! And those two women!

Caro seemed to guess what Alice was thinking, because she added, 'Think of it like an engine. If you don't turn the key, it's not going to rev up, is it? The mistake you and those other silly bitches made was turning the key and expecting nothing to happen. Those women were all over him too, making out like they were up for it.' She sighed. 'As long as you don't – *overexcite* him, Gray's harmless. He won't touch you.'

Alice didn't know what to say to that, so she just walked away, across the gravel, onto the grass and into the mist.

He won't touch you.

It was just the kind of thing the owner of a dangerous dog would say.

Right before it went for your throat.

30

MELANIE - 18 YEARS AGO, 26 JANUARY

Melanie bent over the cot, contorting her face into as good a smile as she could manage.

Alice knew she was about to be picked up. She gurgled happily, fat little legs kicking at the cot blanket. Melanie grasped her solid little body under the arms and lifted her out.

This was the last time.

'Good morning, Alice!'

They were eye to eye. Alice's legs in the yellow Babygro kicked the air, and she beamed, looking right into Melanie's eyes. Her wet Cupid's bow mouth opened, and she chuckled her own *good morning*.

But then her soft face altered into the cutest, most worriedest frown.

'It's all right!' Melanie tried to smile, wiping her face against her shoulder. She'd thought she had no more tears left to cry. 'It's all right, my wee darling! Everything's going to be all right!'

Melanie changed her as quickly as she could.

It was a habit, to rush, although today the flat was warm. Melanie was spending money she didn't have on heating the place properly for once.

But she couldn't do anything about the smell.

No matter how often she wiped the black spots of mould off the walls with diluted bleach, like Gillian the social worker had shown her, every room still stank of it, of rotting wood, rotting carpet, rotting plasterboard. Sometimes it was so bad it made her gag and she'd have to open the windows, even though it was January and the air that rushed in was literally freezing cold and she had to shut them again five seconds later.

Gillian said that was why the mould grew in the first place – because Melanie hardly ever opened the windows. And she dried her washing on the radiators, let the steam from the shower through the house, didn't have the heating on enough, *blah blah blah*. It was all right for that stuck-up cow – she lived in a cottage in Clachnaharry and probably had a wood-burner and an Aga and gas central heating instead of electric on fucking pay-as-you-go that cost an arm and a leg.

Melanie couldn't normally afford to have the radiators on except for short bursts when she needed to dry the washing or it was *really* cold outside. Other than that, the only heat the flat got was from the cooker and the shower, and no way was she going to open all the windows and let that tiny bit of warmth escape.

Gillian said she should *economise* so she could *prioritise* the heating. Get clothes and toys and a buggy for Alice from the charity shops instead of buying new. Use a cloth nappy system instead of Pampers. Breastfeed her instead of buying formula. Stop smoking, like Melanie hadn't been trying ever since she got pregnant, like she smoked around Alice instead of always, *always* going outside the door of the flat before lighting up. Stop drinking, like Melanie was some sort of alkie instead of buying maybe one bottle of cheap cider a week and getting rounds in when she was out with her friends, which was practically never since Alice.

And Melanie wasn't going to dress her baby in manky stuff other kids had vomited and shat on. She wasn't going to put her little bottom in cloth nappies that she couldn't clean properly because she had no washing machine. As for breastfeeding, it just hadn't worked for Melanie and Alice, and the lovely nurse at the hospital had said that was fine, some mums just couldn't, especially very young mums like Melanie, and formula these days was an excellent substitute, especially if you spent a little extra for the good stuff.

She dressed Alice in her best Babygro, the white one with tiny birds all over it, and wrapped her in a warm blanket to give her a feed. This was another habit she'd got into to protect Alice from the cold air, but she thought Alice liked it, being swaddled.

They stared into each other's eyes.

Melanie could look at her forever, this miraculous, perfect little being she'd somehow created and who was part of her. *Literally* part of her. She had never known, until Alice, that feelings like this existed.

As soon as the midwife had laid her on Melanie's chest, she'd been hit by it.

Love.

So much stronger, so much more terrifying than anything she'd ever felt before.

She *had* known love, just once – but that had been the

love of friendship, the love she'd felt for Sadie, the girl she'd shared a room with in the children's home. They'd grown up together. Neither of them had had anyone else, really, and they'd clung to each other like shipwrecked sailors, adrift in the stormy waters of life in care.

That made it sound grim, but it hadn't been at all. For the first time ever, Melanie had had fun. They'd made up silly stories and sneaked out to go paddling in the river, pretending they were children in a book, off on an adventure. They'd made each other little presents for silly made-up occasions, like the pig Melanie had made out of a cone and some wire she'd found on the ground for Sadie's 'half-birthday', 17 June, six months before and six months after her actual birthday on 17 December.

She had loved Sadie, and Sadie had loved her.

But this, the love she had for Alice, was so much more. It filled up her whole head and her whole body, but it wasn't about Melanie at all, really – it wasn't about *her* emotions. It was all about Alice. Melanie was Alice's mum and that was all that mattered. All she had to do was make sure Alice was okay.

As Alice drank from the bottle, her eyelids closed in contentment.

'She's a happy soul, isn't she?' Gillian had said once, not quite able to keep the amazement out of her voice.

It was true, though. Melanie couldn't take the credit, of course, because it *was* amazing that Alice was such a good-natured wee thing and so easily made happy despite living in a manky flat in the Ferry with a mum who couldn't meet her needs.

That was what the boss social work woman had said at the meeting.

We feel you can't meet Alice's needs.

And that was true too. She didn't have enough money to give Alice a nice warm home or lots of toys or clothes. She didn't even have the know-how to keep her safe. One time, Alice had been hospitalised with a bad tummy because, it turned out, Melanie hadn't been sterilising the bottles right. And another time, she'd been changing her and Alice had somehow wriggled off the sofa and fallen on her head on the laminate floor. Melanie had taken her to A&E, and the staff there had called Gillian.

But what had led to Alice going on the 'at risk' register had been Melanie confessing to Gillian that, when Alice had colic and wouldn't stop crying, she'd fantasised about opening the window and dropping her out of it. It hadn't mattered how often Melanie had insisted she'd never have actually done that or anything at all to hurt Alice.

Not long after, Gillian had arrived at the flat one afternoon to find Melanie asleep in bed and Nic and some randoms in the living room smoking weed. That was bad enough, but Alice hadn't been in her cot in the bedroom with Melanie. She'd been in Nic's arms, breathing in the weed fumes.

At the 'safeguarding' meeting, Gillian had made that sound so much worse than it had been. She'd brought up the fact that Nic had convictions for GBH. And she'd gone on about how the room was thick with the stench of the weed because the windows were all shut. Of course. She had to get that in.

And so Alice was being taken away.

Today.

In three hours and forty-six minutes.

'Now,' said Melanie after she'd burped Alice, who was

now wriggling and smiling on the sofa as Melanie tickled her tummy. 'We have to decide what you'd like to take with you.' She managed to smile. She was determined to make this precious time as happy as it could be. 'Let's get your bag, shall we?'

As she packed, she kept up a running commentary. 'Your favourite Babygros. The pink bootees Marion knitted for you.' Marion was the old dear in the flat downstairs. 'They'll maybe fit in a few months' time... Nice warm cardies... Nappies, just in case your new mummy and daddy don't have the right size.'

Alice was looking at her solemnly now, as if she was taking in every word Melanie was saying.

'You're going to have a lovely new mummy and daddy, Alice. That will be nice, won't it? They live in a big posh house in Edinburgh, and they're *millionaires*! Well, they're comfortably off professionals.'

That had been all Gillian would tell her – that they were a 'comfortably off professional couple' who could give Alice a wonderful life. 'But are they *nice people*?' Melanie had begged to know. 'Of course,' Gillian had said dismissively, like anyone would be nice compared to Melanie.

It would be a closed adoption. Melanie would have no contact with Alice until she was eighteen, not even a child any more, and then only if Alice chose to get in touch.

'It's better for everyone,' Gillian had said. 'It's better for Alice.'

Melanie cupped Alice's warm head, moving just the very tips of her fingers to stroke the sweet fuzz of fine hair gently, the way Alice liked her to do. 'You're going to have everything you need. I bet your new home will be really cosy and warm!' She smiled, but Alice continued to stare back at her solemnly.

Melanie picked up Frog and made one of his hands wave at Alice, and slowly, slowly, Alice started to smile. Gillian had said that Frog could come too, and maybe, somewhere deep in her little brain, when she looked at him, when she touched him, Alice would remember her first mummy. Not consciously, obviously. But somewhere inside.

Frog had been Sadie's present to Melanie one Christmas. He was a fat green beanie frog with little black eyes on top of his head and floppy legs. Alice loved to chew him, although Melanie supposed Gillian would disapprove of that too. She would probably ask if Frog's label said he was safe for babies, and Melanie didn't have the label any more. But what was the worst that could happen? Alice couldn't hold things on her own yet, so Melanie was always holding Frog while Alice gummed him. Melanie had started offering her Frog when she'd started chewing on her own hands, which Gillian said could be a sign she was hungry. Gillian was wrong about that, though, because she sometimes did it right after a long feed.

Surely it was better that she chewed on Frog instead?

Would her new parents let her have him?

Of all Melanie's possessions, Frog was the only one that mattered. The only present from Sadie that she'd managed to hang on to. It was important that Alice took him with her.

Because he was the only thing Melanie had that said *love*.

She pressed Frog to her heart, or where she imagined her heart to be.

She could imagine what Sadie would say.

Aw, Melanie. It'll be okay.

And of course it would be.

Because this was the best thing for Alice.

'It'll be nice to have a daddy, won't it?' she said brightly. She sat back down on the couch and cuddled Alice, and sure enough, Alice tried to grab Frog. Melanie held him while she had a good old chew.

She glanced at the clock above the kitchen units.

Three hours and twenty-five minutes to go.

What would happen if she just left? Packed another bag for herself and put Alice in the pram and just took off?

But where would they go?

To Nic's squat?

That was no place for a baby. People shot up heroin there, and there was no heating at all apart from the fires they lit in the extension at the back of the house where there was a hole in the roof for the smoke.

And it was a pigsty. No one ever cleaned.

Could she go to a women's refuge and say her boyfriend had been beating her up? But she had no bruises or scars. And they would check with social services. Even if she didn't give her name, they would tell social services about her, and they'd be able to identify her immediately and take Alice.

If only Sadie hadn't died.

They could have managed, somehow, between them.

But there was no one who cared about her and Alice. That was the real problem – not the flat, because maybe she could start getting stuff from charity shops and afford to have the heating on more. Not the smoking, because if she really tried, she could probably give up. And not the mistakes Melanie made, because she could always learn.

No.

At the root of everything was that there was no one to care. No one to help, no one to come round and just sit with them and listen to all the questions Melanie had, and suggest things, and show her what she should be doing.

No one to catch them when they fell.

Gillian didn't count. All Gillian wanted was to take Alice away, because if she left her with Melanie and something happened, Gillian would get the blame.

Huge tears were dripping off Melanie's face and onto her top, making splotchy dark marks on the white cotton. Alice stared up at her as she fumbled in her pocket for a tissue.

And then Alice started crying too.

THERE WAS another person with Gillian. A big man in a big black jacket. In case Melanie tried to fight it, she supposed. In case she went for the social worker.

But when Gillian took Alice from her arms, Melanie didn't resist. One second Alice was there, solid and warm in the blanket, and the next there was just space. Empty air.

Melanie started to shiver.

'Is that bag to go too?' The man pointed, as if he was just here to collect a few things on a list, a few objects to be transported from one place to another.

'Yes,' said Melanie. 'Her things are in there.'

'You're doing the right thing, Melanie,' said Gillian as she lowered Alice into the pram at the door. 'Better say your goodbyes here. Don't come down.'

Don't make a scene.

Melanie bent over the pram, right over it so only Alice could see her face. But Alice was asleep. Melanie touched her soft cheek with her nose, with her mouth. She whispered close to her ear:

'*Be happy.*'

And then she was gone.

The Yale clicked behind them. Melanie stared at the door, imagining Alice being wheeled along the walkway and into the lift. Settled into the baby carrier, into Gillian's car. Off to Edinburgh and her new mummy and daddy. Off on her big adventure.

But she would be so bewildered. She wouldn't understand where and why Mummy had gone.

And, no matter how much she cried, she was never coming back.

Melanie couldn't stay in the flat. She grabbed her keys and hauled open the door and ran the other way along the walkway, in the opposite direction from the lifts. She ran down the stairs and across the grass and into the little wood between the flats and the industrial estate.

And then she just kept on going.

It was the next morning by the time she got back to the flat. She'd ended up at the squat. Nic hadn't been there, but her boyfriend Mugger had given Melanie a bottle of vodka in exchange for a shag, and she'd spent the night with him passed out on Nic's stinking bed.

But she had to come back to the flat.

She had to check that it really had happened, that Alice really had gone. That it hadn't all been a vodka-induced hallucination, and Alice was here, alone, abandoned, screaming for her mummy.

Dead, mouldy air.

And lying on the floor, half under the couch – Frog.

Melanie grabbed him and flung him across the room.

She couldn't even do that for Alice!

She couldn't even remember to put Frog in the bag!

As she squatted on the floor and howled, as she gave

herself up to the misery, at the back of her mind a voice was saying:

Good.

GOOD!

Alice is better off.

She's better off without *YOU!*

31

ALICE - 20 JULY

Alice couldn't get the darn thing off!

Her nails were too short to get into the knot Gray had made to secure the bracelet to her wrist. In the end, she had to use her teeth, gagging as she did so at the thought of his sweat, his DNA, under her lips.

But finally, it was off.

She didn't want to look at it.

She opened the wardrobe door and hung it in there in the dark, on one of the little hooks, far enough away from her clothes that it wouldn't touch them. Then she sat down on the bed in the Princess Room and looked at the ocean. She wanted to sail away out there, over the horizon, across the Atlantic, all the way back home.

No matter what Caro said, Gray Davidson was a sex offender who needed to be locked up. How could Caro have tried to turn it round on Alice?

But in a way it *was* her own fault!

How could she have been so attracted to him? More than that – she'd seemed to have a *connection* with him. They'd found the same things funny. He'd comforted her that time Tim –

But he was just like Tim. Worse, even.

He was a sexual predator.

And she was his prey.

The way he seemed to see inside her head, to be able to control her, dominate her, always one step ahead, keeping her off-balance – all that had been exciting.

Now it was terrifying.

She needed to leave this place and not look back.

'WHAT'S WRONG?' said Tess.

They were sitting in the dirt, she, Tess and Isabel, in a hole they'd dug in the scrubby ground between the pool house and the rocky shore, out of view of the house itself. There were jobs Alice should be doing in there, cooking and cleaning and laundry and such – and she'd somehow lost her phone, so she needed to do a proper search for it – but the priority was to spend time with the girls. When she'd told Caro she was leaving tomorrow, all Caro had said was, 'Okay, Alice, if that's really what you want.'

Tonight, when she'd found her phone, she'd call Daddy, and he could buy her a ticket home. And then tomorrow morning, Caro would take her to the airport, and she'd be gone.

'Nothing,' said Alice. 'It's just a bit disappointing, isn't it?'

Isabel sighed, sticking her trowel into the earth and pushing back loose strands of hair with muddy fingers, leaving streaks of dirt on her forehead. 'It's too much to expect a skeleton, but you'd think we would have found maybe a jewel or even just a coin.'

So far in their 'test trench', they'd only turned up some nails, a plastic bottle and the top of a tube of Smarties.

'Maybe we should close down this trench,' said Tess. She'd adopted the jargon from all the archaeology programmes they'd been watching.

'Hmm, yes,' agreed Alice. 'It is just a *test* trench, after all. Where do you think might be good to try?'

'Right up near the house,' said Tess at once.

'I don't think your daddy would want us digging up the lawn.'

'They do in *Time Team*. They put all the turf in stacks and then put it all back. We could just do maybe a really small square, and Dad would never know. All the good stuff's going to be close to the house.'

'Okay,' Alice agreed reluctantly. Maybe if they kept away from the side of the house where Gray's study was, they could avoid him. 'We can go nearer the house, but I don't think we should dig up turf, Tess. There's that weedy area by the back door. We could try there.'

'Yesss!' Isabel jumped up.

'We have to fill in this trench first,' said Tess.

They were deciding where to dig the next test trench amongst the weeds when Ken drove up. Isabel ran at him, demanding he come and see what they were doing. As she burbled on about the deeper you dug, the further back in time you were going, Ken nodded and smiled, but he was watching Alice.

At last he said, 'Caro tells me you're thinking of leaving us, Alice.'

Both girls froze.

'*What?*' whispered Isabel.

'Oh, honey, no – I'm not going anywhere,' Alice found

herself saying as Isabel flung herself at Alice's waist and Tess just stood there, her feelings, for once, naked and raw on her pinched little face.

'You can't *leave!*' sobbed Isabel. 'You *can't!*'

'I'm not leaving.' She reached out a hand and pulled Tess into the hug too, squeezing the two of them tight and murmuring reassurances in a calm, gentle voice.

But Alice was mad.

She was pretty sure Ken had deliberately spoken to her in front of Tess and Isabel before Alice had had a chance to break the news to them in her own way and in her own time. He'd ruthlessly backed her into a corner, using the girls as emotional blackmail to force her to change her mind.

'Good, good! Very glad to hear it!' Ken beamed, ruffling Isabel's hair. 'We'd really miss you if you went, wouldn't we, eh, Izz?'

Isabel nodded against Alice's chest.

Alice didn't return Ken's smile. As he strode off into the house, Alice gave Isabel a final squeeze. 'Go wash your face in the kitchen, sweetheart.'

Tess mastered herself quickly, stepping back out of Alice's arms to regard her with a blank but intense look. '*Are* you leaving?'

'No, honey.'

How could she leave these girls?

But everything inside her was screaming, *Go! Just go!*

Murray and the others were right about the Davidsons – Alice was pretty sure of that now. It was more than just Gray being a sexual predator. There was evil in this house. Tess knew it, Christina knew it –

And somehow, at some point she couldn't now determine, Alice had become its focus.

32

MELANIE - 9 AUGUST

On her way back from Inverness, as Melanie drove around the twists and turns of the single-track road that wound its way along the shore of the sea loch, she found the car slowing, as if of its own accord. The sun was shining, the view through the shivering birch trees down to the loch and the hills beyond was achingly beautiful, and the last place on Earth she wanted to be was Scallan Lodge.

While she had believed that Gray was responsible for taking Alice, at least she could be on her guard against him. At least she'd been aware, or *thought* she'd been aware, of what she was dealing with. Now, she was going into the unknown, and all her instincts were screaming at her not to do it, not to go back there.

But she had to pull herself together.

Alice was depending on her.

She stopped the car at a parking area overlooking the loch. There was one other car already there, with a foreign number plate, and a young couple were standing scouring the sky with binoculars. How wonderful, to have nothing more pressing to worry about than ticking an eagle off your 'To See in Scotland' list.

In a bag on the passenger seat were the trackers and phone Nic had brought. She read the instructions for the trackers and made sure the app on the new phone worked. They were satellite GPS trackers, so would be able to send a signal to the app even in places where there was no mobile reception.

'Right,' she said out loud to herself. 'Let's do this.'

At Scallan Lodge, she parked right next to Ken's Range Rover, with the bulk of the vehicle between her and the house. Bending to tie her shoelace, she slipped the magnetised tracker onto the undercarriage.

Getting access to Gray's rucksack was going to be more of a challenge, but was there even any point? As DI Macneil had said, CCTV didn't lie. Gray hadn't abducted Alice. Gray wasn't keeping her somewhere in those woods.

In the Tower Room, she grabbed Frog and sank down onto a chair.

Alice.

She had sat here too, maybe. Not a baby any more, but an eighteen-year-old young woman Melanie had been getting to know, slowly, through her reflection in the impressions of others – Caro, Ken, Christina, but most of all Tess and Isabel.

She'd been getting to know her daughter.

It was obvious that the Snyders had, as she'd hoped, given her a nice life. Alice Snyder was a happy, kind, innocent girl, and you only got to be that way if you'd been cherished and loved and sheltered from life's storms. The problem was that when she'd stepped away from that shelter, when she'd come up against evil, she'd had no defences against it.

Someone in this house had killed her.

Melanie had been kidding herself that it was possible Alice could still be alive. That Gray was keeping her somewhere.

And so all the little, precious things she'd been learning, all the stories Isabel had told her about what Alice and the girls had done together, the games they'd played, the fun they'd had – she'd been putting together a picture of her daughter's last few days on Earth.

There hadn't been a day, an hour that had gone by in which Melanie hadn't thought about Alice, wondered what she was doing, tried to imagine her at two, three, four years old... She had always thought that one day they would find one another again, and in preparation for that, Melanie had worked on herself. She'd got a job at Tesco and attended evening classes, ending up with enough Highers to get a place on a nursing course. She'd lost her rough ways and her rough accent. She'd educated herself by reading and spending time in museums and galleries. She'd even gone to the opera once. By the time she'd qualified as a nurse, anyone meeting Melanie Macfarlane would have assumed she came from a nice middle-class background like the one Alice was enjoying. When she and Alice reconnected, Alice wouldn't be ashamed of her, and Melanie would be able to talk to her about all the things she was interested in. That hope had been at the bottom of everything Melanie had done for the last eighteen years.

But she'd been living in a dream world.

They would never meet again.

This was what was real.

Melanie had known Alice in her first days of life, and was now getting to know her, second-hand, in her last. There was a terrible sort of rightness about that. A punishment, she supposed. What sort of ridiculous, arrogant delusion had Melanie been labouring under, thinking she could ride in to the rescue? Make up for being such a terrible mother all those years ago?

Life wasn't like that.

Life wasn't fair, not even for someone like Alice, someone with a kind and loving heart whose uncomplicated goodness had shone from her even as a tiny baby. A person like that deserved only good things. If Alice's God existed, and if he cared at all, she should still be out there, somewhere, her little flame still burning.

But Melanie knew she was dead.

'No I *don't*!' she said out loud, squeezing Frog to her chest. 'Gray and Ken are going *somewhere*. She *might* be alive.'

As if saying it could make it true.

SHE DIDN'T GET much sleep that night. The app was set to alert her if the tracker on Ken's car started to move. Even so, she kept checking the screen obsessively. But the little blue circle remained stationary.

In the morning, she put the other, smaller tracker into her pocket and hung about at the bottom of the stairs in the hall. If Gray appeared on his way out for one of his walks, that would be her chance to slip it into one of the pockets of his rucksack.

She was rehearsing how she would contrive this when a sudden scream reverberated through the high space.

It was coming from upstairs.

Melanie took the stairs two at a time.

The ear-splitting sound was coming from Tess's room. Melanie burst in –

To find Tess lying on her bed, staring, quite composedly, at a laptop from which the sound was issuing. On the screen, a woman sat screaming in her bed as big red letters appeared on the wall opposite, spelling out '*I'm coming for y*'.

'What on earth are you watching?' Melanie subsided onto the bed, breathing hard.

Tess shut the laptop. 'Nothing.'

'Tess, I don't think that's appropriate viewing for someone your age. It looked very scary.'

'It's not *real*.' The girl's voice was scathing. 'At least – it's a dramatisation.'

'Of what, for goodness' sake?'

After a pause, Tess admitted, 'A haunting. There was this woman, Jessica... A ghost said things like "You're going to *die*" and put cold fingers on her head and wrote things on the wall and stuff, and made things move around. And later she found out that another woman had died in her house under mysterious circumstances.'

'Well, I think Jessica was probably making all that up. Or she had mental health problems or was under a lot of stress or something.'

Tess looked away. 'You mean she was mad.'

'No, I don't.'

'Lots of people have seen ghosts. They can't all be either liars or mad.'

'The mind can play strange tricks. Often we think something's happened, but it hasn't, or at least, not in the way we think. There are usually logical explanations for so-called ghosts.'

'That's what Alice said.'

Melanie's heart contracted. 'Well, she was right. I once started hearing a very strange tapping sound in my kitchen wall, which seemed to move around as I moved, and even though I don't believe in ghosts, it was quite... unnerving. But then my friend Grant was in the house when it happened, and he immediately knew that it was the noise of a pipe expanding and contracting, because the same thing had happened in his house. The noise didn't really follow me around the room – that was just my imagination.'

Tess sat up, pulling her legs under her, to look at Melanie straight on. 'There's this theory, called stone tape theory, that some buildings can replay what happened in them. Like they've recorded it. Like the house can remember. And I'm wondering if it's possible that could work in reverse?'

'What do you mean?'

'Before Alice disappeared, I heard things. I heard a woman, or a girl, screaming. And banging. Dad said it was probably a fox, and Mum said I was probably dreaming. But when I told Alice, she was scared. I know she was. There's that phrase, someone walking over your grave? She looked like that. And... if houses can be imprinted with things that happened in the past, maybe they can be imprinted with things that *haven't happened yet*? Maybe what I was hearing... maybe it was from the future. Maybe it was from the night Alice disappeared.'

'That's not possible,' said Melanie briskly.

Tess's face went blank.

Melanie said gently, 'Don't you think it's much more

likely that what you heard was happening there and then? When you talked to Alice about it, what did she say?'

'She was like you. She didn't believe it could be anything supernatural. She asked if it happened when Tim and Edward were staying.'

Time seemed to slow down. Melanie watched Tess slowly blink at her; the fluffy clouds inch past the window beyond the bed.

Alice must have had some reason to suspect that Tim Gilbey could be responsible for screams and bangs in the night –

'What on earth is going on in here?' Caro was at the door, eyebrows raised at her daughter.

Tess shrugged. 'I was watching a film. Sorry. It was a bit noisy.'

'It certainly was. Use your headphones, darling.'

'Possibly not something she should be watching in the first place,' said Melanie.

Caro looked at her with a blank expression reminiscent of Tess herself, as if the concept of policing her child's viewing was completely off her radar.

The Snyders were right.

There was something not right about this whole family.

Melanie made a decision. 'I have to go back to the dentist,' she said. 'For another emergency appointment. I think they can't have drained the abscess properly.'

Caro's expression changed. 'Let me see.'

'What?'

'Let me see the abscess.'

Shit.

Melanie opened her mouth, and Caro pulled her to the window and put her hands on either side of Melanie's jaw, angling her to the light. Melanie made herself not struggle. Not react.

'There,' she tried to say with her mouth open. It came out as 'Eh.' She pointed.

'I can't see anything. There isn't even any redness.'

Melanie pulled away from the other woman's grip. 'Okay, okay, there's no abscess!' *Donna*. She was *Donna*. 'I'm sorry, Caro.' She blinked and pursed her lips as if battling tears. 'I just – I'm finding it all a bit overwhelming, and I need a break from everything.'

'What do you mean, *everything*?'

Caro grabbed her again.

'*Mum*,' said Tess's strangely booming voice. '*Stop it*. She means what happened to Alice.'

'*Alice?*' Caro's grip on Melanie's arms tightened. 'What's *Alice* to do with you?'

'I know it's silly!' Donna's voice wobbled. 'But I feel her *presence*. I feel she's trying to tell me something. I feel she's always *here*, hovering over me! I just need to get *away*, just for a few hours! *Please!*'

'Oh, how ridiculous, Donna.' Caro dropped her arms.

'I know,' Donna whispered. Then, as if pulling herself together, she said, 'You're in contravention of employment legislation, you know – you don't give me enough time off.' Melanie had no idea if that was true or not. 'I need a break.'

'That doesn't make sense,' said Tess. 'How can Alice's ghost be haunting you if you don't even believe in ghosts?'

Donna lifted her shoulders helplessly. 'I – I didn't mean a *ghost*, exactly.'

But Caro was looking at her too closely. In the end, though, she just said, 'Go! Go, then, and have your "break".

But when you get back, you and I are going to have a serious talk, Donna.'

CHALET 6 HAD no sea view, which presumably explained how the Snyders had been able to book it at such short notice during the summer season. It looked onto trees and a small field, which, anywhere else, would have been considered perfect. But on the other side of those trees was the panorama of Loch Torridon and the hills around it – once you'd seen that, arriving at Chalet 6 would be a big let-down.

Not that the Snyders would care about the view. In fact, not being able to see the sea was probably a bonus.

Melanie parked next to their car and headed for the door, but before she could reach it, Tonya was out on the decking and in her face.

'Have you –'

'I'm no further forward,' Melanie found herself snapping. 'At least – I have some information that I need to talk to you about, but nothing...'

Warren had appeared behind Tonya. 'Come inside,' he said tightly.

Hostility was coming off the two of them in waves, but they were obviously damping it down because they needed her. They needed Melanie to get to the truth about what had happened to Alice.

They looked like they were sleeping about as much as she was – there were dark hollows under their eyes and a defeated slump to their postures. Melanie and Tonya took seats in the tiny, stark living area, Tonya on the faux-leather black sofa and Melanie on the matching chair, while Warren put the kettle on.

'It must have been Gray,' Tonya said. 'I don't care about his so-called alibi. He could have paid some dodgy "investors" to supply that.'

'His alibi is solid,' said Melanie. 'There's CCTV showing him in a nightclub in London at four in the morning on the night Alice went missing. And then again at a meeting at nine o'clock. There's no way he could have got here and back in the time.' She took a breath. 'There's someone else who could be in the frame. Tess, the Davidsons' eleven-year-old, just told me that she heard things at night, screams and bangs – no, no,' she added hurriedly as she saw their faces. 'This was before Alice arrived. But Tess told Alice about it, and Alice asked her if Tim Gilbey and Edward Norcott, shooting enthusiasts who are regular paying guests at Scallan Lodge, were there at the time.' She swallowed. 'Tim Gilbey's a creep. He tried to grab my breast, as if the staff were laid on for his benefit, as if it were almost his *right* to take what he wanted... It's possible, more than possible, that he harassed Alice too. At any rate, Alice must have had some reason for asking that. She must have thought it possible that the noises Tess heard were Tim Gilbey assaulting someone.'

Warren, who'd been rattling mugs about in a cupboard, went very still. Then he came over and dropped to the sofa next to Tonya, putting an arm around her. 'But who?'

Melanie's mouth was dry. She swallowed. 'I don't know. What I do know is that Tim Gilbey was at Scallan Lodge when Alice was, just a few days before she disappeared. He could easily have hung around. Rented somewhere like this.'

Tonya made a wordless sound.

'This is all just speculation,' said Warren harshly. 'For all we know, after Alice – encountered this Gilbey character at

Scallan Lodge, and after what Tess told her about screams in the night, she could have been so freaked out that she decided to disappear.'

'But not without letting us know she was all right,' Tonya whispered, and covered her face with her hands.

'Wishful thinking,' Melanie agreed numbly. She could feel herself starting to lose control too, like the dam holding everything back was about to fail. She dug her nails into her palms.

'I still think Gray's involved,' said Warren. 'He could have set that alibi up somehow, maybe paid someone to tamper with the CCTV. Or he could have got someone to take Alice while he was away. If I could get that bastard on his own, find out what he knows, what he's done... I'll get it out of him, one way or another.'

'But he's unlikely to tell you anything, no matter what you do to him, given the dire consequences of any sort of admission.' Melanie sighed. 'Give me another couple of days. Like you say, we're speculating.' She told them about Ken leaving the house under the cover of darkness. 'We could be barking up the wrong tree completely. Ken might be –'

'Holding her somewhere?' Tonya leapt on this, her ravaged face suddenly alight with hope.

'It's possible. But I doubt it, to be honest. I think you're right, Warren – Gray's much more likely to be involved than Ken. Whatever Ken's up to, it probably has no relation to Alice. He just doesn't seem... Well, when we've got Gray Davidson and Tim Gilbey in the mix, pointing the finger at Ken would be ignoring two massive elephants in the room. But I've put a tracker on his vehicle, and I'm going to try to get one on Gray's rucksack.'

The door suddenly burst open, and a teenage boy came rocketing in. He was fresh-faced, with a muscly physique and a buzz cut.

'I found Gail!' he exclaimed, before doing an almost comical double-take.

'This is Melanie,' said Tonya. 'Melanie, this is Alice's young man, Skip Landry.'

Young man? She meant *boyfriend?*

So Alice had a boyfriend, and this was him?

Skip blinked at her a couple of times. Melanie stood and offered her hand, which he shook, innate good manners obviously getting the better of whatever he was feeling about the woman who'd been such a nightmare of a mother that her baby had had to be taken away from her and given to the Snyders.

'Pleased to meet you, ma'am.'

'Likewise.'

'I finally tracked down Gail Hislop,' he said, pulling a chair from the table and placing it next to the sofa, as if in solidarity with the Snyders.

'The former housekeeper,' said Warren for Melanie's benefit. 'Left Scallan Lodge about a year ago.'

'Yeah, and unfortunately she *kept herself to herself*, according to local folks.' Skip sat, but his right knee immediately started bouncing, as if he had too much pent-up energy to sit still for two seconds. 'So no one knew where she went after she left Scallan. She wasn't from around here. Then yesterday, this guy who'd seen my post on a local Facebook group got in touch, saying Gail was working in another big house a little way down the coast. I've just been there. I've talked to her!'

'What did she have to say?' Tonya was gripping Warren's hand.

'Not a whole lot – she's not the blabbermouth kind. She did say she found Gray *strange*, but she didn't go into any detail. Plus, apparently he used to bring women to the house at night, and in the morning they'd be gone. She never saw them – her room was in a wing at the back of the house away from the family's bedrooms – but sometimes she'd hear them laughing as he brought them or took them away in his car.'

'It's Gray!' Warren suddenly stood. 'He's *got* to be involved!'

'What else did she say?' Tonya found Warren's hand and pulled him back down next to her.

'Oh, she was "let go" eighteen months ago – she said she knew it was coming after the business went belly up. They'd started not paying her wages on time, skimping on things, no more house parties, Christina was pulled out of her fee-paying school…'

'The business failed because of the charges brought against Gray Davidson,' growled Warren.

'Uh, yeah. But just before Gail finished up at Scallan, suddenly there was money for a family holiday to Bermuda, and Ken gave her a bonus to deep-clean the house while they were gone.'

'Well, there's no money to spare now,' said Melanie. 'From what I can gather, there's just what they take in from paying guests like Tim Gilbey.'

Warren turned to Skip. 'He's another monster!' His voice shook on the last word. 'He assaulted Melanie! You need to see what you can find out about him on the internet.'

Skip pulled out his phone immediately. 'How do you

spell that?' When Melanie told him, he started tapping at the screen and scrolling, but then he looked up at her. 'You have to make sure you keep safe. All the digging around you're doing, right under their noses – if they get an inkling of what you're up to –'

Tonya nodded. 'Do you think they *could* be suspicious of you?'

'Oh – no, I don't think so,' Melanie lied. 'I'm being careful.'

'I'm not convinced it's the right course of action,' said Warren.

Before he could elaborate, Melanie said, 'I think I might be close to finding something out.' She had to tell them something to stop them barging in and blowing her cover. 'Christina,' she settled on. 'I think the girl might know something. I'm working on her. I think she might confide in me if I don't spook her. So please – don't come back to the house. Not yet. Give me a couple of days. Keep talking to people, find out if anyone knows anything. Skip, there's a group of kids Alice got friendly with who live in a place called Balnabo. I've had a brief chat already with one of them, Murray Campbell – he's suspicious of Gray too. Maybe you could try to find out what exactly they know? But don't any of you come back to Scallan Lodge. I'll come here if I need to speak to you again.'

'Okay,' said Skip. 'Murray Campbell, Balnabo. I'll see if I can track him and his gang down. Makes sense to leave the Davidsons to you for now.' He started typing on his phone with his thumbs. 'I'll add him to the *To be talked to* list.'

'Skip's so organised,' said Tonya, with an attempt at a smile. 'Lists for everything.'

This was good. This was great. But Melanie couldn't help

feeling a tug of disappointment that Alice's disappearance, the attempt to find her, had been reduced by this boy to lists and boxes to be ticked, as if it were some sort of project for him.

No – that was unfair.

He was just trying his best to find Alice, and making lists ensured nothing slipped through the net.

'Tim Gilbey,' he said, scrolling on the phone. 'Is this the guy?' He held out his phone to Melanie.

Tim Gilbey's ugly, fleshy face leered at her from the screen.

'That's him,' she confirmed.

'Seems he's an entrepreneur, whatever multitude of sins that covers.' Skip started scrolling again. 'Office in Finsbury. Does a lot of charity work.' A pause. 'No mention yet of any convictions...'

'That means *nothing*!' spat Warren.

Melanie stayed another fifteen minutes, getting out her own phone and joining Skip in trawling the internet for information about Tim Gilbey. But neither of them turned up anything significant. There were photos of him at functions, in a hard hat at the opening of an office block he'd invested in, lining up with other sponsors at a classical music festival. If you took his internet presence as a true representation of the man, the worst you could say of him was that he had terrible taste in suits.

'I doubt we're going to find anything online.' She stood. 'I'd better be getting back.'

As they accompanied her to the door, Tonya said, 'If we get Alice back, that's it. Finished. We never want to see you again. We don't want you *anywhere near her*. Okay?'

Melanie just stood there stupidly, clutching her phone.

Tonya got right in her face. '*Okay?*'

'*Tonya,*' groaned Warren.

Tonya turned on him. 'When Alice was a baby, *she almost threw her out of a window!*' She rounded on Melanie again. 'That's why it was a closed adoption, that's why the courts said you couldn't have any contact with her unless *Alice* decided she wanted to know you! And what happens when she comes here looking for you? *It's your fault she's gone!*'

Warren put a hand on his wife's arm. 'That's not fair.'

'I agree,' Melanie managed to get out. 'She's better off with you. I know that. I've always known that.'

'Really? *Really?*' And Tonya pulled away from Warren and ran back into the cabin.

Warren lifted his shoulders helplessly and went after her.

'Do you think...' Skip trailed Melanie across the decking. 'Do you think... Alice...' He choked on her name.

'Is alive?' Melanie finished quietly. 'I don't know. But I think we have to face the fact that it's unlikely.'

'But possible,' he said tightly. 'We have to have faith that our prayers will be answered.'

'Keep praying,' was all Melanie said to that.

On autopilot, she walked to her car and drove slowly back along the winding track to the public road. If only she could believe in their God, in an all-knowing, all-powerful being who would save Alice. Who would let her live.

But she couldn't.

If Alice was alive, if anyone was going to save her, that person had to be Melanie.

33

ALICE - 21 JULY

Alice felt weird, as if her body was going through the motions of life but her head was somewhere else entirely. Her head was flying back along that road to Achnasheen and boarding a train and getting out of here.

On either side of her in the back seat of the car were Tess and Isabel, as if to anchor her down. Caro seemed to be colluding with Alice in her determination never to be alone in the house. She'd taken Alice, Tess and Isabel to a local café for lunch, but only Tess had done justice to the large platefuls of fish and chips. Alice could only eat a few mouthfuls.

As Caro drove slowly between the gateposts and round the side of the house, Tess's hand made its way into Alice's.

Once they'd parked up and were out of the car, Caro said, 'I'd like you to go and supervise Christina and her friends, please, Alice, at the pool house. Stick to them like glue and make sure they behave themselves, okay?'

'I'm not sure how Christina will feel about that.'

'I don't give a fuck how Christina feels about it!' Caro pretty much yelled.

Alice wanted to put her hands over Isabel's ears, but Isabel didn't turn a hair. She looked up at Alice and said, 'Can I come too?'

'Sure!'

'Can I?' said Tess, her hand finding Alice's again.

Alice nodded.

As Caro drifted off towards the house, Isabel said, 'We'll need our swimming costumes.'

'Oh,' said Alice. 'Yes.' She looked up at the high grey walls of the house. She really, *really* didn't want to go in there, into that warren of rooms that interconnected in strange and unexpected ways. So many places a person could be hiding. So many directions from which they could come at you.

'What's wrong?' said Tess. 'Alice? What are you frightened of?'

Alice took a big breath and squeezed Tess's hand. 'Nothing. I'm fine, honey.'

'Is it the ghost? Have you heard her?'

'What? No, of course not, Tess!'

'Because ghosts don't exist,' Tess finished heavily.

'You got it.'

AT THE END of what seemed like the longest day ever, Alice stood in the dim light of the Tower Room stairwell, her hands on the painted wood of the door to the rest of the house. She'd asked Caro if there was a key, and Caro had said no, there wasn't, apologetically, in a way that made it seem like she wished there were.

Well, Alice could improvise, as Daddy would say.

The big old chest of drawers weighed a tonne, and at first she couldn't shift it. But by taking out the drawers, she was able to lighten the load enough that she could drag the heavy piece of furniture across to block the door.

There!

No one was getting past *that*!

At least she could sleep soundly in the knowledge that she was safe.

Alice lay on her bed, staring at the dark.

Something had woken her.

Bang.

Bang bang.

In a second she was out of bed and running across the room, flicking on lights, flying down the staircase to the hallway, where the chest of drawers had already shifted a couple of inches, and, as she stared, the big old door shuddered and kind of bucked against it, like the door was trying to open all on its own.

But of course there was someone there.

There was someone on the other side of that door, trying to get in.

Alice shoved the chest of drawers back against the door with all her strength, but it shuddered in her hands as the door hit it again.

The drawers.

She needed to put the drawers back.

They had things like books and old heavy brass doorknobs in them. She gave the chest another shove and then had to leave it while she ran to where she'd left the drawers against the wall. She tried to lift one of the long ones, but it was too heavy. She dragged it across the floor and managed to manhandle it into place in the bottom section of the chest just as the door banged and juddered against it again.

It was him.

Gray.

It had to be.

She imagined him there, on the other side of the door, his flashing pirate eyes and his strong hands. There was something terrible about the fact that he wasn't speaking. That they were engaged in this completely silent, voiceless struggle, he to possess her, she to keep herself from him. There were no words, she supposed, necessary now.

No more pretence.

She pulled across the other long drawers – she had to take out some of their contents to make them light enough for her to lift them into place – and then the two smaller ones.

All the while the door *bang*, *banged* against the chest, but it was no longer moving with each *bang*. And finally, now that she was pretty sure he couldn't get in, she found her voice, but not for him.

'*Help me!*' she screamed. '*Help!* He's trying to get *into my room!*'

The door just kept on banging.

She ran up the stairs, to the nearest window. But none of them opened! Ken had said he'd look for the key to the catches, but if he had, he hadn't found it, and like an idiot, Alice hadn't asked again. She put her face right up to the window and shouted:

'*Help meeeee!*'

She slapped her hands on the glass, hard.

But the family bedrooms were all in a distant part of the house, a whole other wing.

If only she had her phone!

The banging from the hallway had stopped.

Did that mean he'd managed to push the chest clear?

Was he coming upstairs *right now*?

She wanted to hide, under the bed, in the wardrobe, but that wouldn't work – he would know she must be in here. He'd find her in five seconds!

Slowly, slowly, she edged her way to the top of the stairs and peeped down them.

No one was there.

Not that she could see, anyway. She edged her way onto the stairs, descending one step at a time, looking around each bend with her heart in her throat. *Help me Lord, help me Lord*, she repeated in her head. *Please help me!*

At the last bend she stopped, and listened, and when there was no sound she looked around it –

Oh, thank you, thank you, thank you!

The section of hallway she could see was empty. The chest was still in front of the door. The door wasn't moving. All was still and quiet.

But he could have got in and then put the chest back in place! He could be hiding down the hall, behind the sideboard, in the shower room –

Slowly, slowly, she edged down the last steps, her heart hammering as she reached the hall and swung around quickly, her hands bunched into fists, scanning the rest of the space.

Empty.

She flung open the shower room door.

Empty!

'Thank you, thank you, Lord,' she whispered.

Suddenly, into her head came church, her very own church in Branchfield, Indiana, filled with all the people she loved, but most of all Mom and Daddy, standing either side of her with their shoulders just touching hers. That feeling of peace, of love, of being as safe as a person could be – it suddenly swept through her and she knew she had to get out of here, she had to leave this place *right now* if she was ever going to see any of them again.

34

MELANIE - 10 AUGUST

Christina, Tess and Isabel were in the kitchen. There was a bowl of jelly beans on the island and a few on the marble surface. When Melanie appeared, Isabel ran up to her. 'Can you be the judge? We were going to get Mum to do it, but she's... not well.'

'She's in the library getting rat-arsed,' amended Christina. 'She wants to see you, by the way, but good luck getting any sense out of her.'

Isabel's little hand was on Melanie's sleeve. 'Can you do the judging first though, *please*?'

How could she resist those sad blue eyes? These poor kids.

Melanie nodded. 'Judging of what?'

'Jelly Bean Masterchef!'

'The contestants choose any three jelly beans,' explained Tess, pointing at the little groups of three colourful beans on the worktop. 'You have to try to get the most interesting and delicious combination of flavours.' And then she added what

Melanie had been hoping and dreading she would: 'Alice showed us.'

'Okay... so let's see what we've got.'

Isabel ran around to the other side of the island. 'Do mine first!' She crouched down until she was eye level with the jelly beans, like an artist assessing her work. She poked the bright green one in her group of three closer to the other two, as if titivating a plateful of cordon bleu cuisine.

Melanie stood at the island, facing the three sisters.

'Mine's peppermint, cola and peanut butter!' squealed Isabel.

The other two made faces.

'Oh dear,' said Melanie.

'You have to put them all in your mouth at once!'

'Really?'

Isabel giggled and then held her breath as Melanie chewed on her selection. It was sickly and very unpleasant.

'Interesting combination,' said Melanie. 'I'm certainly getting all three flavours.'

Christina had gone for blueberry, vanilla and lemon, and Tess for peach, tangerine and pear. As Melanie watched the girls' faces – even Christina seemed invested in her decision – she felt Alice's presence so strongly that she had to turn away for a second.

'Do you need a drink of water?' said Tess.

Melanie awarded Star Cook to Christina, who grinned, looking surprised, before settling her face back into its habitual expression of indifference. Melanie supposed Alice would probably have awarded the prize to Isabel, who was scowling up a storm.

'The mint and peanut butter combination is particularly disgusting,' Melanie pointed out.

'It really is,' agreed Christina.

'You're innovative, I'll give you that,' she told Isabel, who finally smiled.

In the library, sure enough, Caro was sitting at the desk, a glass of wine in her hand and a bottle on the embossed leather surface next to her. She had both elbows on the desk, and her chin was propped on her hands. Light was falling through the big bay windows into the otherwise gloomy room, illuminating the thousands of dust motes that swirled in the space between them.

'Donna,' Caro said carefully, straightening and making an attempt to look as if she weren't drunk.

Melanie came straight out with it. 'Alice was afraid of Tim Gilbey. What do you know about him?'

'*You*,' said Caro, 'need to be very careful. *Very* careful. Timothy Gilbey is a powerful man.'

'I – *what?*'

'*You assaulted him!*'

'No, I defended myself against him when *he* tried to sexually assault *me*.'

'Managed to talk him down.' Caro nodded, as if to herself. 'Not easy. He was going to make a complaint against you to the police.'

'Oh, I very much doubt it,' said Melanie. 'I very much doubt whether Tim Gilbey wants any police attention anywhere near him.'

Shit.

'I mean – I doubt if a busy man like him would want the hassle of it.'

Caro stood. 'If you queer our pitch with Tim and Edward, Ken's going to be *absolutely livid*, Donna. And you *really* don't want to make Ken angry.' But it was Caro's cold eyes that sent Melanie's stomach plummeting.

As she turned to leave the room, suddenly Ken was there, like a big bear, his body blocking the whole doorway.

'Ah, *Donna*.' He smiled down at Melanie, then looked past her at his wife. 'Why should I be angry?'

'She's still going on about Tim and Alice,' Caro drawled.

'What about them?' He was too close.

Melanie took a step back, but he grabbed her arm.

'What about Tim and Alice, *Donna*?'

He spoke her name with exaggerated care. Why was he repeating it like that? And why couldn't she think of a bloody thing to say? He was still smiling at her, his rather large mouth quirking at the side whimsically, as if she were a naughty child he was humouring, but his eyes were steely, unblinking, his gaze seeming to bore right through her.

'Nothing,' she muttered.

'Oh, *nothing*. I see.' He stepped back, with an exaggerated sweep of his arm to indicate she could go past him, as if he were some Regency buck and she a Jane Austen heroine.

As she made her escape, she found she was shaking.

Was it Ken who had taken her toothbrush and hair?

Did he know that she was Alice's birth mother?

IT WAS ALMOST as if Gray were deliberately making it easy for her. There was his rucksack, abandoned on a fallen tree trunk. Melanie hadn't even been looking for him. She'd left the house to clear her head, striding along the track beyond the old stables, not knowing or caring where she was going but needing this time alone to think.

What should she do?

Should she go back to the police, maybe take Murray along with her, try to make them take some sort of action? Or should she wait and see where the trackers might lead her?

And there it was, Gray's blue rucksack, a sitting duck on an old tree trunk next to a tumbledown building.

She put her hand in her pocket and closed it around the small plastic disk. Eyes scanning the vegetation, she walked over to the rucksack and undid its clips. Inside, there was a plastic lunch box, a hat, and a rolled-up waterproof. The rucksack had two zipped pockets inside, a big one and a smaller one. The bigger one wasn't zipped up – a map was poking out of it.

Glancing around again, she pulled the map out and unfolded it.

It was a map of this area, covered in red crosses.

What the *hell*?

She wrestled with the damn thing, eventually managing to fold it up and shove it back in the pocket. Unzipping the smaller, empty pocket, she pushed the tracker inside, hoping he wasn't in the habit of using this compartment.

She was just zipping it up again when she saw movement out of the corner of her eye.

'Find anything interesting?'

Gray was standing watching her from the doorway of the ruined building. How long had he been there?

'Sorry!' Donna simpered at him. 'I was just... I thought someone had lost it.'

'Ah.' He came towards her with a smile. 'Easy thing to lose, after all, isn't it? Easy to drop a rucksack without noticing.'

Melanie's heart pumped. This was a secluded spot. She

was reasonably fit, but Gray had the advantages of height, weight and, let's face it, being a man. He would probably be able to catch her if she ran. Overpower her if she fought.

But Melanie had lived a hand-to-mouth existence for years when she was little more than a child. She knew a few tricks.

And she had one advantage he couldn't guess at.

She was a mother.

Almost before she knew herself what she was going to do, she was on him, one foot hooked behind his leg, pushing him hard so he fell full length onto his back. She heard the air puff from his lungs.

She jumped on him, straddling his chest, her knees on his arms, her hands around his throat.

'Where is she?' she spat at him. 'Where's Alice?'

His eyes were huge, and she could feel his legs scrabbling about behind her. His hands were pulling at her feet, trying to free his arms from where she had them pinned.

'*Tell me!*'

'Nugh,' he choked. '*Nuh.*'

She loosened her grip. 'Tell me,' she said again, her voice harsh but, now, controlled. She needed to know this. She couldn't just kill him.

'*I* haven't – done – anything to Alice!' he gasped, staring into her eyes. 'Wasn't even – here when she – went missing!' He coughed, and flecks of spittle spattered her face. 'I'm *looking* for Alice! I think – I hope – he might be – keeping her nearby. Had her elsewhere until the police – finished searching – then brought her nearer to hand.'

'Who are you talking about?'

He swallowed.

'*Who?*' she screamed.

'Ken!' he shouted back, his eyes filling. 'All right? *Ken!*'

Melanie sat back, but she didn't break eye contact. 'You're telling me Ken took Alice. So why didn't you go to the police?'

'I don't know – for sure. If I'm wrong... He's my brother! This family is all I have. If I go to the police... accusing Ken of – abducting Alice... that's gone. I'll lose them all. I have to be certain.'

Melanie suddenly pushed herself off him, staggering to her feet. She went back to the rucksack and pulled out the map. The red crosses, she saw, marked small rectangles and squares and L-shapes on the map. Buildings.

'You've been searching buildings?'

Gray, propping himself on one elbow, nodded. 'Abandoned ones. There are a lot of them around here –'

'From the time of the clearances,' Melanie finished distractedly.

'No. The dwellings then...' He coughed. 'They would have been primitive affairs, turf houses or cruck-framed ones... with low stone walls and –'

'Spare me the history lesson!'

He sat up and put his hands through his hair. 'There are a lot of more intact buildings dating from – abandoned more recently,' he finished hurriedly, with a ghost of a smile, holding his palms out towards her as if to ward off another attack. 'Wind and watertight – and with potential to lock someone in a room or cellar.'

'This place hardly fits the bill.' She gestured at the tumbledown building behind him.

He shrugged. 'I'm running out of options. Sometimes places like this – they have intact portions.'

Melanie was staring at the map. There must be dozens of

crosses. And the map was wrinkled, as if it had been soaked in the rain a few times, and torn along one of the creases. It had seen a lot of use.

His story added up.

'Okay,' she said slowly. 'But *you're* the brother with the criminal record for sexual assault.'

Gray blinked at her. 'Christina said she thought you could be a journalist masquerading as an au pair, digging around, trying to find out about Alice's disappearance. Is she right?'

'No,' said Melanie shortly, and waited.

'I never did anything to those women.' He coughed again, then sighed. 'Anika Benson, who accused me of groping her at that event – we'd been flirting all night, and I thought she was... shall we say, receptive to my advances. Turns out I was wrong. Anyway. When that allegation came out in the press, one of our events team – she said I tried to rape her in the office one night. The power went down, and someone attacked her in the dark. But it wasn't me.'

'So what made her think it was?'

'I'd just left the office. When she heard someone – she thought I'd come back. But I hadn't.'

'You're saying it was Ken?'

He nodded. 'There have been... other incidents. At university, he took advantage of girls when they were drunk. A couple of them reported him, but who would believe that good old Ken, everyone's best friend, would force himself on women?' He sat up, taking a gasping breath into his lungs. 'That set the pattern.'

Melanie's stomach was roiling. 'Pattern for what?'

'Getting away with it,' said Gray grimly. 'Everyone thinks I'm the clever one, but Ken has always been able to run rings around me. He – I don't know – he makes people feel *comfortable*, makes them think he's such a great guy, so much fun, so they just can't see his other side.'

Melanie's brain was reeling. Was he telling the truth or not?

After a little silence, she said, echoing Skip, 'Do you think Alice is still alive?'

He put his hands through his hair again. 'I've no idea.'

'If she is... What are you intending to do once you've found her?'

'Oh *God*, I don't know! But the important thing is to *find her* – wouldn't you agree?'

35

ALICE - 22 JULY

Her suitcase would be too heavy, too unwieldy if she had to run. Instead, Alice decided to take a small floral shoe bag. Into it she put some underwear and toiletries, her toothbrush, a fresh T-shirt and the 'Welcum Alice' card Isabel had made.

Then she slung the strap of her purse across her body and checked inside it for her passport and wallet.

She was ready.

One last time, she looked around the Princess Room in the cold early-morning light as tears started again. She had thought she would be so happy here.

Poor Tess and Isabel! Poor Christina, even. She couldn't help but feel she was abandoning those girls. It wasn't just Gray who was *off* here. It was the whole place, the whole set-up. She hated to leave them.

Maybe she could go to the police?

And tell them what?

She felt herself blush at the prospect. Would they think she had *led him on* too?

Well, she could decide about that later. Right now, she needed to get out of here.

She removed each drawer from the chest that was blocking the door, trying to do it as silently as possible. What if he was right there on the other side? Would she have time to run and lock herself in the shower room?

When all the drawers had been removed, she pulled the carcass of the chest away from the door and, her heart bumping, eased the door open a crack. Then a little wider, wider...

No one out there.

She tiptoed along the corridor, through the silent house, wincing at each creak of a floorboard under her feet. And then she was in the big space of the main hall, feeling small and exposed as she ran lightly down the stairs, glancing up at the stained-glass window as she passed it and remembering her first encounter here with Gray.

Across the hall and into the empty kitchen.

Along the corridor to the back door.

The key was kept on a hook on the wall. She fumbled it into the lock and turned it, and then she was running across the grass and onto the driveway that led around the side of the house. It occurred to her belatedly, as she ran down the drive and between the big stone gateposts, that this was a stupid way to come – anyone looking out of a window that faced this way would see her. She should have gone past the pool house and down the other track to the beach.

Maybe, subconsciously, she'd wanted to leave the same way she'd arrived, to hit rewind on everything that had happened here.

She bunched the floral bag in her right hand and

powered up the track towards the trees. She'd go to Balnabo, find Murray's or Katie's house, call Daddy...

A whining noise made her falter; turn around.

It was a car engine.

The SUV was coming around the side of the house.

Coming after her.

And there was no place to hide. No trees here, just open moorland. He would catch her before she made it up the track to the woods.

Her feet had made the decision before she was conscious of it. They took her off the track and onto the heathery, tussocky ground to her right. She had a good head start. She could get to the trees this way, and then she could make her way through them to the public road, hitch a lift, maybe... Or just lie low until nightfall.

The heather was hard to run through, the ground under it uneven and treacherous. She tripped on a root and, trying to stay upright, stepped sideways into a pool.

Her foot kept on going.

Down and down, into the water, into the cold, stinking mud under it, right up to her hip, pulling her down onto her ass. The mud seemed to suck on her left leg, to close around it. Frantically, she kicked and got the knee of her right leg under her on the solid ground as a kind of lever. But still the bog held onto her other leg.

She looked around.

The SUV had stopped on the track.

The driver's door opened.

A tall figure got out.

'Ali, Ali,' said Gray. 'I thought I warned you about these bogs? What *are* you doing?' With a laugh, he flicked back his hair and started loping over the heather towards her, his long legs eating up the space between them in seconds.

36

MELANIE - 10 AUGUST

'Donna, I need to talk to you,' said Gray out of the corner of his mouth.

Melanie, with Isabel's help, was setting the table for dinner.

Isabel frowned at her uncle in disgust. 'Whisper, whisper!'

'Okay,' said Melanie brightly as Caro appeared from the direction of the utility room. 'Who's hungry? I've made a big pot of stew!'

'After dinner,' muttered Gray, and Melanie nodded.

It didn't sit right with Melanie, this alliance she seemed to have formed with Gray Davidson. But she believed that he really had been searching for Alice. Which, along with his alibi, exonerated him from any involvement in what had happened to her.

As she dolloped out the stew, Ken joshed Christina about her obsession with some reality TV show where members of the public were put through their paces by the SAS, threatening to totally embarrass her by applying to go on it himself. As he ran with this idea, speculating on how many hours it would take him to complete the assault course, everyone around the table, even Christina, was soon laughing.

Gray was right – you would never suspect this jolly, slightly buffoonish family man of having a dark side. Not unless you gave him reason to reveal it, as Melanie had this morning in the library. He'd shown it to her then, after Caro had told him that Melanie was asking questions about Alice; it had been there, in the way he'd looked at her, the jolly mask slipping to reveal the real man beneath.

Had he taken Alice?

Did he have her somewhere still, as Gray believed, or had he –

'Donna?' said Tess.

Melanie realised that she'd frozen, a ladleful of stew poised above Tess's plate.

'Sorry.' She smiled at the girl. 'How much would you like?'

'A lot.'

'Ask a silly question!' Ken guffawed.

Melanie looked at him stonily and then met Gray's gaze across the table, registered the very slight widening of his eyes at her, as if to say, *Be careful.*

And so Donna smiled at Ken and then at Tess, saying, with Donna-like banality, 'I don't know where you put it all, Tess!'

When dinner was over, Melanie loaded the dishwasher and wiped the table and worktops. As she was rinsing the cloth at the sink, Gray's voice said from behind her, 'I need to show you something,' making her start and whip round to face him.

He was standing right there, looming over her.

She could smell the sweat on him, see the sheen of it on the skin at the open neck of his shirt. He grimaced. 'I think it could be significant. Ken's in the library – we'd better go out the back.'

She followed him away from the house onto the track that led inland. He was striding ahead of her, not talking, and she had to trot to keep up. Soon the old stable block came into view, and he stopped abruptly, pushing a hand through his hair.

'What?' she said.

Suddenly, she was very aware of where they were – out of sight of the house. There was no one around. What if he went for her? What if she'd got it all wrong?

But she hadn't had a problem overcoming him before, had she? He wasn't likely to try anything, surely, after that? Gray might look dangerous, but he was a big girl's blouse, as Nic would say.

He looked past her. 'No one's followed us, have they? Tess is a fucking stalker.'

'Just tell me where we're going,' she said. 'What have you found?'

'There's a cellar under that building.' He jerked his head at the stables. And he must have seen something in her face, because he added quickly, 'Alice isn't there. Not now, anyway. But I think she recently could have been.'

The stable buildings were arranged around a cobbled courtyard. There was a run of arched double doors in one range, which would originally have housed carriages and then cars, she supposed, and in the other ranges were a variety of doors and windows, all with peeling green paint. Gray opened one of the old doors, which stuck a little on the floor as he pushed it.

Inside was a large room with some boxes stacked up against one wall.

Gray pointed at the floorboards, and Melanie saw that there was a trapdoor secured with a long iron flange and a padlock. Next to it was a white plastic switch. Gray bent and flipped the iron flange open, lifted the trapdoor and flicked on the switch.

'Ken had this cellar kitted out a while ago for storage, but get a whiff of that.'

Melanie peered down into the space below. There were proper steps, she saw, rather than a ladder, which made sense if you were going to be lugging things up and down.

'Bleach,' she said.

'We won't be needing any of the storage space in this building until the glamping business is up and running. As far as I know, no one has used this basement area since the workmen finished renovating it. So why does it stink of bleach? Why would Ken need to be using bleach on an empty, unused cellar?'

Melanie shrugged. 'Maybe just cleaning up after the workmen?'

Gray started down the steps. 'Possible, I suppose. But they were the type to take pride in their work. Taking a piss or a shit in the "build", as they called it, would have been frowned upon, to put it mildly.'

'They might have had their lunches in here and spilt some Pot Noodles or something.' Melanie followed him down the steps.

'Donna, they finished work *over a year ago*.'

The floor of the cellar was concrete, smooth, well made. Melanie walked across it, the smell of bleach making her want to gag. Was it possible? Could Ken have kept Alice in here?

In one corner of the room were a big blue plastic drum, a white plastic tank and two red plastic buckets, one full of water. In one of the buckets was a pack of toilet paper.

'Toilet facilities,' said Melanie.

'And look at this,' said Gray.

She turned. He was pointing to the bare stone wall, at the mortar joint between two large stones.

She walked across and peered at it. 'What?'

Pain arced through her, and the next thing she knew, she was looking up at the ceiling, up at him as he stood over her and said, 'Sorry.' In one hand, he held what looked like a kids' black and yellow water pistol.

He bent over her, and she could see the gleam of his eyes as he said, '*Not sorry*, you silly bitch.'

It was a Taser.

She could feel two pinpricks of pain in her neck. That would be the barbs. And dangling from the weapon in his hand were the wires attaching it to them.

Her whole body had gone completely limp, floppy, her arms and legs failing to respond as she tried to get up. She tingled all over, like biting ants were everywhere, under her skin, in her eyes, her mouth, even her teeth. He fiddled with the end of the Taser gun and detached part of it, which he tossed onto the floor – the cartridge, she realised, to which the barbs were attached. Kicking it away, he came over to her and pulled her phone from her pocket. 'I'll have this, thank you.'

Get up, get up!

She managed to push herself onto her elbow, but he was already on the steps, already up them, already slamming the trapdoor shut.

The lights went out.

37

ALICE - 22 JULY

'*Don't touch me!*' screamed Alice, thrashing her arms about in a hopeless attempt to fend him off.

'Whoa, whoa, *whoa*,' said Gray. 'I'm trying to help you. Or do you want to stay stuck in this bog all day?'

He caught her in a bear hug from behind, so she couldn't move her arms any more, and hauled her up. Her leg made a horrible sucking noise as it came out of the mud. The material of her jeans was now black and stinking and stuck to her skin. He lifted her bodily off her feet, and she struggled, she kicked back at his shins, she wriggled, but he just tightened his grip.

'I don't want to hurt you,' he growled in her ear.

When they reached the SUV, he hauled open the rear door and flung her inside, before slamming the door on her and getting into the driver's seat. Alice lunged for the door catch, but by the time she'd found it with her fingers, he'd engaged the central locking.

'Gotcha!' he said, like this was some game they were playing.

Alice couldn't think of a single thing to say. She should be talking to him. Trying to make him let her go. But whatever she said could make him angry. Maybe it was better to stay quiet?

'Buckle up, Ali.'

Numbly, she reached for the seat belt.

She should try to get away.

But how?

She was locked in. He was so much stronger than she was.

'Here we go – hang on!' He revved the engine and executed a sharp three-point turn on the track, and then the vehicle was hurtling back the way they'd come. 'Home again, home again, jiggedy-jig!'

Oh thank God, thank God, he was taking her back to Scallan Lodge!

Maybe it hadn't been Gray who'd tried to get into the Princess Room. Was it possible that, despite everything, he really was trying to help her?

Then she remembered the track that wound on past the house, and a little sob escaped her. But he turned in through the gateposts and up the drive, round the house to the parking area. Before the car had even stopped, she'd unbuckled and was trying the door.

'Hold your horses!' He got out and opened the door for her with a flourish, grinning and holding his nose as she got out. 'Ripe, Ali, *ripe*! I don't think Ken's going to be too happy about the state of the upholstery!'

'Sorry,' she muttered.

Should she make a run for it?

No. He would catch her.

'Maybe take off your shoes and socks at least before you go inside.'

Alice slipped them off at the back door and left them there. In bare feet, she made her way along the corridor to the kitchen, Gray walking behind her, and then through the silent hall and up the stairs.

'You're shaking,' said Gray, putting his hands on her shoulders.

'I'm cold.'

'A hot shower will soon fix that.'

When they reached the landing, Alice opened her mouth and screamed.

She choked on that scream as pain seared across her scalp, and her whole head was yanked back so hard that she found herself looking up into his eyes. His face was upside down, like the whole world had tilted. He clamped a hand over her mouth and hissed, '*No.*'

He kept one hand over her mouth and the other pulling back on her hair as they moved across the landing and along the corridors. When they arrived at the stairs to the Princess Room, he put his hands on her shoulders again. 'Let's get you cleaned up before you go dragging half the bog around your nice clean room.' He steered her past the stairs and into the shower room. 'Clothes off, Ali!'

Alice just stood there. She should scream again, try to attract attention, but she was scared of what he might do. Gently, he pulled the strap of her purse over her head and put the purse down on a table outside the shower room. But when he took hold of the zip of her hoodie, she stepped back. 'I can do it myself. Leave me to do it myself, please.'

'You're in shock, Ali.'

'No I'm not. I don't need you to undress me. I can do it myself.'

'*You*,' he said with sudden energy, 'need to learn what's good for you!' And he ripped the zip of the hoodie down and started wrestling it off her shoulders, down over her arms –

'No!' Alice yelled, pulling off the hoodie and pushing it at him, making him stagger back a pace. She managed to slip by him, out into the little hall, but she'd only taken a couple of steps when she felt her hair being yanked back again.

'*Gray!*' It was Caro, still in her dressing gown, face fierce. '*Let her go!*'

Immediately, her hair was released. Alice grabbed Caro's arm, babbling, 'He was trying to *take my clothes off*! I need to get *out of here*!'

Gray lifted his voice over her. 'She was halfway to the road.'

'I need to call my daddy! I need to go *home*!'

'Oh, Alice, I'm so sorry!' Caro caught her in a tight hug. 'I don't know what to say. Of course you can go home, you poor love!' And to Gray: '*Get out!*'

For two, three seconds, there was a charged silence. Then Gray flounced past them, hair swinging, long legs taking him in a few strides through the doorway and out of their sight.

'He scared me so much!' Alice sobbed.

'Oh, Alice. Why didn't you come to me, rather than running off on your own like that?'

Why *hadn't* she? 'I don't know,' she admitted in a small, shaky voice.

'Well, I'm here now, and I'm not going to let Gray touch you! But where on earth have you been? Look at the state of you!'

'I fell in the bog.' Alice gulped. 'At least – my leg did. Gray pulled me out. But then he – then he –'

'You're safe now, sweetheart. You get yourself showered and changed, and then you can call your parents, okay? You've some wages owing, and presumably they can transfer the rest of the money for a plane ticket?'

Alice nodded.

What in the world were Mom and Daddy going to say?

'I'm so sorry, Alice, that this has happened.' Caro patted her back briskly, in a *pull yourself together* kind of way. 'But I did warn you, didn't I, about how Gray might take your behaviour? Now, I'll leave you to get cleaned up, and I'll go and get dressed myself.' She held Alice away from her and looked into her face. 'We're all going to miss you very much, but I think maybe it is for the best that you leave.'

ALICE STOOD under the hot shower for a long time. Then she wrapped herself in a big towel, with a smaller one for her hair, took a breath, and eased open the bolt and then the door itself.

The little hallway was empty.

She scooted up the stairs and into the Princess Room. No time to blow-dry her hair. She just towelled it and pulled it back in a scrunchy, then dressed quickly in a knitted blue cotton top, wide beige linen slacks and sneakers.

Where was her purse?

She remembered Gray had put it on a table downstairs. She would need to clean that up too. She hoped the passport and wallet inside weren't messed up. But when she got downstairs, she found nothing on that table. She couldn't remember Gray going off with her purse. Maybe Caro had taken it to clean?

She went to the door and turned the handle, but it wouldn't open. It was stuck. She jiggled it and pulled harder. It didn't even move a millimetre.

It was locked.

Gray had locked her in?

But why would he do that?

What could he gain by doing that?

Alice pounded on the painted wood.

'Help!' she yelled. '*Help!* I'm *locked in*!'

She kept yelling for what seemed an age, but no one came. The Princess Room was far from the family's bedrooms, of course, and it was unlikely anyone would hear her. But surely Caro or Ken or one of the kids would come looking for her soon.

Until then, she had to stop Gray getting in.

She unloaded the drawers from the chest and pulled it across to block the door, then added each drawer back into it.

Ha!

He couldn't get to her now. And when Caro or Ken came, she was going to stick to them like glue until she was on that plane out of here.

38

MELANIE - 10 AUGUST

In the pitch dark, Melanie managed to pull the Taser barbs out of her skin. Then she shuffled around the walls of the cellar, fingertips grazing the rough stonework, until she found the stairs. There was a shaky banister on one side, so she wasn't in danger of falling. But she hit the top of her head on the trapdoor when the height of the cellar proved to be lower than she remembered.

She spent a long time feeling all over the trapdoor. It was smooth – plastic of some sort, with screws sunk into it attaching it to the wood. Around the edges of this plastic covering were indentations, gouges and cuts.

Someone had tried to prise it open.

Someone locked in here, as she was.

Alice?

She tried to push the trapdoor up with her hands. Then she turned around and used her shoulders, pushing and then barging at it until her whole body ached and she accepted that it was useless. There was no give at all. In addition to the iron flange, there must be something heavy on top of it.

She found and used the empty bucket and toilet paper in the corner, and tipped some water onto her hands from the other bucket, sloshing more than she'd intended onto herself. The big tank contained water – there was a tap on the side, which she could use to fill the bucket. And the drum, presumably, was for waste.

Panic rose in her at the thought of being trapped in here for hours, days even. Might Gray just leave her here? Who knew about this cellar? Ken, obviously, and Caro. But when they realised that Melanie was missing, why would they come here? Would they assume that she'd just left?

Gray must have taken Alice and made it look like she'd drowned.

Would he set up a similar scenario for Melanie? Pack up her things and dispose of them? Leave a note saying she resigned, that she was being exploited, that she hadn't signed up for this?

He was clever.

He'd somehow set up that alibi in London. The CCTV.

But how?

She explored the rest of the cellar systematically, starting with the wall furthest from the stairs. Then she took two paces away from it and walked gingerly, in what she hoped was a straight line, parallel to the wall but not touching it. As she moved, she stared ahead, as if by staring hard enough she could penetrate the darkness. She was very conscious of the space around her, the black air, as she swept her hands through it, ahead and to the sides; very conscious of being surrounded by it, exposed by it, somehow, despite the pitch dark.

Her ears, she found, were straining, her skin prickling, as if all her other senses were reaching out into the cellar to make up for her lack of sight.

When she reached the side wall, she took another couple of paces away from the end wall and walked back the way she'd come, repeating this process until she gauged she was near the stairs. There seemed to be nothing else in the room, as she'd expected from what she'd seen of it before the light went out. Now, care was needed to avoid bashing into the stairs. She swept her hands up and in front of her as she walked slowly forwards, and soon found the wooden steps.

She crouched to investigate the area under the stairs, and stumbled as her feet encountered something on the floor. Stooping, she ran her hands over it. It was a small, thin mattress, the kind that people took camping. And on top of it, the slippery softness of a sleeping bag. There was something inside it – the crinkle of plastic wrappers. Small bars of some kind. She tore open a wrapper and put her tongue, gingerly, to the contents. Cereal bars.

This and the buckets were good signs, weren't they?

Gray had thought about her comfort. That had to be a good thing. That meant he hadn't just locked her up and thrown away the key, surely? If he'd wanted her to die, he wouldn't have bothered with all this.

She carefully removed the cereal bars and stacked them against the wall at the bottom of the mattress. Then she wriggled inside the sleeping bag and lay down. What colour was it? Weird thought to have, but it was strange, not knowing. She buried her face in the material, breathing shallowly through her nose. Was there any trace of Alice's skin?

No – it had the slightly chemical smell of newness.

Or was that wishful thinking?

If Alice had been here, the one sure thing was that she wasn't any more.

Of course she'd been here. Those gouges on the trapdoor told their own story. She'd tried to get out, but hadn't succeeded. And now she was gone.

But Melanie had to hang on to one sliver of hope – those crosses on Gray's map. They were another thing that didn't make sense if her reading of the situation was correct. Why would Gray have been searching if he was the one who'd taken Alice and locked her up? Had it all been an elaborate ruse to gain Melanie's trust, to lure her here?

She made herself lie down and close her blind eyes; breathe slowly and evenly. She had to sleep. When he came for her, she needed to be, physically and mentally, as strong as she could be. She thought of Alice as a tiny baby, and repeated in her head the old Scottish lullaby she used to sing to her, the lullaby that Marion, her old neighbour in the flats in the Ferry, had taught her long ago.

O, rest my ain bairnie,
Lie peaceful and still.
Sleeping or waking,
I'll guard ye from ill.

Sleep now, my bairnie, sleep now, my dear.
Until dawns the day for ye, new, bright and clear.
No devil shall fright ye,
Nought shall ye fear.
I'll sing a sweet cantrip that none may come near.

Eerily gathers the mist on Ben Shee,
Coldly the wind now sweeps in from the sea.

But terror or storm
May come east or come west,
Warm will my ain birdie bide in the nest.

O, rest my ain bairnie,
Lie peaceful and still.
Sleeping or waking,
I'll guard ye from ill.

She woke to the sound of muffled voices.

Scrambling out of the sleeping bag, she stumbled through the dark, hands held in front of her, shouting:

'Help! I'm down here! HELP ME!'

Her left hand hit the banister, and then she was up the stairs and pounding on the trapdoor, all the while shouting at the top of her lungs.

As she paused for breath, straining to hear what was happening up there, a man's voice said, low and hard, 'At least lock the door! I can hear her!'

'I would if we had the fucking key.' That was Gray. 'They were all on hooks in the tack room. *Someone* seems to have decided there was a better place for them.'

She set her ear to the smooth plastic on the inside of the trapdoor.

'Well, *I* never touched them. And don't start! Don't fucking start trying to deflect blame for *any* of this! You knew Alice was off-limits.'

'Oh, come on.' Gray sounded faintly amused. 'When a peach lands in your lap, it would be an offence against nature not to show it some appreciation. Stop stressing, Ken.'

Melanie stood, tensed, straining to hear. She recoiled as a

squealing sound ripped through the trapdoor and vibrated against her ear. They were moving something across the floor. Something that had been on top of the trapdoor...

She turned and felt her way back down the stairs, heart pounding.

A weapon. She needed a weapon.

The buckets.

She ran blindly across the cellar, hands outstretched, until she came to the far wall. Feeling her way along it, she found the corner where the buckets were, but had only just reached it when the trapdoor banged open and the cellar was flooded with light.

'Hello, *Donna*,' said Ken.

He came halfway down the stairs and then stopped, staring at her.

Melanie cleared her throat and lifted her chin. 'Where's Alice?' The words came out as a croak. '*Where is she?*'

Ken grimaced. 'I'm sorry. I'm sorry any of this had to happen.'

'*Had* to?' She was shaking. 'Two au pairs going missing one after the other isn't going to look good, is it?'

'Just one,' said Ken, quite calmly. 'Poor girl drowned. Donna MacKenzie, her replacement, didn't last – she was freaked out by her predecessor's disappearance and left. No one's going to report Donna missing, are they? *Because she doesn't exist.*'

Melanie stared back at him. 'Of course I *exist*!'

'Melanie Macfarlane is already missing – went AWOL after discovering Alice was probably dead. Quietly having a breakdown somewhere. There's no suggestion she was ever here.'

So Ken had had the hairs and toothbrush DNA tested.

It was on the tip of her tongue to say that the Snyders knew who she was – that they'd come looking for her when she didn't make contact as arranged. But if she prewarned them of that, they'd be more likely to do away with her here and now. And they'd work something out, some tale to put the Snyders and the police off the scent. They'd done it once, successfully, with Alice. They'd do it again.

No.

Her best chance was to keep her contact with the Snyders quiet; let them come looking for her.

'Are you going to kill me?'

Ken seemed to consider the question. Then he gave a rueful little laugh, shaking his head. 'What a thing to ask anyone, Melanie. Have we hurt you, thus far, in any way?'

'You're keeping me locked in a *cellar!*'

He waved a hand around the space. 'It's dry, it's clean, you have food and water and a bed. Don't worry. Everything's going to be fine.'

'Is that what you told Alice? What have you done with her?'

She was just reaching for one of the buckets when there was movement behind him; a face, looking down through the open trapdoor. She expected to see Gray, but –

'Caro!' she shouted, leaving the bucket and running across the cellar towards the stairs. '*Caro!*'

The other woman made eye contact just for a fraction of a second before her face disappeared.

'*Caro!*' she screamed. 'You can't let them do this! *Please!*'

Ken raised his eyebrows and pointed the Taser at her. 'Behave yourself, Melanie, stop screaming and shouting and carrying on, and things will go a lot better for you.' He turned and stomped up the steps, and then the trapdoor thunked back in place, and the lights went out.

39

ALICE - 22 JULY

Alice couldn't shout any more. Her throat was dry and sore, her voice all but gone. And her wrists ached from pounding her hands on the windows and the door.

Why was no one coming?

Why was no one looking for her?

She'd been locked in the tower for almost two hours. She went from one window to the next in the Princess Room, looking down at the roofs and garden below. Where was everyone? As she stared down at the front of the house, she saw a movement – Caro, lighting a cigarette, walking away from the house over the lawn.

She needed something hard, something robust.

The wooden chair by her bed.

Holding it by its back, she ran at the middle window overlooking the front of the house, smashing all four legs into the glass. The window shuddered but didn't break. She did it again, and again, gasping with the effort.

The glass suddenly turned opaque, and Alice realised it

had shattered, but in the way safety glass did, fragmenting not into shards but into a mosaic of thousands of tiny pieces. One more whack with the chair legs sent them raining down onto the roof below.

Air rushed in. Lovely fresh air!

She chucked the chair aside and leant out of the gap.

'Caro! Caro! I'm *locked in!*'

Slowly, Caro turned and lifted her face. She shielded her eyes from the sun with the non-cigarette hand.

'Gray's *locked me in!*'

Caro flicked away the cigarette, and her voice drifted up to Alice. 'All right, I'm coming! I'm coming, Alice!'

When she heard Caro's voice on the other side of the door, and the key turning in the lock, Alice removed the drawers and pulled the chest away. Had Caro got the key from Gray? Or maybe there was more than one key?

But it was Ken who came through the doorway first, his thatch of hair standing on end and giving him an agitated look that matched how Alice was feeling.

Caro said, 'You poor thing!' and pulled her into a hug.

And then Ken's big, meaty hand was between Alice's face and Caro's shoulder, and he was putting a cloth over her nose, a damp cloth that stank of something acrid and awful, and Alice tried to pull away, but Caro tightened her arms around her.

Everything swam about, and her head seemed to drift upwards into nothing.

'Well, help me with her,' said Caro.

40

ALICE - 22 JULY

Alice opened her eyes.

Her head hurt, in sharp pulses, as if her brain were being shoved against her forehead over and over again. She was lying on her side in a strange bed. In a strange room, flooded with harsh artificial light. She could see the wall opposite, painted white. The ceiling, also white, with a strip light in the middle of it. A table and chair. A rug. A sofa with several tweedy throws over it and a faux fur one on top.

A bookcase filled with paperbacks.

A little kitchenette with a sink and a worktop and cupboards. A fridge. A microwave.

The bed was a king-size one with smooth sheets and a silky grey quilt. She turned her head, and pain screamed through it.

'*Ow!*' she said aloud.

The bed had a padded pink headboard, set against the wall.

To her right there was a door, and there was another in the wall opposite.

She slung her legs over the side of the bed and tried to think.

What was this place?

Was it one of the bedrooms at Scallan Lodge?

What had happened? She remembered Ken and Caro –

As her whole body started to tremble, her thoughts scrambled, tearing through her sore head until she was gasping as if she'd just run a race.

Ken had given her something to knock her out!

Caro had told him, 'Help me with her.'

They had *kidnapped* her?

So it wasn't Gray she should have been most afraid of but *Ken and Caro*?

What was this place? It smelt of dust and cement and chemicals, like the builders had smelt who'd been working on the renovation next door at home. Mom would take pity on them and ask them in for a home-cooked lunch. They'd carefully sit on newspapers around the kitchen table, and this same smell had wafted off their work clothes.

At the thought of that kitchen table, Alice wanted to curl up and sob.

But she couldn't break down. She had to think.

There were no windows – just those two doors. She stepped across to the one on the right. It was made of metal, not wood, its surface completely smooth. There was no handle. Not even a keyhole. She pushed it, but of course it was locked.

The door straight ahead led into a tiled en suite bathroom. There was a bath, a shower, a bidet, a toilet and a sink with a big mirror over it and a shelf with a toothbrush in a mug. A tall cabinet in the corner contained packs of toilet tissue but also a dizzying array of toiletries and products, all new: shampoo and conditioner, body wash, moisturiser, wipes, a hairbrush, dental floss, tampons, a grooming set containing tweezers, a nail file and a hand mirror, a waxing kit, bubble bath, essential oils, deodorant, a skincare set with toner and cleanser and serum, and one of those fancy make-up boxes like an artist's paintbox with lots of shades of foundations and lipsticks and mascaras and eyeshadows.

Her gaze rested on a cute, squat bottle of Chloé eau de toilette, sitting there on the shelf with a jaunty little orange ribbon tied around its neck.

What was this?

All the time she was looking at that stuff, a voice was screaming in the back of her aching head:

Get out! Get out! Get out!

She attacked the metal door. She kicked it, she screamed, she barged her shoulder against it like she'd seen in films. It didn't even move. Not one millimetre.

Her head ached *so bad*.

She sat down on the bed. There was obviously no way out of here unless they *let* her out. And they weren't going to do that, were they, because she'd go straight to the police and they'd be arrested.

Her heart was pumping. Her mouth so dry she couldn't swallow.

That meant...

That meant...

And now she did curl up on the bed and cry. And she must have slept again, because the next thing she knew, something had woken her.

She shot upright and out of the bed.

The door was open. Just a tiny crack.

Ken's voice said, 'Stand against the wall opposite the door, Alice.'

Numbly, she did so.

The door opened wider, and Ken came into the room. He was pointing a yellow gun at her!

Alice couldn't help it – she started to cry again.

'Don't worry – it's just a Taser,' said Ken with a sickly smile. 'Now, now, Alice. It's okay! I know you must be shocked and frightened. But this is for your own good.'

'*What?*' She almost laughed.

'You're here because we have to keep you away from Gray. My brother – I'm afraid he's a sex maniac.'

'You can keep me away from him by letting me out of here and letting me *go home!*'

'All in good time, Alice, all in good time.'

Really?

They were really going to let her go?

'You'll be here a few days, and then you'll be winging your way back across the Atlantic.'

She tried to control her breathing. 'Why?' she got out.

'It's complicated,' he said with a grimace. 'But please don't worry. Make yourself at home. There's food in the cupboards and the fridge. I'll come by every day to check that you're okay.'

'Oh, *please* just let me *out of here*,' Alice begged. 'I won't tell anyone. I won't tell the police.'

He laughed. 'And what is there to tell the police, I'd like to know? We've changed your accommodation for a few days after you decided to leave, that's all. We need your room for the new au pair.'

'I'm *locked in!*'

'The door may malfunction from time to time.'

She should play along with this! If he thought there was nothing for her to tell the police, he was more likely to let her go, wasn't he? Could it be true that she was being locked up here to keep her away from Gray?

Of course not!

Caro could have driven her to the airport like she'd said she would. They were keeping her here for some other reason that sat at the back of Alice's head and wouldn't let her look at it straight on.

But she should play along. Lull him into thinking she accepted it.

'Okay,' she said in a small voice.

He nodded, like she was a good kid who'd given him the right answer.

'How long will I be here for?'

'Like I said, just a few days. Relax and enjoy the peace away from the littlies! Sorry there are no screens, but there are books.' He waved the yellow Taser at the bookcase. 'Is there anything else you need?'

She shook her head.

'When do you expect to have your period?'

'*Excuse* me?'

'Do you need, um, products...?'

'There are tampons in the cupboard.'

'Yes, but I'll need to bring you some bags, a bin...' He smiled and raised his eyebrows. 'When is it, Alice?'

'I –' She was trembling now, her back pushed against the wall to hold herself upright. 'I'm not sure. It's not regular at the moment.'

'You must have some idea.'

'Soon,' she said. 'It's due soon.'

He grimaced. 'Well, let me know when it starts.'

She nodded.

And then he stepped back, and the metal door clunked shut, and she was alone.

SHE BEGAN to lose track of the days. Each one was the same – she'd wake up late in the morning and immediately check the door to see if by some fluke it had been left open, find she was still a prisoner and panic, screaming, pounding on the door, then straining her ears to try to detect anything beyond it.

When that got old, she would quickly shower, then wrap the towelling robe they'd supplied around herself. The en suite had no lock on the door, and she always dreaded being surprised when she was undressed, even though Ken usually came at night. She didn't bother with waxing her legs or plucking her eyebrows or any of the other parts of her normal grooming routine. She didn't even wash her hair, in case he came when she was standing under the shower with shampoo in her eyes.

The drawers and wardrobe were filled with her own clothes. She dressed in something comfortable, like joggers and a T-shirt and fleece. And then she would make breakfast – cornflakes and milk and a cup of coffee.

That was followed by some more screaming for help and pounding on the door and the walls. She walked round and round the room and the en suite, keeping herself fit in case she got a chance to make a run for it. She did stretches and press-ups and lunges, and used two big bottles of milk as improvised weights.

Then lunch – one of the microwaveable pouches of

lentils and some vegetables from the fridge, or a can of soup and a slice of bread. In the afternoon, she did more fitness stuff and read a book, forcing her brain to leave her prison for a few hours so she could lose herself in another world. Then more yelling and pounding. Her evening meal was generally a ready-made one from the fridge, again with vegetables, all cooked in the microwave. And all the time she was going through the motions of this daily routine, she was biting down on the same panic she'd woken up to that first day.

What's going to happen to me?
When will it happen?
What are they going to do?

She had been so, *so* wrong about the Davidsons. She had thought Caro was this cool, funky lady. And Ken a big friendly softie. And Gray –

She had been halfway to falling in love with that creep.

Daddy had been right all along.

Alice couldn't be trusted out in the world on her own.

But not even Daddy could ever imagine *this* happening to her! There was something almost ridiculous about it, like Alice had deliberately gone out of her way to get herself into the worst possible trouble. When her thoughts took that line, she would find herself laughing, hysterically, until the laughter turned to tears and she flung herself down on the bed for an energy-sapping cryfest.

When she started her period, she had to set the bin liner and its contents next to the door each evening for Ken to take away that night.

He almost always came at night. Usually she would be asleep and not know he'd been until she woke and saw the stuff he'd left by the door, like he was Santa Claus gone bad.

Sometimes it would be fresh fruit, milk, bread. Juice, cheese. Sometimes salad stuff, lettuce or tomatoes. A quiche. Some cookies. Once there was a Tupperware container of homemade soup, but Alice poured it away down the toilet. Who knew what might be in that? She only ate stuff that was sealed.

She started to stay up until he arrived. She'd sit up in the uncomfortable chair with a book, making herself stay awake until the door clicked open, just a crack, and the end of the yellow Taser gun appeared and Ken's voice told her to get back against the wall.

When he left, she would press her ear to the door and listen to his steps receding. It sounded like there were stairs.

Was it possible that she *was* in Scallan Lodge? In the north wing, maybe? She'd only ventured into a couple of rooms in that part of the house – they weren't interesting, just lumber rooms. But houses like Scallan Lodge often had secret rooms, didn't they? Maybe this was one such, sealed up and soundproofed so no one would know she was in here.

The only way she was going to get out was when Ken opened that door.

So she made a plan. Ken never came far into the room. He just left whatever he'd brought at the door. But he always bent to place it on the floor, and as he did so, he was looking down and not at Alice.

That was her only chance.

It must have been at least two weeks in when she decided she had to do it. She had to rush at Ken when he bent over. So that night, instead of the slippers they'd supplied, Alice was wearing her sneakers when the door opened and Ken appeared.

'Hello, Alice,' he said, all fake niceness as usual. 'How are you today?'

'Okay, I guess.' She was standing, as instructed, with her back against the wall facing the door. She felt sure he must be able to see how tensed she was, her leg muscles ready to explode, her hands pressed against the wall behind her, ready to push off.

But he was burbling on. 'I've brought you some chicken salad. And a laundry bag. If you put your dirty clothes in this, I'll get it next time.'

As he stooped to place the Tupperware and the large striped cotton bag on the floor, Alice launched herself at him. He was straightening, his face registering surprise, as she barged into him, sending him sprawling against the doorframe. But he was such a big guy that there was hardly room for Alice to get by him. She pushed herself into the space between his body and the other side of the doorframe and wriggled out into a short passageway with crude wooden stairs leading upwards. She could smell the night air.

Pain exploded across her back, and she went down.

41

MELANIE - 11 AUGUST

The trapdoor opened, and the lights came on.

'Stand back against the wall,' said Ken, taking a couple of steps down the staircase. He was carrying the yellow Taser.

Melanie, blinking in the light, did as he said.

He reached up to the floor behind him and pulled a cardboard box onto the stairs, which he pushed down the steps. 'Supplies,' he said. 'Food and cleaning products. You need to use them on your toilet area. I'll leave the light on, shall I?'

She nodded, and stepped forward.

'*Don't move!*' he snapped.

He backed up the steps, never taking his eyes off her, and slammed the trapdoor shut. She heard something heavy being pulled across the floor above, presumably on top of the trapdoor.

There was no way out of here other than past whoever came down into this cellar.

In the box were a cleaning cloth and a bathroom spray,

plus a box of oatcakes, a block of cheese, and a large fruit cake. She ate some oatcakes and cheese, making herself swallow each painful mouthful. Her throat was raw from shouting.

She had to take advantage, now, of the light. There was no telling how long they would leave it on. She quickly cleaned the concrete around the buckets and tipped the waste one into the blue drum, which had a lid to contain the smell. She refilled the other bucket with water from the tank.

And then she examined every inch of that cellar.

An hour later, she had one object that could be used as a weapon, which she secreted under the mattress: a lump of mortar. But it was only a couple of inches across and wouldn't do enough damage, unless, she supposed, she could mash it into an eye.

The buckets were a better bet, but hardly something she could conceal about her person.

Eventually, they were going to come for her.

And she had to be ready.

The next time the trapdoor opened, it was Gray leering down at her. But he didn't even come onto the steps. He just called down:

'How are you doing?'

'Oh, *I'm* okay,' said Melanie. 'Relatively speaking, anyway.'

That threw him. The leer slipped a little.

She kept her tone conversational. 'I'd rather be locked in a cellar for a few days than spend a lifetime as a sick, twisted psychopath.'

She needed to lure him down here. She needed him within striking distance. She had the lump of mortar in her right fist. She would mash it into his eye, knee him in the groin and hopefully avoid that Taser.

But he laughed. 'Each to his or her own,' he said. 'Personally I wouldn't fancy it. Being locked in here, I mean. Are you wondering what we're going to do to you?'

'Oh, I imagine you've got plans for me. And then you'll kill me. You can hardly let me go now, can you?'

'It would be a little tricky,' he agreed, and slammed the trapdoor shut.

The lights went out.

And as she listened to him hauling whatever it was they put over the trapdoor, she realised she'd missed a chance. Between shutting the trapdoor and locking it – that was her opportunity. She could rush up the stairs and barge the trapdoor open, taking him by surprise.

Next time.

But she needed something better than a lump of mortar.

The buckets were plastic, with plastic handles. She felt them with her fingertips, forming a picture in her head. The handles were the kind that popped into holes in the top of the bucket, and a small amount of brute force was enough to pull one of them free. Jamming one end under her foot on the concrete floor, with the other foot she forced the other end of the horseshoe shape back and back and back until it snapped off.

Now she had two pieces, the smaller straightish with just a slight curve to it and a jagged break at the end. A sharp shard of reasonably strong plastic.

Perfect.

She pushed it into the pocket of her jeans and concealed the other piece behind the water tank.

No one came for two days.

She was asleep when a bang woke her, and she sat up, instantly alert, her hand going to the pocket of her jeans to check that the shard of plastic was still there. The lights snapped on, and she screwed up her eyes against the glare, heart pounding.

You can do this!

There were voices. Ken and Gray.

It would be hard to get past both of them, but she had to try.

'I'm very much getting the raw end of the deal, though, amn't I?' said Gray.

Ken laughed. 'You're lucky there's any *deal* at all after the bloody mess you've made.'

'Yeah, yeah. Give me the Taser, then. She's liable to go for me.'

'Would serve you right if she did. But you'd probably be better to Taser her first. Then do what you like to her, but don't try coming after us. I mean it.'

Didn't they realise she could hear them?

Her stomach roiled as it hit her: they didn't care if she heard them or not. Because this was it. Melanie wasn't supposed to survive what was about to happen.

The arrogant bastards. To them, she was little more than an object, something to be incapacitated with a Taser and then –

Gray was going to rape her.

Her thoughts were flying at a hundred miles an hour.

She stood, tensed, ready, but then quickly got back into the sleeping bag on the mattress. Gray needed to believe she was passive and vulnerable.

She curled herself up into the foetal position and closed her eyes.

Footsteps on the stairs, crossing the concrete floor towards her, and then Gray's voice. 'Hello there, Donna. Or should I say Melanie?'

She didn't move or say anything or open her eyes.

'Melanie?'

Should she say she was ill?

No – that might put him off.

Slowly, she opened her eyes.

He was bending over her, the Taser pointed right at her face.

'Hello,' she whispered, bunching the silky material of the sleeping bag up under her chin. She kept her eyes wide and scared.

'Been having a refreshing sleep? I must say, you've kept the place nice.' The form of words made her heart pound faster: *you've kept*, not *you're keeping*. 'Quite the domestic goddess.'

She offered him a little smile.

Was it in any way believable that she'd be so accepting, so amenable? Especially after the insults she'd flung at him last time? But maybe he'd be expecting two days spent terrified and alone in a dark cellar to have broken her spirit. Maybe that was what he was counting on.

'Thank you,' she breathed.

He squatted down next to her, his right hand aiming the Taser at her head. With the left, he touched her face; pushed her hair back from her forehead. He cupped her shoulder, and then he was running the hand down the length of the sleeping bag, ending at her feet, one of which he grasped through the layers of material.

'You've still got your shoes on, dirty girl.' He gave the foot a little admonishing shake.

'I was cold,' Melanie breathed.

He grimaced. 'I'm sorry. We can't have that. Do you need me to warm you up?'

She left a little pause before shyly nodding. 'But – what are you going to do to me?' she whispered, letting her eyes film with tears. 'Please don't hurt me.'

Oh, he liked that. His pupils were dilating as he brought his face close to hers. 'I'm afraid I can't make any promises.'

Melanie's face collapsed. Her lips wobbled. She gasped, '*Please!* I'll do anything you want me to. *Anything.*'

'Anything, eh?' He grinned. 'Well, first things first. Get out of the sleeping bag.'

Slowly, slowly, Melanie pushed it down her body, wriggling herself free of it, but continuing to lie passively on the mattress, now on her back. Gray twitched the sleeping bag free of her feet and then ran his left hand up the inside of her right leg, all the while maintaining eye contact.

She tried to look back at him with nothing but a sort of frozen horror, terrified that he'd see something else whilst their gazes were locked like this. Out of the corner of her eye, she tracked his right hand, the one holding the Taser, as it drifted away from her head, his instinct obviously being to set that hand on the floor for balance as he moved the other one over her.

'*Please*,' she whispered, tears overflowing. 'Gray, please –'

She grabbed his left hand with hers as it pushed into her crotch.

He laughed.

With her right hand, she stabbed the shard of plastic as hard as she could into his eye.

He screamed.

She rammed it home.

He shrieked and slumped back, the Taser clattering to the concrete floor. In one swift movement she was up off her back and onto her feet, grabbing the Taser, aiming it at his face and firing the barbs into his cheek at point-blank range.

His body spasmed and then was still.

She stood over him, breathing hard, watching gloop and blood seep out of his eye and down his face.

Had she killed him?

She hoped so.

Nic had shown her how to kill that way. The eye socket was the most vulnerable part of the skull – 'There's a useful fact that could come in handy,' Nic had told her, demonstrating on a pig skull that one of the mad bastards in the squat had got from somewhere and used as a hat stand for his collection of beanies. 'Straight through to the brain.'

Unsurprisingly, Melanie had never put that knowledge to the test.

Until now.

She hadn't killed him, she realised. He was still moving, just a little.

Groaning.

The shard of plastic was sticking up from his eyeball. She supposed it wasn't deep enough. For a second she considered shoving it all the way in, but she might need him. The police might need him.

The barbs in his face were still attached by wires to the Taser cartridge. She ejected it, remembering something else

Nic had said – after the cartridge had been used, a Taser could be deployed again in what was called drive-stun mode. She pressed the Taser muzzle to Gray's crotch and zapped him in the balls. Just because she could.

He twitched; groaned louder.

Melanie crept up the steps, the Taser held in front of her. At the top, she poked her head out, half expecting Ken to pounce. But the storeroom was empty. The door to the courtyard was standing open to the night air. She slammed shut the trapdoor and padlocked it in place.

42

ALICE - 10 AUGUST

Alice was helpless, lying just outside the doorway to her prison. Her muscles didn't work. As Ken bent over her, she tried to wriggle away from him, but she couldn't. She felt two sharp stabs of pain in her back.

'There we go,' he said. 'That's the barbs out.'

He hefted her up into his arms, like she weighed nothing. She struggled, and he said, 'It's okay, it's okay, I'm not going to hurt you.'

You just have! she wanted to yell at him.

And then he was setting her gently on the bed.

'Silly girl,' he said mildly.

Alice could only lie there as he looked down at her.

'Wash your hair,' he said eventually.

And then he was gone.

THE DREAM HAD MORPHED into something strange. She wasn't on the outside looking in any more – she was inside that cottage, but she was alone, locked in. She wasn't afraid, though. In fact, she was enjoying it, like it was a game. There were dozens and dozens of doors, and Alice had to run around the house trying them all. She was against the clock, which ticked away in the background like on a game show.

It was awful to wake up and realise, yes, she really was locked in, but she wasn't in the cute cottage.

'And it isn't any fun,' she said out loud to the ceiling.

She curled up in a ball and shut her eyes. All she wanted to do was go back to sleep, but thoughts were going round and round in her head. How were the Davidsons explaining her disappearance – to the kids, to Murray and Katie and the others, maybe, when they came looking for her? To the *police*?

Would the police be involved yet?

Ken, Caro and Gray were bad people.

Had they done bad things before?

Did the kids know, on some level, that the adults in their family were...

'Psychopaths,' she said into the pillow.

That would explain Tess's behaviour, maybe. And Christina's. The way they each seemed to have detached themselves, in their own ways. Did Tess know that that wasn't a ghost she'd heard?

She shot upright.

They'd done this before!

Tess had heard some *other* girl that the Davidsons had locked up! Banging on a door. Screaming...

Or maybe the screaming had happened when they –

'Don't think about it,' she whispered.

But did that mean that she was in Scallan Lodge?

If she screamed and banged loudly enough, maybe someone would hear her?

All that day, she alternated banging and shouting and resting and eating. It felt good to know that there was a possibility of rescue out there. As she banged away with the chair on the door, she imagined Tess lying on her bed and hearing the muffled noises and thinking, clever girl that she was, 'Maybe that isn't a ghost. Maybe Alice is trapped somewhere.' And then going off in search of the source of the sound...

But maybe she'd tell her parents, and they'd fob her off, tell her it was workmen doing some repairs and listening to the radio, or Christina and her friends messing around.

If the noises became a problem...

What would they do about it?

She paused, the chair in her hands.

She set it down.

Next thing she knew, she was back on the bed, not wailing, not crying, just staring, dry-eyed, at the ceiling.

THAT NIGHT, Ken came again. Why was it never Caro or Gray?

He brought her new clothes, with the tags still on them. The clothes were too young for her – a little top with a bunny on it, the kind of patterned leggings kids wore, two short summer dresses and a couple of cardigans. White socks and sandals.

'Wash your hair,' he said again. 'And do something about the shadows under your eyes. You need to look after yourself, Alice. Keep yourself nice.'

She washed her hair, but there was nothing she could do about her face. She peered at it in the mirror in the en suite. She did look bad. Being in a state of constant terror would do that to you, she supposed, although the terror had now receded. Today, all she felt was a sort of hopeless numbness.

'Fear exists for a reason,' she remembered Daddy saying when she was maybe twelve years old and too afraid to go out in the backyard in the dark to collect the rug and book she'd left out there, which Mom had told her to go get. 'If there really is danger in the yard, your fear will make you so alert you'll pick up on it, and make you run so fast that nothing can catch you.' He'd taken her hand, and the two of them had gone out into the yard together with the flashlight. Alice had picked up the book and Daddy the rug, and the two of them had sprinted side by side back through the dark to the warm yellow safety of the open door. With Daddy alongside her, of course, she hadn't really been afraid at all.

'Daddy,' she said out loud.

But it was Mom's voice she heard.

Don't you dare give up on yourself, Alice Snyder!

Which was weird, because she didn't think Mom had ever said or would ever say such a thing. She couldn't think of a situation where she'd needed to. Alice had never been a quitter. She was the classic overachiever who hadn't needed pushy parents to excel either in sports or academically. She used to love tests in class, because she knew she'd be the one to ace them, and she liked that smug feeling, she liked the way the teacher said, 'Excellent, Alice!' with the *as usual* left unsaid but still hanging there in the air; she liked how the other kids looked at her with either an admiring sort of wonder or open disgust. Alice the straight A student.

Mom hated boastfulness more than anything, but at graduation, Alice had overheard her get as close to it as she ever did. Another parent had been saying how proud she must be of Alice being valedictorian, but in a kind of surprised way. 'She must have worked very hard,' the guy had added, like this was the only way to explain it. And Mom had said coolly, 'Oh, no more than her friends – not so much, if anything. Folks underestimate Alice because she downplays her intelligence, but she's a very smart girl.'

You're a very smart girl, honey, she imagined Mom saying now. *And this is the test of your life.*

43

MELANIE - 14 AUGUST

Gray must have brought a torch with him, but where was it? Melanie looked around the storeroom but couldn't see one. Maybe it was down in the cellar. Maybe he'd left it on the steps. But no way was she opening that trapdoor to look. She imagined him crouched there, just under it, blood and jelly congealing on his cheek from the ruined eye, the plastic shard still sticking out of it...

And anyway, it wasn't a good idea to advertise her presence with a light. She slipped out of the door into the courtyard. The night was overcast, but there were breaks in the clouds, and there was a moon there somewhere. It felt late, probably after midnight. She crossed the cobbles on silent feet and edged around the stable building and onto the track. Its line was just about visible, wending back towards Scallan Lodge in one direction, and in the other between the verges that bounded the fields before heading off over the moorland.

She decided to take the way she knew, back to the house. She had the advantage of invisibility in the dark. It would be easy enough to slip past the gates and up the track to the public road. She'd walk to the village and get help there. Call the police. There was no way they could fail to act against the Davidsons now.

Ken had told Gray, *Don't try coming after us.*

What had he meant by that?

Who was 'us'?

Where were they going?

When she reached the house, she stopped at the gateposts and looked up at the grim slab of granite wall facing her. There were lights on in the drawing room. The curtains were pulled across the windows, but she could see the shape of someone moving around in there.

What if they'd brought Alice here?

She slipped between the gateposts and across the lawn, but then she heard it.

The sound of an engine, up the track. Coming closer, at speed.

Instinctively, she dropped, flattening herself on the damp grass. But no – they might see her, out here in the middle of the lawn. She stood and sprinted for the line of rhododendrons edging the grass, and had just dived under one of them when headlights raked past.

Had they seen her?

She lay still, watching the moving headlights sweep across the porch, the shadows cast by its stone arches moving disconcertingly across the front door as it came open and Ken appeared, foursquare, his big body blocking the entrance.

Car doors opened, and two shapes emerged.

'You've made good time!' said Ken, rubbing his hands, his face eerily smiling in the light from the headlights and from the hall behind him, like a sinister character in a black-and-white film. 'Come in, come in! We've got the fire going, and there're a couple of drams with your names on them!'

'Later,' barked one of the men.

That was Edward Norcott!

'You've stalled enough,' said the other.

Tim Gilbey.

'Let's go,' he added.

Ken's smile froze on his face. 'You don't want to...?'

'We don't want a whisky, we don't want a sandwich, we don't want to go pee-pee,' snarled Tim.

'Where is she?' said Edward.

'Not far,' said Ken.

Melanie smothered a gasp. They were talking about Alice?

She was still alive?

'Let's go.' Edward was already turning back to the car. 'You lead and we'll follow.'

'But I need to – prepare her.'

Tim lunged at Ken, grabbing the front of his shirt. 'What do you mean *prepare* her? Why should she need to be *prepared*? I hope we're not going to find she's deteriorated since we last saw her, because if that's the case –'

'No, no, no.' Ken gave a strangled laugh. 'I think you'll find she's everything you've been hoping for.'

Deteriorated? Like she was a product they were anxious had been stored correctly?

Melanie clamped down on her rage. Ken, Caro and Gray were procurers for these sick bastards? After they'd had their 'fun' with Alice – what were they going to do with her?

They couldn't let her live.

Of course they couldn't.

And this wasn't the first time. What Tess had heard... That must have been other girls, other poor souls they'd lured to Scallan Lodge for these perverts, other young girls for them to abuse and discard. Edward Norcott and Tim Gilbey were friends of Gray's, presumably, other sick psychos he'd met online, maybe.

That must be why Ken and Caro had kept Alice's location from Gray – he couldn't be trusted not to avail himself of what was on offer before the 'clients', rendering Alice 'damaged' goods they might no longer be interested in. And so Ken had given Melanie to Gray as a fop.

Edward suddenly shoved Ken back against the door. 'She'd better be everything we're hoping for *and more*. Get your vehicle and let's go.'

44

ALICE - 13 AUGUST

The drawers in the kitchen units contained no knives, for obvious reasons, but they didn't have forks either, only spoons. All of the meals they had supplied, Alice could eat with a spoon: macaroni cheese, lentils, tuna pasta, ready meals...

But there were the nail file and tweezers from the grooming set.

She selected the nail file, digging it into the grout around the tiles in the end wall of the en suite. The tiles were rectangular and small, the size of bricks, which meant there was a lot of mortar to get through. But on the plus side, the tiles would be relatively easy to prise off. She hoped.

If there was an outside, stone wall underneath, of course, she was out of luck. In that case, she'd try one of the others. If she was in Scallan Lodge, once she'd found an interior wall, she could knock through the plasterboard, or more likely an old-fashioned plaster and wood wall, and get through into the next room. And just hope she could get out from there.

Ken never came into the en suite, so he wasn't going to discover what she was doing.

The mortar was quite crumbly, and she soon realised that she didn't need something as pointy as the tweezers – a bigger, blunter implement would be just as good and quicker. She got a spoon from the other room and used it to scrape and scoop the mortar around the tile she'd selected, at chest height. Sooner than she had dared hope, she had gone all the way around the tile.

Now to remove it.

She dug the end of the spoon into the grout between the side of the tile and the wall underneath and wiggled. Soon, she had the spoon's handle halfway under the tile.

She got another spoon and did the same thing from the top of the tile. Wiggling and levering the two spoons at once, she tried to pop the tile off the wall, but only succeeded in snapping off the corner.

Progress, at least.

She'd get another spoon to make a sort of three-way lever and try to get the whole tile off at once. At this rate, she could have enough tiles off to tackle the wall today!

45

MELANIE - 14 AUGUST

The line of rhododendrons extended right around the side of the house, so Melanie was able to crawl and push her way through them until she was out of sight of the men at the front door and well away from the illumination cast by the headlights.

Then she left their cover to run across the back lawn to the parking area.

Adrenaline was coursing through her body, heightening her senses, sending one thought after another chasing through her brain. Alice was alive, and they were going to her. To do unspeakable things. But she was *alive*, and Melanie could save her.

Ken's Range Rover was positioned between Caro's car and Gray's. Melanie crouched behind Gray's car and waited.

Soon, she heard the back door open and Caro snap, 'I know that! But if you keep rolling over for them, they'll come to expect it. They need to start having a bit more respect. They're not the only fish in the sea. When demand exceeds supply, it's the suppliers who should be calling the shots, but you've allowed the opposite to happen.'

'It'll be fine. After tonight –'

'It's not *fine*!' Caro hissed. 'The kids were really fond of that girl!'

'I can hardly help it if Gray –'

'Oh yes, Gray's always a convenient scapegoat, isn't he? But if you had any backbone, you'd have told them no, sorry, there's been a mix-up and she's not available. *Our own fucking au pair!* How much closer to home can you get? There was *no need for it*, Ken! It's not as if the streets of Glasgow and Dundee aren't overflowing with silly little drunken randoms ripe for the picking –'

'They're waiting,' said Ken hollowly. 'Can we play the blame game later?'

The door slammed.

Melanie ducked down, trying to compose herself as terrible images leapt into her mind's eye. It was almost too horrible to believe, what Caro and Ken were doing.

The Range Rover bleeped and the lights flashed on as Ken used his key fob to unlock it. Melanie crawled around the back of Gray's car into the space between it and the Range Rover. When Ken opened the driver's door, she opened the offside rear door at exactly the same time and slipped inside the vehicle. As Ken closed his door, she closed the rear door too, trying to synchronise it exactly.

She crouched behind the driver's seat and held her breath.

Ken's big sausage fingers reached behind his seat, but only for the seat belt. He clicked it into place, and then the vehicle was moving smoothly off.

Would he sense her here?

She had the Taser, but she needed him to take her to Alice.

Fortunately, there was nothing on the back seat, no coat or hat or anything else he might decide he needed. But she was sure he would hear her breathing. The only sounds were the wheels on the gravel and Ken huffing and puffing to himself.

He had *sold* Alice to those psychos, but it was all about poor me, poor Ken and his bad day at the office.

Monster.

Melanie tensed as light washed the backs of the front seats. Headlights, from behind. Edward Norcott and Tim Gilbey were following them.

Three men to overcome. But Melanie's whole body was zinging with adrenaline.

No way were they getting to Alice.

Ken made a wordless sound, and the Range Rover leapt forward. They must be on the track now – Melanie had to brace herself against the seats as they weaved from side to side and bounced around on the potholes and ruts at a crazy speed. The light from behind soon fell away.

Ken seemed determined to get ahead of them.

Which would play right into Melanie's hands.

She felt the Range Rover make a sharp left turn, and then they were on an even worse surface, the vehicle tipping and jolting, but Ken didn't slow down. At one point they went into a skid, and the top of Melanie's head banged against the side of the vehicle, but Ken, grunting, brought the wheels back under control.

She rehearsed what she'd do once they'd stopped. She would Taser Ken. Free Alice. Run with her in the dark –

If Alice could run.

She'd just have to play it by ear.

The Taser, of course, was no longer armed with a cartridge and barbs. She'd have to use it in drive-stun mode, which would mean, ideally, pressing it against bare skin. And drive-stun mode did not incapacitate – it only delivered pain for 'compliance' purposes. Nic had delivered a whole lecture on Tasers, a lifetime ago, as she and Melanie had sat on a roof watching, far below in the street, a running battle between the police and a gang of yobs.

'Ah, unlucky!' Nic had commiserated, like an impartial commentator on a sports fixture, as a hapless policeman had deployed his Taser in drive-stun mode but failed to follow through quickly enough with the cuffs, and the miscreant had scrambled up from the pavement and made off after his pals.

Melanie wished Nic could be here now.

Or Grant.

But *she* was here, and that had to be enough.

The light that had washed the interior of the vehicle from behind had gone. Ken must be well ahead – the other two men didn't know these tracks and where the ruts and potholes were. In the dark, they'd have to take it slowly.

She seemed to have been squashed in the cramped space behind the driver's seat forever when the Range Rover finally stopped. Ken sighed and opened his door. The interior light came on, and when he left the vehicle, Melanie risked peeping up between the front seats.

The first thing she saw was that he had left the key in the ignition. And then the interior light went off, and she was able to see beyond the windscreen.

Ken was trudging across through the headlights' beams

to a door set in a granite façade. The door was painted red but peeling badly to reveal layers of other colours underneath. On either side were large windows and above three more, all boarded up. Rising into darkness, the wall met a roof that sagged in the middle, a gutter dangling free.

What was this place?

Now, Ken was shining a torch on the door as he brought something from his pocket. Keys, presumably.

Melanie eased the door catch towards her.

Fortunately, Ken seemed too intent on fumbling with the keys to hear the click. Melanie slipped out of the vehicle. The night air was still. An owl called, faintly, somewhere over the boggy fields that surrounded them. She could smell the bog, stagnant and pungent. Beyond the house, a few pine trees loomed against the slightly lighter sky.

She was aware of all this, of being on such high alert that her senses were gathering information from her surroundings at lightning speed, but, like a cat stalking her prey, she tuned it out almost immediately, all her focus on the man standing at the door of the derelict building.

He was tall, bulky, in dark trousers and a waxed jacket, a couple of inches of skin visible at his neck between the corduroy collar of the jacket and his hair.

The soles of her feet almost caressed the ground as she crept up behind him, as if she weren't wearing shoes at all, as if she were feeling every little lump and bump under them on her bare feet. *Closer, closer –*

He began to turn –

She exploded into a sprint, sprang on him before he could complete the movement, shoved the Taser into his neck and fired.

His body jerked and he cried out.

Quick, quick, quick!

She snatched up a piece of the heavy iron guttering lying by the door, raised it above his head and brought it down as hard as she could.

He slumped forward onto his knees, his face thunking against the door.

'*You bastard!*' she yelled, whacking him again.

And again.

And again.

As he slumped lower and lower with each blow, she was able to get a better and better swing at him, more force behind each whack.

Blood spurted. He made a strangled, wordless sound and was quiet.

Melanie grabbed the keys he'd dropped and, after two attempts, found the one that opened the door. She could hear an engine, somewhere off across the moor. The other men would be here in, what, five minutes? Less?

She snatched up Ken's torch and pushed the door open.

The high-ceilinged hall reminded her of Scallan Lodge, although it was on a smaller scale, and the floor and the staircase stretching up into darkness were splattered with birds' droppings. It smelt of damp old dust and wood, and there was a low humming noise, like there was a wasp's nest in the wall.

'Alice!' she shouted.

She ran from room to room, the torchlight bouncing around crazily, illuminating fireplaces with cascades of twigs and debris spilling from them, peeling wallpaper, curtains hanging off their rails, broken tables and chairs and even a grand piano, covered in dust.

As she ran back into the hall, she glimpsed, through the open door, moving light.

Headlights, slowly approaching down the track.

'Alice!' she screamed. '*Where are you?*'

She stood in the middle of the hall, quite still, straining her ears.

And was rewarded by a very faint sound.

Someone calling back!

It was coming from under the floor!

She dropped to her knees. '*Alice!*' she screamed again, and stamped with her feet.

'I'm here,' came a stronger call.

Oh thank God, thank God!

'Okay, I'm coming! It's okay!'

There must be a cellar here too. Scallan Lodge, the stables, this place... They must all have been built at the same time. Scallan Lodge was too vast to need a cellar, perhaps, but they'd added one to the stables and must have done so here too. So she was looking for a similar means of access, perhaps. A hatch in the floor.

The kitchen. Or the utility area. That was where it would be.

She hadn't seen a kitchen. It must be through the door in front of her. She threw it open.

Beyond was a corridor, which, unlike the rest of the house, seemed to have been swept clean. At the end of it was a kitchen, 1970s units and ancient orange and brown linoleum on the floor, but again free of dust. There was a table and chairs, a kettle on the worktop and a Tupperware box. A tea towel over the rail of the Aga. The humming noise was louder – not insects. Machinery of some kind?

Two more doors.

'Alice!' she screamed over the humming.

'I'm down here!' came an answering cry, closer now, under her feet somewhere...

The linoleum was stuck to the floor – there couldn't be a hatch in here.

The first door she tried led to a utility room. The humming was much louder now, and she realised there must be a generator somewhere, maybe in an outbuilding on the other side of the wall. There was a heavy door to the outside with small glass panels above it. Again, the floor was covered in linoleum.

She ran back to the kitchen. How long now before the men arrived? Finding Ken slumped unconscious – or dead? – at the door would, she hoped, give them pause. Who would want to venture into a dark, abandoned house with some maniac on the loose who'd just staved in a man's skull?

She pulled open the other door and found herself in a small room with no windows.

And there it was: a hatch in the floor, with a metal flange across it just like the one in the stables, secured with a padlock hooked around a loop set into the floorboards.

She dropped to her knees.

The keys!

What had she done with them?

Had she dropped them?

No – her fingers touched cold metal in her jeans pocket. She must have thrust the keys in there unthinkingly. There were four keys on the ring, three for mortice locks and one tiny one. This she shoved into the padlock, making a wordless sound of relief when it sprang free.

She heaved the hatch open and shone the torch into the void.

Like in the cellar under the stables, there were steps leading down. But this staircase was enclosed by walls, giving the space a claustrophobic feel. She ran down the steps and found herself facing a metal door.

46

ALICE - 14 AUGUST

As the door opened, Alice stood back, the jagged piece of tile she had snatched up held out in front of her. The sharp point of it danced in the air with the shaking of her hand.

A woman.

About Alice's own height, quite young, with lovely eyes.

The woman said, 'I'm not going to hurt you! My – my name's Donna. They had me locked up too. I managed to get out and...' She lifted her left hand, in which she held the yellow Taser gun. In her right was a torch. But she set both down on the floor and came forward and gently, gently took the tile from Alice.

'We have to go. We have to run.'

Numbly, Alice nodded.

The woman – Donna – made a little noise, like a sob was trying to get out, and pulled Alice into a hug. 'Did they hurt you? Are you all right?'

Donna was shaking too.

And that was what gave Alice strength. She hugged her

back and said, 'I'm fine,' and then she managed to say, 'Are *you* okay?'

Another little noise, this one almost a laugh. 'I am now.'

For a moment Donna held her, and then she let her go and grabbed up the Taser and handed it to Alice. Donna herself snatched up the torch. 'We have to go.'

She started up the stairs and Alice followed, finding herself grabbing onto the material of Donna's fleece, and at the top of the stairs Donna took her hand, and they ran like that along a dark corridor, as if this human contact were vital for both their survivals.

There wasn't time to think, to examine what was happening. It didn't seem real. One second Alice had been locked in that room, and now she was out, rescued out of nowhere by this woman. Donna.

There was something familiar about her.

Who was she?

But all that mattered was that they were both free.

Now they were in a hall, and in the open doorway in front of them she could see a man slumped.

Alice gasped. 'Is that Ken?'

Donna snapped off the torch, and now Alice could see light washing the trees outside, and then the weedy gravel in front of the open doorway. Headlights.

'We have to hide!' Donna hissed, and pulled her towards the stairs that led up from the hall.

A car door opened, and someone cursed.

Was that Edward Norcott?

Alice stumbled on the first couple of steps, but Donna hauled her upright and the two of them clambered up the stairs in the light from the headlights and lay flat on the landing just as Tim Gilbey's voice said, 'Is he dead? What the hell's happened?'

'How the fuck should I know? Is he breathing?'

A pause. 'Don't think so.'

'Must have been Gray,' said Edward. 'He must have come with Ken – there's no other vehicle. Get a torch! And keep your eyes open! He could still be here, although chances are he's gone off with her.'

'That *fucking* maniac!' Tim was almost sobbing. There was a pause, a car door opened and closed, and then he said, 'You're not calling an *ambulance*?' His voice quivered, rising in alarm.

'Hardly!' Silence, and then, in a different voice, 'We've got a problem. That lunatic Gray's done for Ken... No...' He must be talking on a phone. 'We've only just arrived. Give us a fucking chance!' A long pause. Then, 'I've no idea. But I expect he's taken her.'

Her. Did they mean Alice? Or Donna?

'If he has,' Edward went on, 'they can't be far. We were just behind Ken. Can only have happened five, ten minutes ago. Get over here *now*.'

'She could still be in the house. He might have seen us coming and taken off before he had a chance to get to her.' Tim's voice was louder. He must be in the hall. And now torchlight was moving about down there.

Alice felt Donna, lying next to her, move.

Alice grabbed her.

If Edward and Tim found them, what would happen? They had a Taser, but maybe the men did too. And they were big. Alice and Donna were both slight.

Could they make a run for it? But out there in the bog...

What if they got sucked down into it, as Alice almost had before?

The torchlight was moving away into the house, but in the background light from the headlights, she could still see the outline of Donna, her hair tied back in a ponytail. She was peeping through the banisters.

And now she turned to Alice and brought her lips right up to Alice's ear.

'We're going to go down into the hall and hide behind the door. Then when the other one comes inside, we're going to run out and get into Ken's car. The key's in the ignition.'

No.

No.

Alice couldn't move from this dark, safe place.

But it wasn't safe, was it? Sooner or later those men would come up the stairs and find them. Maybe they could hide somewhere, though, in some dark corner of a wardrobe or –

'We have to do this,' Donna breathed. 'Okay? Give me the Taser. Let's go.'

47

MELANIE - 14 AUGUST

They were halfway down the stairs when a voice just below them boomed, 'Where the hell are you? Come back here with that torch!'

Melanie grabbed Alice, hugged her close, pressed the girl's face into her fleece to muffle the tiny little whimpering sounds she was making. Edward Norcott was striding across the hall, the beams of the headlights behind him casting his shadow, hugely elongated, over the floor and up the wall in front of him, like some enormous sinister puppet with its own enormous Taser gun. As his feet moved, the massive shadow legs went up and down.

'There's a hatch and a cellar or something!' came a call from through the house.

Edward Norcott went through the door into the corridor.

Melanie shoved the Taser into the pocket of her fleece and let Alice go.

'Now!' she breathed, but Alice immediately grabbed her hand.

Ruthlessly, Melanie yanked her down those steps,

making the girl half-stumble as they hit the floor of the hall. And then they were running, through the door and –

She had the keys in her pocket.

'Wait,' she said, pulling Alice to a halt. Then she let go her hand and heaved at Ken's shoulders, dragging his upper body free of the doorway.

The front door key was the largest one. She remembered that. She thrust it into the lock and pulled the door to, turning the key in almost the same movement.

The windows were all boarded up. Both the front and back doors were sturdy Victorian ones. Those bastards weren't going anywhere.

'Donna?' said a man's voice behind her.

48

ALICE - 14 AUGUST

Alice grabbed Donna's hand and tried to pull her away from the man, but he had Donna's shoulders grasped tightly, and Donna was staring at him, not even trying to get away.

'*Donna!*' Alice yelled.

'It's okay,' said Donna, and at the same moment the man let her go. 'He's a policeman. DI Macneil. He – how did you know? Did Caro call you? Or was it Tess? How did you know where we were?'

The man was tall, lean, the planes of his face angular in the eerie light from the car headlights. He shook his head as he took something from his pocket and held it out to Alice. It was some sort of ID, with his photo on it. 'My warrant card,' he said. 'We've been carrying out surveillance on Scallan Lodge for some time. I followed the vehicles out here.'

'Oh. Thank goodness!' Alice's legs were shaking so much she had to sit down, suddenly, on the hard ground. 'They're in there. The men who – are there other policemen? There are two of them! And Gray! He's somewhere...'

'This is Alice,' said Donna, squatting next to her and putting an arm around her. 'It's okay. It's all okay now, darling.'

The policeman stooped over them. 'Shock,' he said briefly. 'Thank God you're all right, Alice. To be honest, I never expected to... Well, all's well that ends well, eh? Let's get you two out of here. My colleagues will be here in five or ten minutes – they've been stationed up on the road, so they've got a bit further to come. They'll deal with this.' With a wave of his hand he indicated Ken's body and the house behind him. 'What happened here?'

'The Davidsons,' said Donna. 'They've been keeping Alice in a cellar under this house. The men they *sold* her to are in there. The men who were going to – to abuse her and –'

Alice hugged Donna close. 'But they didn't,' she choked out. 'Thanks to you.'

'The priority now is to get the two of you to a hospital. I'm afraid it will be quite a drive. I'll just let my colleagues know what's happening.'

'I suppose you'll be getting an ambulance for Ken?' said Donna, her voice suddenly harsh.

'Well, yes. But he's dead,' said the policeman briskly. 'I'll make the call. Get into my vehicle – it's the Alfa Romeo over there, under the tree – and we'll soon have you in a nice warm hospital eating terrible food.' He smiled.

Donna got shakily to her feet and the two of them, still with their arms around each other, started walking towards the vehicle he had indicated, the one without its headlights on. But as the policeman turned away, Donna whispered, 'Get in the Range Rover. *Now!* We can't trust him!'

'But –'

'There's no time to explain, Alice. Just do it!'

Alice looked from Donna to the tall figure of the policeman strolling away from them as he talked on his phone.

What in heaven's name should she do?

That was a *policeman* – he had ID and everything, and Donna herself had confirmed his identity. Whereas Donna...

She could be anyone. Any random person.

She could even be in league with the Davidsons. How did Alice know that *anything* Donna had told her was true? Where had the Davidsons been keeping her? How had she so conveniently escaped? How had she known where Alice was?

Did she kill Ken?

49

MELANIE - 14 AUGUST

As Alice hauled open the passenger door of Ken's vehicle and jumped in, Melanie ran around the bonnet and got in at the driver's side, just as DI Macneil turned to stare at them.

She revved the engine and slammed the Range Rover into reverse, hauling at the wheel. The big vehicle slewed, spitting gravel under its tires, and then she was flooring the accelerator and bumping onto that potholed track.

In the rear-view mirror, she could see DI Macneil heading for his Alfa Romeo.

It looked like it was an SUV model, but Ken's vehicle was bigger and presumably more powerful.

Headlights blinded her for a second – he had them undipped, probably hoping to dazzle her. She batted the rear-view mirror so the lights from behind wouldn't hit it.

'He's a policeman!' Alice's voice shook. 'Why can't we trust him?'

Melanie slalomed between two pairs of huge potholes and then pressed her foot to the pedal as the surface improved for a bit. 'A few things. First of all, he didn't seem at all surprised to see you. And why was he on his own? The police always do surveillance in pairs, don't they?'

'They do on TV.' Alice breathed out on a little laugh that sounded close to hysteria.

'But I think they really do. And why would the police be watching Scallan Lodge anyway? The family haven't ever really been under suspicion. That was the whole problem. Gray had an alibi for the time you went missing –'

'But Gray was there!' Alice exclaimed.

'He must have set it up somehow, probably with the help of DI Macneil. He's in cahoots with the Davidsons. He's part of it. Maybe they give him a cut of the profits, or maybe he's one of the abusers.'

Melanie wasn't about to tell Alice, but she'd been hit by another suspicion – that it was probably DI Macneil who had arranged for a DNA test on her toothbrush and hair. Then he would have told the family who she was, and left it to them to get rid of her.

The front passenger wheel suddenly bounced into a pothole, and Alice was flung against the window.

'Put your seat belt on!'

Melanie negotiated the next bit of bad road and then reached for her own, but the catch was taken out of her hand as Alice pulled the belt across Melanie and clicked it home. She felt tears threaten at the small act of thoughtfulness in the midst of this awful situation that would have most teenagers thinking only about their own safety.

But then, she should have expected no less of Alice.

She blinked away the tears. 'DI Macneil's involvement explains how the Davidsons have miraculously managed to sail through the investigation into your disappearance completely unsuspected. I bet he was leading the search for you. I bet he personally covered this area and managed to deploy the other searchers elsewhere while he supposedly examined that house himself.'

'But – a *policeman*...' Alice's voice was small.

'You're safe,' Melanie said almost harshly, risking a look behind. She couldn't even see following headlights. 'Unless he's driving without lights, which would be really stupid, he must have either come a cropper in the potholes or he's fallen well back. He's not going to catch us.'

'But we can't go to a police station.'

'No,' agreed Melanie. 'I'm taking you to your parents, and then we're all going with you to the nearest hospital, wherever that is.'

'My parents?' Alice choked. 'They're *here*?'

'Well, of course they are. And you're going to see them very soon.'

50

ALICE - 14 AUGUST

Mom and Daddy!

Donna was taking her to *Mom and Daddy*!

Alice could feel it bubbling up inside her, all the emotion that had been threatening to overwhelm her while she'd been locked in that room, and took a lungful of air to push it back down. She had to keep strong just a little bit longer.

Strong like Donna.

There was something about this woman that had made Alice trust her and not the policeman. Was it just that she *was* a woman? No. Something deep in her gut told Alice that Donna was on her side. And when she had first appeared at the door of that terrible room, when they'd fallen into a hug, Alice had felt her shaking. You couldn't fake that.

Donna was fighting to hold it together just like Alice was.

They seemed to have got away. Alice kept turning in her seat to look behind for the policeman's car, but there was just darkness.

'You can slow down a little, can't you?' she said as they bounced through another set of potholes. The track was now raised up a metre or more above the level of the surrounding moorland, and Alice was worried they could bounce right off it and into that bog.

'Not until we're out of here.'

In the beams of the headlights, Alice could see rain falling, lines of silver slanting into the light from the darkness above.

'Be careful,' she urged. 'It's getting wet out there, and we don't –'

'*What's that?*' Donna suddenly shouted, her head jerking to the right. 'Oh *fuck!*'

Alice looked past her.

Headlights! In the bog!

But how was that possible?

'How can he be driving *through the bog?*' Alice gasped.

'There must be another track parallel to this one.' Donna's voice was grim.

The Range Rover leapt forward. Donna was glaring out of the windscreen at the rough surface in front of them, and Alice didn't want to say or do anything to distract her, so she sat perfectly still, hands clasped together, gazing in horror at the headlights that were, what – a hundred yards away across the bog?

Drawing level with them...

Drawing ahead...

'Does that track join up with this one?' Alice whispered at last.

'I don't know.' Donna's hands were gripping the wheel so tightly they looked like claws. 'Let's hope not. I think this track we're on comes off the main one, the one that goes to Scallan Lodge. If the other track also meets it, he'll have to come some distance along the Scallan Lodge one to cut us off. If we can get to that main track first...'

'If we don't, we'll be trapped.'

But it was worse than that. The taillights of the other vehicle, now ahead of them, were veering across the bog, converging on the track ahead.

'So his track joins ours before the main track,' said Donna briskly. 'Okay. Hold on, Alice!'

She floored the gas, and Alice cried out as she was flung back against her seat. The Range Rover bucked and then seemed airborne for a second before it slammed back onto the hard, rutted surface, rocking crazily and then surging forward again.

Oh please God, please God.

But the policeman's car was turning, turning... And now its headlights were bearing down on them.

Alice jerked forward as Donna slammed on the brakes.

'Get out,' she said.

'What?'

'We need to get out. We can't get past him, there's no room, not on this raised track. We need to get out, slip along the edge of the track on foot and get past him, get to the main track, the public road... *Go*, Alice! Keep low!'

Donna undid Alice's seat belt and then leant across her to open her door. She shoved at Alice's shoulder. '*Go!*'

Alice slid out of her seat, stumbling as her sneakers slipped on the wet surface. She slammed the door shut and slithered to the weedy margins of the track, crouching low as Donna had instructed. She lifted her head, expecting to see Donna.

But the vehicle was moving.

Fast.

Donna was driving straight at the headlights accelerating towards her.

51

MELANIE - 14 AUGUST

She had finished running.
She had finished hiding.
She had finished with all that.
Because Alice was safe.

She jammed her foot on the accelerator and let out a yell.

On either side of the track was a steep bank down into the bog. The bastard had two choices – either veer off the track down one of those banks, or keep going and crash head-on into the Range Rover.

The headlights hurtling towards her on full beam flooded the windscreen with light. Half-blinded, she screwed up her eyes and kept the steering wheel steady, aiming straight for the light.

At the last second, the light slewed off to one side, and there was nothing in front of her, just the track stretching away.

She slammed on the brakes and jumped out.

The Alfa Romeo was on its roof, wheels spinning. The headlights were still casting white light across the reedy bog, the engine still turning over. Faintly, she could hear groaning from inside the car.

'Alice!' she called, running back down the track. '*Alice!*'

'THIS IS IT,' said Melanie, pulling up outside Chalet 6, but Alice was already out of the Range Rover and running for the door, calling out for her parents.

Melanie got out slowly and just stood for a moment watching as the door came open, and Warren Snyder, in striped pyjamas with his hair standing on end, bellowed a wordless sound and caught Alice up in his arms. And then Tonya was there, and Skip, and they were all crying and laughing and talking over each other, but Alice broke away and came running back to Melanie.

Her face was wet with tears, her eyes alight with happiness. She took Melanie's hand and said simply, 'Come.'

Inside the chalet, Alice tried to explain, tried to tell them what had happened, that 'Donna' had saved her, but it was too much for them to assimilate. All they seemed to want to do was look at Alice, touch her, drink her in.

'Do they know where you are?' Alice said at one point, turning in her mother's embrace. 'The Davidsons? What if Gray or Caro comes here?'

'You know, honey?' said Warren, his face suddenly grim. 'I hope they do.' And something wordless passed between him and Skip.

'You have to get Alice to the hospital, though,' said Melanie, taking advantage of this hiatus in the emotional reunion. 'Get her checked over. Then we have to make statements, but not to anyone who worked closely with DI Macneil.'

'That cop was in on it,' Alice explained.

'A *cop?*' Skip shook his head.

'Donna – Donna was so brave.' Alice was choking up again. She grabbed Melanie and pulled her into a hug. 'Thank you. Thank you for saving me.'

Over Alice's shoulder, Melanie met Tonya's gaze. There was a question in it.

Very slowly, Melanie shook her head.

She wasn't going to use this moment of vulnerability, when the Snyders would do anything for the woman who had saved their daughter. There was enough emotion flying around without adding the revelation of Donna's true identity to the mix.

Alice had enough to deal with.

If she eventually decided she wanted to find her birth mother, everything would come out, but until then, it was best to leave things be. It should be Alice's decision to go looking, rather than Melanie's to spring the truth on her at the most traumatic moment possible.

In the cold light of day, the Snyders would no doubt revert to their default position of not wanting Alice anywhere near her dodgy birth mother, especially when they found out that 'Donna MacKenzie' had killed Ken and possibly also Gray. She'd proved herself to be exactly the violent, dangerous person Gillian and the other social workers had no doubt described to the Snyders when they'd adopted Alice. And so the Snyders and Skip weren't likely to reveal Donna's identity to anyone – not the police, not their lawyers, not the press – because if they did so, Alice would find out about it.

Donna MacKenzie could just disappear.

'I have to go,' said Melanie.

But Alice clung tighter.

Despite her days locked in a stuffy room with, presumably, rudimentary facilities, she still smelt of *Alice*, that cottony, sweet smell she'd always had.

But the experience was bound to have changed her.

Alice had no doubt had enough adventures to last a lifetime. There was no guarantee that she'd want to go searching for her birth mother – especially here in Scotland. Her family, Skip, his family, their friends, the whole community of Branchfield, Indiana, were going to wrap themselves around her and never let her go, and who could blame Alice for wanting just that?

Melanie was never going to see her again.

And she didn't want Alice's only encounter with her, albeit unknowingly, to have been full of nothing but fear and tension and raw emotion.

It was the hardest thing – no, the second-hardest thing she had ever done, to gently ease the girl away from her, to find a smile, to say, 'Next time you run away from home, try to keep out of trouble. Join the circus or the Foreign Legion or something.'

And to be rewarded with a little smile in return.

52

ALICE - ONE YEAR LATER, 18 SEPTEMBER

Alice sat on her bed, watching the light at the window and the leaf shadows from the little maple tree shaking around in the breeze out there. She would have liked to have gone for a walk, but Skip had more photographs to show her. He was sitting next to her, scrolling through them on his phone.

'The surveyor thinks there may have been a little termite action,' he said. 'We'll have to get a specialist to go take a look. But it's probably nothing serious.'

'Uh-huh,' said Alice.

He'd stopped on a photo of the porch, taken from one end and showing the long expanse of wooden floor and rail, the grey-painted clapboard and cute white windows, the porch swing at the end, a glimpse of the pretty front yard with its flowering shrubs. It was just a little place, but perfect for a young couple starting out together in married life. And just two blocks away from Alice's parents and three from Skip's and church.

Number 149 South Polston Drive.

The two sets of parents were clubbing together to buy it, and it would be rented out until Skip and Alice had finished college. The question of the timing of the marriage was all that remained to be decided. Skip didn't want to wait, but Alice felt they should get college done first. She was about to start the second year of her history degree and Skip ditto in theology.

Skip wanted to have sex.

He hadn't exactly said so, but he kept on about how, even though they were engaged now, they couldn't *do it* outside of marriage or his parents would have a conniption. What if their birth control went wrong and Alice got pregnant? If they were *married*, though, that would be a whole different ball game. They wouldn't have to worry about birth control at all!

'But I don't want to be a mother at nineteen!' Alice had protested.

'My mom was nineteen when she had me,' Skip had countered – and what could Alice say to that?

He was still talking about the house. 'I thought maybe... the basement's not been used for decades, looks like, but I thought I could fit it out as a den once the tenants have left and we're doing it up for ourselves.' Skip kept scrolling. 'If those windows were cleaned and proper lighting installed, a few rugs, a couch, a TV, maybe even a pool table... Then the guys and I could watch sports and make a hullabaloo without disturbing you.' He gave her a little smile. This was obviously something he'd been working up to broaching with her. 'But if you have plans for it yourself...'

Alice grimaced. 'I think I've had enough of basements to last me a lifetime.'

'Oh, good grief, I'm *sorry*, Alice!'

'It's fine,' she almost snapped.

She still couldn't go down to the basement even in her own home.

It seemed the Davidsons had decided to keep Alice in the cellar of the abandoned house, rather than in the one under the stable block where they'd kept most of those other poor girls, to stop Gray 'getting' to her, as he'd gotten to some of the others, and 'spoiling' her for the clients. Gray didn't know that the cellar under the abandoned house existed. Ken and Caro had told him that they'd decided not to keep Alice under the stables because it was damp down there, and that they'd found a better location, but didn't tell him where the new place was.

So Gray had gone looking, eliminating the possibilities one by one. Ken, though, had realised what his brother was doing and put him off the scent by telling him he had decided to use the abandoned house in their glamping business. He'd even taken Gray there to discuss the renovations, and shown him the new generator and the newly functional, although still basic, kitchen, claiming it was for the tradesmen's use while they carried out the work. Faced with this evidence that tradesmen were in and out of there all the time, Gray had evidently crossed the house off his list. Presumably Ken had covered up the hatch with something when he'd shown Gray around.

He'd have had to, because it was just like the hatch in the stables.

She kept thinking about that cellar under the stables, the cellar she and Isabel had innocently explored, little thinking that terrible, terrible things had happened there to those other girls. They'd all been kept there – all except Alice, the last girl, and Jenna, the first.

It was bad enough thinking about the girls in the cellar under the stables. But when the Davidsons had first started up their new 'business', the initial idea had been to keep their captives in the Princess Room. They'd changed the windows for lockable ones with toughened glass, although Alice supposed that even if a girl had managed to break one, as she had, there was no way out from there. It was too high up to try any tricks with bed sheets.

The first girl who'd been their victim, Jenna Bain, had been shut up in the Princess Room, but the Davidsons had soon come across a problem. The tower was remote from the other bedrooms but not, it turned out, remote enough. Tess had heard Jenna banging on the door and shouting.

How could Alice not have sensed that something terrible had happened in that room? The day she'd arrived at Scallan Lodge, she'd run around the Princess Room in glee, little thinking –

'Come here,' said Skip, and pulled her against his sweater. 'You need to try to put it out of your mind. You're safe now.'

'*I'm* safe!' She really did snap this time, pulling away from him and standing up. 'But Jenna Bain isn't. Or Morven McBride. Or Heather-Louise Evans. Or the girl they're still trying to identify, and goodness knows how many others they couldn't find a trace of.'

The forensics team had gone all over Scallan Lodge and the two cellars. Jenna Bain's DNA had been picked up in the Princess Room, and DNA from the other two missing girls in the cellar under the stables, despite the fact that the Davidsons had slopped bleach everywhere down there. The team had managed to find a hair belonging to Morven, and Heather-Louise's skin cells on a nail, which it looked like she'd used to gouge around the edges of the trapdoor.

Their bodies had been found in the bog near the stables, together with the remains of another girl who was yet to be identified. All three of the identified girls had gone missing on nights out – Jenna in Dundee just two months after the Davidsons had been declared bankrupt, Morven in Glasgow six months later, and Heather-Louise, again in Glasgow, about four months after that.

It was almost unimaginable, what the Davidsons had done. The thinking was that Gray had always been a predator, perhaps even as a teenager. When he, Ken and Caro had lived in London, it seemed he'd been involved in a network of wealthy men preying on vulnerable girls. His DNA had now been matched to rapes and murders carried out in the city over the course of the seven years he'd lived there, and to another murder of a girl in Glasgow after the family had moved north.

Ken and Caro knew about it and did nothing. Worse – when their business had gone belly up, they'd tapped into Gray's network and started procuring for the men involved, snatching and selling young girls to them for abuse and murder.

Caro had made a supposedly complete confession in which she'd described their 'business model' – and yes, Caro had actually called it that! She'd described how Gray would prowl around Glasgow or Dundee or Inverness city centre on a Friday or Saturday night, looking for a likely victim, a drunk young girl who'd become separated from her friends. He'd charm her into his car and drive her to Scallan Lodge, where she'd be locked up ready for the 'clients'.

The 'event' would involve one or more clients being

given *carte blanche*, as Caro had put it, to do as they wished to the girl and then murder her. The fact that they got to kill her at the end had been a huge part of the attraction for those monsters and had had the side benefit that there was no risk of their victim subsequently identifying them to other clients or, if she were somehow to escape, to the police.

It was never intended that either Alice or Donna would be involved – the whole idea was that there should be nothing to connect the Davidsons with the missing girls. But Gray forced their hand by sending photographs of Alice to Edward Norcott and Tim Gilbey – apparently, as an innocent, untouched virgin, she had been regarded as a 'premium' product, and Gray had priced her accordingly. Tim and Edward had come to the house to inspect the goods and had not only offered Ken a million pounds each to 'buy' Alice, but issued an ultimatum – either Ken let them have her, or they would take their custom elsewhere in future.

'They should never have made you testify,' Skip said. 'It's brought it all back.'

She'd had to return to Scotland last month to testify at the trial. Caro had pled guilty and given evidence against the others, but Gray, DI Macneil, Tim Gilbey and Edward Norcott had entered 'not guilty' pleas and had all been in the dock. The court had given Alice the option of a video link, but she had decided to face them.

It hadn't been easy, but she was glad she'd been able to look them all in the eye as she condemned them. *Eye*, literally, in Gray's case.

He only had one now.

She'd half expected him to be wearing a pirate's eye patch, but he had a glass eye that gave him a weird, deadpan look. Every time she looked at him, she thought of Donna jabbing a sharp piece of plastic into that eye – and it was terrible, but it made her feel a whole lot better. She hoped he remembered it, too, every time he put in and took out that false eye.

All his easy charm, all his confidence, all his attractiveness had gone. He'd stood there in a white shirt with his greying hair pulled back from a pasty face and stared at Alice like he'd never seen her before, like he couldn't understand what was happening.

But that was likely all an act too. He was trying to look as pathetic as possible, trying to make out that it had all been Ken. Even in London, Gray had claimed, long before they'd started their sex trafficking business, depraved Ken had blackmailed Gray into picking girls up off the street and having sex with them while Ken watched. Sometimes Ken would then murder them. The jury, though, had seen straight through this flimsy explanation for Gray's semen being present on the clothes and bodies of those raped and murdered girls in London.

Gray, and each one of the other defendants, had been found guilty on all charges.

The lawyers had been pleased with Alice. They said the jury had warmed to her at once, and she'd stood up to cross-examination 'magnificently'.

'Of course she did,' Mom had said, an arm around Alice. 'She's a very smart girl.'

It all seemed like yesterday, but a whole month had gone by since they'd left Scotland. Alice curled herself up in the big armchair by the window and pulled a cushion onto her lap.

'The trial didn't *bring it all back*, Skip – it's never gone away. I can't just erase it all from my memory. I don't *want* to erase it. It happened, and I have to live with that.'

They'd all had therapy last year, and Mom had suggested Alice should have some more after the trial, and maybe she would. But everyone at church had been so great, and Alice preferred to talk to people there. Surprisingly, it was Mrs Miller who had come up trumps in that regard – she was a good listener and quite insightful, and she didn't let Alice wallow in too much angst and self-pity.

She took a long breath. 'Compared with what *could* have happened if Donna hadn't... Compared with what *did* happen to Jenna and Morven and Heather-Louise...' She hugged the cushion against herself. 'I've been so lucky.'

Skip nodded, tearing up. 'I don't know what I'd have done if...' He gazed down at his phone and said quietly, 'Those bastards.'

Mrs Miller had told Alice that Skip was going to have a hard time accepting that he had been so powerless, that he'd been there, just a few miles from where Alice was being held, for days and days, but he might as well have stayed home for all the good he'd done.

'That's not fair,' Alice had said.

Mrs Miller had grimaced. 'But your knight in shining armour played no part in your rescue. He can't deal with that, so I guess he's taking refuge in anger directed at Those People.'

That was what Mrs Miller called them, *Those People*, and always with a little sneer, like they didn't merit the privilege of their names on a decent woman's lips.

Now, Skip was talking about Caro again, about how she'd been handed a lesser sentence because she'd pled guilty and *supposedly* told the authorities all she knew.

'She's pure evil,' he said, glaring at Alice like he expected her to contradict him.

Caro, like Gray, had put all the blame on Ken and claimed she was a victim herself. The words 'coercive control' had been used a lot. She'd told the police that, after Edward and Tim had put down a 'deposit' on Alice, a date had been set for the 'event' – August 5. They were busy people, and this was the first mutually convenient date they could manage. Ken had intended to snatch Alice on August 4 and take her to the abandoned house, meanwhile preparing a grave in the bog. But Alice had tried to get away on July 22, and Ken had ended up having to keep her in that cellar for a lot longer than planned.

But by August 5, Alice's parents were turning up the heat, and Caro was able to use this fact, or so she claimed, to delay the 'event' – she persuaded Ken that it was too risky to kill and dispose of Alice while the Snyders were sniffing around. Edward and Tim were furious, insisting that Alice was as much a risk to them all alive as dead, but Caro and Ken had prevailed, and the date was put back. Caro had been hoping that it might be possible to save Alice, but in the meantime the replacement au pair, Donna, was ferreting out the truth and, from the Davidsons' point of view, signing her own death warrant. Gray was told to have his fun with her while the clients had theirs with Alice. The plan was then to dispose of both bodies at the same time.

But Donna had jabbed that shard of plastic in Gray's eye and not only got away herself but rescued Alice.

Skip was still frowning at her. 'Caro Davidson might not have physically raped or murdered anyone, but she was no victim! She was in it for the money just as much if not more than Ken was! Surely that makes her just as bad as any of them?'

'It sure does,' Alice agreed quietly.

She got up and joined him on the bed. She took his hand. 'Skip... If you and Mom and Daddy hadn't gone to Scotland and kicked up such a rumpus, hounded the Davidsons and the police... Ken and Caro would have given me to those men just as they'd planned on August 5 and I'd be dead.'

He just shook his head.

No matter how often she said it, in a dozen different ways, he would never accept that he'd come through for her.

'It was your parents who made all the fuss with the Davidsons. I just ran around doing my amateur sleuth act. It was – that woman who saved you.'

Donna. Yes it was.

Alice glanced up at the shelf where Frog sat, and he looked back at her with his little worried face. When they'd all got back to Chalet 6 after Alice had been discharged from hospital, they'd found Frog on the doorstep sitting on an envelope, looking so cute and lonely, and Alice had immediately snatched him up and hugged him, even before she'd read the note he'd been left with.

The note from Donna.

Dear Alice

I'm sorry not to say goodbye, but I have to leave now. This little frog is called Frog! He is something of a lucky mascot. Maybe you would like to keep him.
I feel as if I've got to know you a little from Tess and Isabel, and from being at Scallan Lodge in your place.

Please, please don't let what's happened derail your life. It is, I think, possible to choose to be happy, and you seem to be one of those lucky people who finds that choice easier to make than most. Above all, though, you have the knack of making <u>other people</u> happy. Don't lose the joy in life that makes that possible.

You are braver than you know – I will never forget how much courage you showed on that awful night.

Be happy, Alice.

With best wishes for the future,

Donna

Alice had been looking forward to seeing Donna again at the trial – in fact, it was the only thing that had made the prospect of the trial bearable. But, after giving her statement to the police, Donna seemed to have vanished into the ether. And they hadn't been able to trace her to testify at the trial because, for some reason, she'd been using a false identity. She wasn't called Donna MacKenzie at all.

The police had put out appeals for her to contact them, but she hadn't.

Maybe she was worried about having to reveal why she was using a false identity, and also about having killed Ken, even though no charges had been brought because it had been deemed to be 'reasonable force'.

Donna's absence didn't affect the outcome of the trial – there was more than enough evidence for convictions without her. The police had extracted videos from Gray's computer, horrendous films of the abuse they'd perpetrated and even, in one case, murder. Some of it was shown to the court, but the Snyders were strongly advised by the judge not to attend that day, and of course they didn't.

Tess gave evidence via a video link. She spoke about the screams and bangs she had heard in the night, and Alice, who had held it together until then, found herself weeping uncontrollably as that brave little girl testified against her own family.

The girls were living now with their grandparents, Caro's parents, in Linlithgow. Caro had fallen out with her parents when she was a teenager and had had no contact with them since, so they were effectively strangers to their grandchildren, which couldn't have been easy for Christina, Tess and Isabel – although Alice believed that Tess and Isabel, at least, had always had a stronger bond with each other than with their parents. As long as they were together, they'd be okay, wouldn't they?

That was what she liked to hope, but it didn't stop her worrying.

They had stayed in touch by Zoom and email, and Alice had spoken with their grandparents, who seemed lovely. But the girls were always begging Alice to come visit.

The problem was that Alice never wanted to go back to Scotland again. She'd completely given up any idea of getting in contact with her birth mother, and she hadn't had the dream for months.

She had other dreams, though.

Not, weirdly, about that cellar.

About Tess and Isabel.

And Donna.

Where was Donna now?

She stood and went to the shelf and took down Frog,

running her fingers down the raised seam where someone had repaired him – badly. She smiled as she imagined action-woman Donna frowning in concentration as she ham-fistedly sewed up the gap.

She would always remember what Donna had done – making Alice get out of the SUV and then driving straight at Macneil's car on that dark track. Maybe they would meet again some day, although she didn't see how that would be possible, as no one even knew *who* Donna was, let alone *where*.

She thought again about the note Donna had left her, what she'd said, or implied, about the importance of bringing happiness to others.

'When we have our own place, maybe Tess and Isabel can come visit,' she said.

Skip blinked. Alice could tell from his expression that he'd forgotten who Tess and Isabel were.

'The kids? The Davidson girls?'

'Oh, no, Alice,' he said at once. 'I don't think that would be appropriate. It's not like you're related or anything. They're not your concern.'

'I'm not biologically related to Mom and Daddy, but I hope you wouldn't try to say *I'm* not *their* concern?'

'That's completely different and you know it.'

Alice didn't bother to argue.

Skip was back scrolling on his phone. 'This little room upstairs – it's really just a box room, although it has a nice big window. Mom thought maybe you'd want it as your sewing room.'

Alice snorted. 'I don't sew. I can't sew.'

'Mom can teach you. It's a good skill to have. Dad always says that Mom saved our family a bundle by making a lot of our clothes, and she'd always fold extra material into the seams, so when we grew, our clothes could grow too.'

Alice was aware of that. The whole of Branchfield was probably aware. Other moms were always talking about whether Mrs Landy realised how terrible her kids' homemade clothes looked, because actually she wasn't that great a sewer. All the extra material ready to be let out and let down made the clothes weird and lumpy, and often the seams and hems were squint.

'I don't want to learn to sew,' said Alice. 'If it's such a big deal for you, why don't *you* learn?'

'Okay, okay!' Skip grinned. 'It could be your studio, and you could... paint watercolours or some such.'

Alice guessed that would be a nice little hobby for a minister's wife.

Skip kept scrolling through the photographs. 'While we're in college, I guess we'll need someone to keep the yard in shape, because the tenants sure won't. We could get one of those robot mowers for the grass. Uncle Jay has one, and it's pretty neat, but I like stripes on a lawn. Makes a place look classier. Don't you think? Do you suppose there are robot mowers that do stripes?'

Oh good merciful heaven!

Alice exchanged a long look with Frog. He seemed to share her sentiments.

'I need to go to the bathroom.'

Five seconds later, she was striding down the street with Frog, not quite knowing where she was going but not really caring.

'A little tour of the neighbourhood,' she told Frog.

Oh my goodness, she was cracking up!

She waved at Mrs Martinez on the opposite pavement,

ignoring the elderly lady's rather searching look, as if she suspected that Alice could be running away again. As if Alice would put everyone through that! If she ever did go travelling again, it would all be entirely above-board, and she would let Mom and Daddy know where she was probably a dozen times a day.

She smiled at Mr Richardson mowing his lawn. Skip would not approve of the lack of stripes, she reflected with a little hysterical laugh.

She had thought she wanted this.

The comfort, the safety of her life back here in Branchfield.

She *did* want it.

Didn't she?

She looked down at Frog, and he looked up at her.

Donna hadn't hesitated. She'd floored the gas and driven straight at that bastard. Maybe Alice needed to have that sort of courage too. *You are braver than you know*, Donna had said in her note. And yeah, maybe she *had* been pretty brave, given that those psychopaths had locked her up alone in a room for three weeks, and all that time she'd known something really bad was going to happen to her. She hadn't just meekly given in to her fate. She'd tried to get out of there. She'd run at Ken and almost got past him, and then she'd prised those tiles off the wall, even though it had been a useless endeavour. The wall behind had been solid stone.

And then she'd trusted her instincts and gone with Donna and not the policeman.

There was a big world out there. Why should she let what *Those People* did to her stop her from enjoying it?

Be happy.

Would she be happy with Skip in that claustrophobic

little house? She loved him, sure, but he didn't really *get* her like Daddy got Mom. Or was it just because they'd been together so long that, as Mom put it, Daddy knew what she was thinking before she'd even thought it?

Alice didn't think so.

Sometimes you just had a connection with a person, like she had with Tess and Isabel. And if she didn't have that with Skip, what was the point? It wasn't fair on either one of them to settle for what was comfortable.

What was safe.

From nowhere, the shadowy figure of her birth mother popped into her head.

Alice knew that her name was Melanie Macfarlane. She knew her address. She knew every inch of the outside of that little cottage from examining it on Google Streetview and from the dream.

But maybe Melanie Macfarlane wasn't a nice person. Wasn't that what the dream had been trying to tell her? What Mom and Daddy obviously believed? It was better to leave well alone.

And she knew she never, ever wanted to go back to Scotland again.

EPILOGUE
MELANIE - 15 OCTOBER

Melanie took big lungfuls of crisp autumn air as she raked up the leaves that had accumulated on her handkerchief of a lawn. The exercise felt good. She'd been horribly restless lately, as if her body were full of excess energy she wasn't burning. And yet she wasn't sleeping. And she'd lost weight.

This in particular worried Grant. To keep him happy, she'd seen her GP and gone through a general 'MOT', but when she'd reported her clean bill of health, Grant had just frowned and said, 'So what does he think the problem is?'

'There's no *problem*,' Melanie had insisted, waving the printout of her blood results.

She hadn't told Grant what had happened or where she had been for those weeks last year when she'd gone AWOL, but maybe it was time. He had suggested they move in together, and Melanie wanted that too. But she knew she couldn't be around him all day, every day with that sort of secret lying heavy between them.

This should be a happy time.

The blossoming of her first proper relationship.

Moving in with the man she loved.

But all she could think about was Alice.

She'd followed the trial and pored over the photographs, in the press and online, but had wasted the minimum of time and headspace on the Davidsons and those other psychos. She only wanted to know about Alice.

She was paler and thinner in the photographs, in the footage. Head bowed, her parents' arms around her. Obviously it was a horrendously stressful thing to do, give evidence in such a high-profile trial, face Gray Davidson across a courtroom, but Melanie sensed something deeper.

Alice wasn't happy.

She stopped raking and stood for a minute, gazing unseeingly at the trees across the road, the ploughed field beyond them and the scrubby hillside of Leitch Craig rising to a china-blue sky.

It wasn't her place to worry about Alice. That was Warren and Tonya's job, and they were brilliant at it. Melanie couldn't have hoped for better parents for her child. Alice was safe and well and cocooned in the love of good people. She would get over this. She *would* be happy.

Wouldn't she?

Melanie had no right to be a part of her life.

She'd given that up nineteen years ago.

But *Alice, Alice, Alice.*

Everywhere there were reminders of her: in the inflection of an American voice on TV; in the innocence of a baby's eyes; in a patient's long caramel-coloured hair, swinging over her shoulder as she stooped to unfasten her shoes.

Alice.

Even that girl walking down the road, a rucksack dangling casually from one shoulder in a way Grant would not approve – even she reminded Melanie of Alice. Something about the shape of her and the way she walked. Something about the set of her shoulders. Her hair was shorter than Alice's, though, cut in a neat bob.

Melanie realised that she was staring, that she would be making the girl feel uncomfortable. She resumed her work, looking down at the leaves, wielding the rake so vigorously that the prongs scored parallel lines in the mossy grass.

She heard the girl's footsteps approaching down the road.

Slowing.

Stopping.

Melanie raised her head.

For a long moment she looked into wide, shocked eyes.

And then a look of wonder, of joy, came over Alice's face as she laughed incredulously, as she said something, as she ran through the open gate and into Melanie's waiting arms.

FROM JANE

I started the story that became *The Au Pair* several years ago. It featured a mysterious island, a missing housekeeper and a psychopathic child, but wasn't nearly as good as that makes it sound. I soon gave up on it, but was encouraged to revisit the general plot by my ever-enthusiastic writer friends Lesley McLaren and Lucy Lawrie.

I'm very lucky to have so much help and support from them, and from Brian Lynch and Alice Latchford at Inkubator Books, who helped me turn a collection of ideas into an actual book. (Sorry, Alice, for subconsciously stealing your name and then putting poor Alice through such an ordeal...!) Many thanks are due to them and to Shirley Khan and Pauline Nolan for all their excellent suggestions and corrections. Thanks also to Claire Milto for her formatting expertise and Lizzie Bayliss for another great cover, and to the whole team at Inkubator Books for all the work they do to give my books the best possible chance of reaching readers.

My sister Anne has recently also discovered the joys of

writing and has already had a lot of interest in her work from some big names in the publishing industry. It's been fun to share our writing dilemmas and problems, and also a few 'smug' moments! We both have to thank our mum, Grace, for nurturing our love of stories from an early age, and for her endless enthusiasm for everything we write (regardless of quality!).

It never fails to amaze me that people I don't know are buying and reading my books – thank you all!

Finally, reviews are so important to us authors. I would be very grateful if you could spend a moment to write an honest review (no matter how short). They really do help get the word out.

ABOUT THE AUTHOR

As a child, Jane spent a lot of time in elaborate Lego worlds populated by tiny plastic animals and people. Crime levels were high, especially after the Dragon brothers set themselves up as vets and started murdering the animals in their 'care'. (They got away with it by propping the victims up with Plasticine and pretending they were still alive…)

As an adult, she is still playing in imaginary worlds and putting her characters through hell – but now she can call it 'writing' and convince herself that she is doing something sensible. In real life, she has a PhD in genetics and copy-edits scientific and medical journals.

www.janerenshaw.co.uk

ALSO BY JANE RENSHAW

INKUBATOR TITLES

THE CHILD WHO NEVER WAS

WATCH OVER ME

NO PLACE LIKE HOME

THE STEPSON

THE LOST BOY

THE OTHER SISTER

THE AU PAIR

JANE'S OTHER TITLES

THE TIME AND PLACE

THE SWEETEST POISON

Printed in Great Britain
by Amazon

37789765R00209